Lost to Alice

By: Cassandra Crull

LINE BY LION
PUBLICATIONS

To my husband and the unending support you give.
My soul needed you

Alycytraline Extended Release 5 mg
"Alice"

Take one tablet by mouth every 12 hours.
Take with food or a full glass of water

Side effects may include:
Dry mouth
Fatigue
Giddiness
Dizziness

Contact your doctor immediately if you experience any
of the following:
Homicidal tendencies
Loss of all inhibitions
Oily sweat
Physical changes like excessive sweating or the ability to run
at high speeds
Loss of memory
Taste for human flesh

Alycytraline… Feel more you

Prologue

"GOOD morning, everyone, and welcome to the 1996 Annual Pharmaceutical and Biotech Summit! My name is Sophie Howard, and I am head of sales and marketing for RTO Pharmacies, and we are so excited to tell you about a new medication that could change the lives of those suffering from depression. From the years of 1990 to 1994 alone, 154,444 people were victims of suicide. That statistic is staggering and tragic. We are a 20th-century company, and we need a 20th-century solution - Enter Align.

Align is a newly formulated SSRI that has shown tremendous promise in treating the chemical imbalance that causes most major depressive disorders. In the clinical trials, patients reported improved mood, energy, and overall well-being with just the initial low dose. Most major insurance providers have already committed to covering this revolutionary drug. Therefore, we are offering major incentives to physicians who prescribe Align in the next six months! We are offering samples to everyone in attendance today! We cannot wait to see the amazing things we do together and the lives we save!"

PART ONE

1999

Chapter One

Aria

ARIA chewed her lip nervously as she entered the front doors of Serenity Springs High School. The freshly waxed floors shined as hundreds of kids she didn't know flooded through the front door. Her stomach was in knots, and she felt tears threatening to spill down her cheeks. But she would be damned if she let any of these people see her cry. She'd cried enough in the last three months to last a lifetime.

"Hey," her cousin Jude nudged her, "it'll be fine." he smiled warmly down at her. He was tall and lanky in stature, with dark hair and amber eyes. His ebony locks tousled over his forehead, his neck was donned with multiple necklaces and chokers, and his ears were decorated with several studs that crowned the curve of his ear. From behind her, she heard Jonah enter with a cough as he tossed his cigarette at the last second.

"Yeah, Aria," Jonah rasped. "It's not like it isn't the worst place on earth," his words dripping sarcasm.

"Nice, Jonah," Jude snapped.

Jonah was an identical copy of his twin brother except for his long, shaggy hair and bad attitude. Aria's aunt had adopted the twins when they were 8, the same age as Aria. She had been so excited to have more kids in the family, and luckily, they all had loved each other immediately. She would see them during the summer when she and her parents could make the trip to the mountains. They had kept in touch through letters, though. Jonah wrote more often than Jude, but his words were always like dark poetry, whereas Jude told of their adventures, hiking, and places they promised to take her the next time she visited. Jude focused on the future, Jonah always the past.

None of them knew how their lives would collide.

Her Aunt Marnie tried her best to help Aria adjust to her new surroundings; a small, secluded town in the mountains offered a thousand new ways to occupy oneself, but there were dangers: bears, mudslides, snowstorms, avalanches, driving the twisty roads. And Aunt Marnie made sure the twins taught her the rules of living in the mountains: always tell someone what direction you're headed, never approach a bear, get big if you do and scare it away, lock the garbage cans, and never throw a still burning ember into the sagebrush. Aunt Marnie was a single mom to three teens now, so money and emotional availability were tight. Even so, when she arrived in Serenity Springs mere weeks after her parents died, they welcomed her with open arms. The twins both swept in and gave her a safe place to grieve. Before coming to live with Aunt Marnie, Jude, and Jonah had lived with an extremely abusive father. They never told Aria the specifics, but the way their eyes darkened when they talked about it made a part of her heart shatter. What was clear is whatever they had endured, Jonah had made sure the worst of it was focused on him, not his brother. And Aria could see it. She could see it in the way Jude smiled without sadness in his eyes, the way Jude laughed and spoke without an edge of anger. Jude was truly good, and Jonah had made sure that it stayed that way. But the cost to Jonah seemed to be part of his soul. Though the boys were like brothers to her now, Jonah could be possessive and mean. No one else was allowed into their bubble of trauma.

When Jude had started spending time with a boy, he refused to name him because Jonah had a habit of scaring people off. Even in middle school, Jude would have a gaggle of friends after the first day, but it was never long-lived as Jonah would alienate them, and soon Jude was alone again. So, Jonah had paced all night in his room, as he felt control over his brother slipping again. Aria shared a wall with him and could hear the fervent muttering and angry steps around and around his room. When Jude finally came home that night, Jonah had interrogated him only to be met with a slamming door. Aria listened as Jonah came back to his room and recognized the squeak of springs as he threw himself on his bed… and cried. The three of them were all broken, being held together by nothing but themselves and sweet Aunt Marnie.

Now, walking into her new school with the twins at her back, she realized how secluded she'd let herself become, but she had never felt lonely. Aunt Marnie had taken the three school clothes shopping the weekend before, getting what they could at the second-hand store. Aria didn't mind wearing Goodwill clothing and hand-me-downs from the twins, but now she tugged at her sleeves self-consciously as she looked at the other girls wearing shiny new clothes for a shiny new year. Aria hated shiny things. She wanted to be home in her room curled up on her bed with Jude flopping across the foot, trying to steal her blanket, and Jonah crisscross on the floor next to her, gaming or getting lost in a movie. They'd protected her for almost three months now, it was like jumping from a nest.

A boy across the hall caught Jude's eye, and suddenly, he was saying goodbye as he merged into the mass of bodies. Aria squinted at the boy, trying to see who had captivated her cousin so. He was tall and muscular with tanned skin and startling dark eyes. Ebony curls fell past his ears, just dusting the shoulders of his varsity jacket. Jude was a skater, and in the world of high school cliques, the two clashed. Nonetheless, Jude beamed as they met against the far side of the hall and then disappeared around a corner.

"That isn't very discreet, is it?" Jonah joked. Only Aria and Jonah knew Jude's secret - that Jude was gay - and they protected that secret viciously. But Aria saw her cousin finally stepping out from the shadow of fear and stigma and finding someone who made him smile. This was a small town with some small minds, so Jude had to be careful; sneaking off during school hours probably wasn't the best idea, but Aria wouldn't take that glow she saw in his eyes away.

Serenity Springs was a beautiful yet secluded valley in the Rockies. Boxed in on all sides by mountains, sometimes Aria had to remind herself that they weren't walls pressing down on her. She had never lived somewhere where you couldn't see the horizon, that place where the sun dipped below the earth. That magical moment before night takes over. But the valley was small and sheltered and offered a girl like Aria countless adventures in the backcountry if only she had the will to do anything other than sleep. The boys had pulled her from her bed and sadness and taken her to places where roads barely existed, just dents in a grassy trail. Where stars were so vast and clear that you almost couldn't believe it was real. They'd explored caves that dipped cool and dark into the earth until Jude realized he was claustrophobic and swore off underground spaces forever. They'd explored old mine shafts… from a safe distance. Waterfalls that only the elk had seen in decades. It was like a balm on all their souls, bringing them together and giving them a purpose and a reason to get out of bed.

"C'mon, I'll take you to the office," Jonah put his hand between her shoulder blades gently and led her to the left against the current of moving bodies.

At some point in the aftermath of Jonah and Jude's childhood and Aunt Marnie finding them in a group home, Jonah had taken it upon himself to be the 'man of the house' and his brother's keeper. After some time, that meant bringing in money. Aunt Marnie worked as a patient advocate at the local hospital. The hours were long, and the pay wasn't great, but she loved helping others, so someone had to help. Jonah refused to let his brother work and insisted he could take care of Jude and Aunt Marnie on his own. After struggling with fast food work and shoveling popcorn at the local movie theater, Jonah met Carlos. In the two years since, Jonah shuffled drugs up the valley to the neighboring town for a man out of Denver, a few hours away. And he sampled plenty along the way, becoming a connoisseur of all the things he peddled. Jonah was a walking pharmacy, and it was no secret amongst the youth of the valley.

"Hey, Jonah!" a pimply-faced blonde boy yelled, running to catch up with them. "Hey man, you carrying?" Jonah stopped mid-stride and eyed the kid angrily. The kid's eyes fell on Aria. "Oh, hey, what's up?" Jonah pushed the kid away roughly against the row of lockers.

"Hey! I don't deal here, man!" Jonah hissed at him, looking back with something like shame in his eyes, "And don't talk to her! In fact, don't go anywhere near her!" Jonah threw the kid against the lockers again and rejoined Aria, making a hasty retreat down the hall.

"Who was that?" Aria asked.

"Some douche who doesn't know the right time to buy…" They stopped short outside the office door. Jonah looked down at her. "Ready?" he said softly, squeezing her shoulder encouragingly. Jonah knew how much she'd dreaded this day; they shared a wall, so he heard her crying from nightmares or her worried conversations with the mirror about being the new girl senior year. And he kept her secrets, too. She took a deep breath and pushed through the door to the office, pulling out of Jonah's comforting grasp.

The office was like a beehive, as people buzzed from task to task with focused anxiety. The secretary spotted them standing just inside the doorway and waved them over to the counter. They let the door shut behind them and stepped up to the counter.

"Hello dear. You must be Ms. Delgado. I'm Mrs. Baker," she said as she slid Aria a schedule, fumbling through a small filing box of papers, handing her a slip with a series of numbers printed neatly on it. "You're in locker #354, this is your schedule and locker combination. Your Aunt already sent in all the paperwork, so you're all set!"

"How did you know who I was?" Aria asked, reaching for her schedule.

"Well, we only have one new student this year, so it was an easy guess," Mrs. Baker smiled nicely, but Aria's stomach dropped.

The ONLY new student?

Suddenly, Aria noticed all the other students in the office were staring at her. Staring in that way people stare but are trying not to get caught. She was furious with her cheeks for getting red and her eyes for welling with tears.

"Hey, it's okay," Jonah said quietly, noticing her stiffen next to him. Aria pulled away slightly, wanting to disappear into herself.

"Oh, Mr. Forrester!" The secretary chirped towards Jonah, "You owe me an hour of in-school suspension from last year." The secretary clucked, turning her attention to a clipboard with a list on bright yellow paper. Jonah sighed at her and looked anxiously at Aria.

"Mrs. Baker, can I please walk Aria to her locker? It's her first day," he pleaded to the secretary.

"You tried to sell a substitute teacher marijuana, Mr. Forrester… You're lucky you're not in jail."

"I thought he was a senior!" Jonah said defensively.

"Yes, well, you're lucky Mr. Burton didn't press charges," Her eyes softened, "I'm sure Ms. Delgado will find her way…. Oh, Mr. Gorski!" Mrs. Baker called to someone over Aria's shoulder as the office door closed again. "Would you please show our new student where her locker is?"

Aria turned and looked up at a 6-foot-something blonde-haired boy with soft blue eyes. He had high cheekbones and a pointed nose atop broad shoulders. He looked down at her and froze in her gaze. He handed something to Mrs. Baker around Aria without taking his eyes off her. Aria's heart raced as the noise around her seemed to fade. All she saw were those blue eyes.

"Uh… yeah. I needed to turn this form in…" he finally broke his gaze and looked at Mrs. Baker, smiling politely. Aria watched as the boy's eyes fell on Jonah, as he was being ushered to the ISS room by another secretary. A mean smirk spread across his face.

"Damn Jonah, isn't that a new record? ISS on the first day?" he laughed condescendingly.

"Language!" Mrs. Baker chided. Aria, this is Chase Gorski. He can show you where your locker is," Mrs. Baker said while ushering them out.

Chase was still smirking in Jonah's direction when he looked down at her, but Aria rolled her eyes at him, pushing past him into the hallway. He quickly followed.

"What's your locker number? I can show you where…" He began, but Aria spun on him, suddenly furious with this boy. Did making other people feel small make him feel good? She hated bullies and hated condescending douchebags more. Jonah was her family, and for all his faults, she was protective of him because the twins and Aunt Marnie were the only family she had left. They protected her and had given her a safe place to fall when the world had gone dark. She wasn't going to entertain some small-town jerk who reveled in Jonah's failures.

"I can figure it out, thanks," she spat, spinning on her heel and walking confidently down the hallway.

"That's the cafeteria," Chase said, Aria turned and cocked her head at him.

"Down that hall… you're heading towards the cafeteria," he smirked, flushing Aria's cheeks. She angrily changed directions and stomped confidently in her new direction.

"That…. is the gym…" Aria stopped and fumed in place. Chase sighed. Why did he have to be so cute? And what was this pull she felt?

"So, I finally get to meet The Orphan Girl," he said, dodging students.

Orphan Girl?….

"My name is Aria," she corrected.

"Okay," Chase said, "You live with Jude and his brother?"

"His name is Jonah," she snapped.

"Yeah… I know." Chase said in a tone that indicated he was not a member of the Jonah Fanclub. Aria's temper flared again, and heat rose up, flushing her neck and cheeks.

"You don't know him!" Aria said, stepping boldly toward Chase, who almost stepped back in surprise. She furiously glared up at him, yanking her bag back up her shoulder. She took her finger and firmly poked him in the chest, emphasizing each word, "He. Is. My. Family." she took her hand back, "and you know absolutely nothing about what any of us have been through," Chase held his hands up in submission and stepped back quietly. Aria took a steadying breath, trying to get a handle on her anger.

"You're right," Chase conceded, putting his hands up. "I'm sorry."

They stood quiet a moment longer, and Chase put down his arms.

"Can we start over?"

Aria side-eyed him. He was trying hard to be charming, and damnit if it wasn't working. She knew that Jonah rubbed people the wrong way. It was in his nature. Where Jude was liked by everyone, Jonah was always being suspected of things or judged. It was her first day, and she had already made an enemy on Jonah's behalf… this new enemy made her feel… and the feeling wasn't anger or despair. But it was something. Aria just hadn't decided what yet. She rolled her eyes and sighed, offering her hand to him.

"I'm Aria Delgado: Orphan Girl and New Kid." She smiled sweetly knowing her dark joke hung in the air like acid. Chase hesitated then took her hand.

"I'm Chase Gorski," he smiled. His hand was warm against her usually cold hands but not sweaty - for which she was glad. That might have killed his charm.

"Sorry... I let my temper get the best of me," Aria said, embarrassed, wrapping her arms around herself.

"Nah... I'm sorry. You're right, I don't know shit. Truth is, Jonah and I have never gotten along. We went to middle school together and he was a dick even then!" Chase joked, eliciting a laugh from Aria. "Jude is cool, though. We used to play soccer together actually,"

"Yeah? I didn't know he played" Aria said sadly.

"I mean... in like fifth grade. Don't feel bad," Chase smiled, "Okay, so you wanna tell me where your locker is now?" Aria agreed and they made their way to the far hallway where Aria struggled with the combination. Chase took the paper from her, their fingers grazing as he did. Electric warmth crawled up Aria's hand, and her pulse quickened again. She wondered if he felt it too.

Probably not.

Chase turned the dial, and after a fair amount of desperate jiggling, the locker popped open.

"Thank you, Chase Gorski, former soccer player," Aria said lightly.

"You're very welcome, Aria Delgado, former orphan and new girl," He smiled back, turning to go, but he stopped, and Aria's heart caught in her throat. "I…" he hesitated, "I hope we have some classes together."

"Me too," she smiled.

"Oh yeah?" he joked, "So I didn't make too bad of an impression?" He had dimples when he smiled, and she noted the blush across his cheeks.

"No… I've seen worse."

"Um… if you uh… need any more help, you could give me a call."

"Chase Gorski, are you asking for my number?" Aria acted offended, grasping imaginary pearls. He reached around into his own backpack and took out a pen. He reached over gingerly and took Aria's hand. Above the electric buzzing of his touch, she felt the feel of a pen against her skin, looping out numbers.

"No, I'll give you mine," he said, concentrating on the back of Aria's hand. She studied his face. He had some of the bluest eyes she'd ever seen, but under the brightness of those eyes were dark circles and a form of tired Aria was well acquainted with. The emotional tiredness that saps the energy from you. Then he was meeting her eyes again. They stayed like that for a long moment, caught in whatever web they had stumbled into. Chase cleared his throat and dropped her hand.

"Yeah, give me a call… or let me know, ya know?" Chase said, quickly turning and leaving her standing next to an empty locker in a crowded hall of strangers.

Chapter Two

Chase

HE knew it when he saw her.

It was like breathing for the first time, not realizing you'd been holding your breath. Then she turned and looked up at him through thick dark lashes above light gray eyes.

Chase had heard about "The Orphan Girl" who had moved in with the Forrester's, but he hadn't so much as seen a glimpse of her. But now, here she stood, with storm cloud eyes and strawberry blonde hair. She had a tendril of freckles draped across her nose, and Chase wondered if he could count them all. Mrs. Baker brought him back to reality, and then he saw Jonah. Chase had hated Jonah since he caught him torturing Mrs. Taylor's cat in sixth grade; Chase had tried to stop him, but Jonah only laughed at his efforts. Jude eventually had talked Jonah into letting the cat go, but Chase never trusted him again. And now, this freckled wisp of a girl was living in the same house with him.

Chase tried to shrug off the thought.

What is this pull?

Before he knew it, he was walking next to her in the hallway. His heart was thumping in his ears…

Chapter Three

Aria

AS it turned out, Aria did have some, most, classes with Chase. Which was almost worse than having none. These kids had all known each other their entire lives, there were well-defined lines in the cliques, and Aria found herself existing outside of those. She missed her friends from home, but... they had stopped calling when all Aria wanted to talk about were her dead parents. Aria hid herself in the back of chemistry class, trying not to look too pathetic with no one to talk to; having to sit at a two-person lab table alone was especially pitiful. She doodled on her notebook, sketching a wavy sun and moon interconnected with a swirl of stars.

"That's really good," a girl's voice said from behind her, then a tall, slender brunette sat down next to her.

"Um... Thanks," Aria said, embarrassed.

"Are you the orphan Girl living with Jude and Jonah?" she asked excitedly.

Oh god....

"Yeah... My name is Aria," Aria said warily.

"I'm Dana! I'm so excited to have new blood in this town! Ugh, everyone suuuuuuuucks." She groaned, dropping her head back dramatically, eliciting a laugh from Aria.

"I probably won't live up to the hype." Aria said, smiling despite herself.

"You already dress better than 80% of them," When Dana noticed Aria's confused expression she continued, "Look at all these preppy girls, they wear the same shit just in different shades of boring. YOU, on the other hand, have kickass jeans with patches and a flannel I'm pretty sure I saw at the consignment shop downtown - I know because I was going to buy it, but it definitely looks better on you."

Aria wasn't sure how to respond, so she stayed silent.

"Can I sit with you? I hate everyone else. I'll tell you who to stay away from." Dana smiled so brightly that Aria couldn't help but accept.

"Yes," she laughed. "Please help me survive this,"

"Oh girl, I got you." Dana began naming every person in chemistry, and when she got to Chase, Aria interrupted.

"What's his deal?" she asked carefully, but Dana saw it all over the blush in her cheeks.

"Oooohhhh Chase, huh? Nice guy, doesn't really date…. Maybe he's waiting for someone new too?" Dana smiled devilishly at Aria, making her face heat again.

"Hey, it's the Orphan girl," a stocky boy with startling green eyes and blonde curls said, smiling at her.

"Get bent, John," Dana said, flipping her hand at him dismissively.

"Whatever, Dana," John walked back to his desk dejected.

"That's John, he's a dick. The short one sitting with him is Drew, also a prick. They're all jocks. Chase hangs with them, and Miguel - he's the guy in the varsity jacket," As Dana pointed the boys out, Aria recognized Miguel as the boy who disappeared with Jude earlier in the day. Aria smiled. She couldn't wait to tell Jude she'd figured it out.

The teacher entered, and the dreaded introductions started. Every. Single. Teacher. Made her stand and introduce herself: her name, where she is from, why she moved. Imagine their surprise when she met their eyes and said.

"My parents died,"

Most cleared their throats and then awkwardly welcomed her to the school. By the end of the day, she was exhausted. Geometry was her last class. She hated math on a good day and today was NOT a good day. Again, she sat at the back of the class and slumped into her desk, putting her head down on her arms. She just wanted this day to end. Every class had been like being on stage, a hot spotlight trained right on her. She wanted to go home and hide away with movies and games and the twins.

"That bad, huh?" a familiar voice said over her shoulder. She turned her head to the left, not bothering to lift it from the table.

"I've had better," she groaned. Chase had seen her do the introduction torture three times already; she was sure he would never be seen with her again, and really, she couldn't blame him. Each one had been more awkward than the last. It was probably painful to watch.

"You've probably had worse, though, so... there's that," Chase said, taking the seat to her left.

"HA!" she said sarcastically into her arms, "Thanks so much, you can go now."

Chase laughed softly.

"Sorry," he said, leaning towards her, his elbows on his desk.

"I'm sorry you had to witness it!" she laughed.

Chase looked at her hand; under his number was Dana's number, and he smiled.

"Looks like you made at least one friend. that's good,"

"Just one?" she asked almost shyly.

Chase reddened and sat up.

"Yeah… or something," he muttered, trying to play off the redness in his ears and cheeks.

Aria smiled.

The last introduction wasn't so bad.

***

ARIA sat in the kitchen, staring at the phone. Should she call him? Should she call Dana? What if they both were just being nice and only wanted to get to know "The Orphan Girl" because she was a new shiny toy? They couldn't help that many people didn't move here, though. Was it bad if they WERE excited?

"What are you doing, my dear?" Jude asked as he entered from the living room and opened the fridge.

"Um…" she chewed her lip. Jude turned, seeing the look on her face.

"Hey, are you good? What's up?" he pulled out a chair and sat down, opening the pudding he'd pulled from the fridge.

"I got a couple of numbers today, and I don't know if I should call them," she admitted.

"Like from potential friends or potential something else?" he raised his eyebrows playfully.

"One of each,"

"Holy shit! Who is the something else? You HAVE to tell me!" Jude exclaimed.

"Tell me who your guy is first," Aria responded. It bothered her that he hadn't told her yet.

"First of all,… I can't yet. I can't out him. Second of all, don't deflect. Let's go! Who is it?" Jude snapped his fingers at her, which she batted away.

"What if I think I knew who your boy was," Aria asked with a devilish smile.

"Then I would ask that you respect my privacy and keep it to yourself," Jude said with an asking smile.

Don't tell.

Aria sighed.

"Chase Gorski gave me his number," Aria finally admitted.

"Really?" Jude said, surprised, "He's cool. Hates Jonah though, so good luck with that," Jude took a bite of his pudding, "He's gonna lose his shit," Aria sighed and slumped back in her chair.

"It was weird," Aria began. "I felt like… a… feeling with him. An electric pull or something." Then she shook her head. "It's dumb. And he and Jonah don't like each other anyway. I won't call him."

"No!" Jude said quickly, taking Aria's hand. He said, "Jonah doesn't get to control it all," There was an emotion in Jude's eyes that Aria hadn't seen before. Like the sadness that comes from finding someone you love can't be trusted. Someone whose broken pieces have created toxicity that leaks and stains everything and the realization that you can't let that happen anymore. That you're sick of cleaning up stains just to have them reappear. Aria put her other hand over Jude's and smiled.

"I'm glad you found someone who makes you smile," Aria said genuinely.

"Me too," Jude beamed. "It's new and fun, and I'm... happy, I think." Aria smiled back at him and squeezed his hand. If anyone deserved a happily ever after, it was Jude. Aria was quiet while Jude took his hand back and began scraping the bottom of the pudding cup loudly with his spoon.

"Can you not?" Aria asked.

"I have to get it all," Jude said, concentrating.

"IF I call him, what do I say?" Aria asked shyly after another moment.

"Just say 'Hi,' Chase will take it from there," Jude winked. He stood and kissed her head. He left her in the kitchen to stare at the phone some more. She sat silent and then grabbed the handset on the phone.

"Fuck it"

Chapter Four

Chase

"HELLO?" Chase said flatly.

His dad was passed out on the couch, so he talked in a low tone even though he doubted anything would wake his dad now. He'd hit the bar after his shift, then the liquor store. Luckily, by the time Chase got home, his dad was already sleeping it off, but he didn't want to wake him. He'd rather not deal with that bullshit tonight.

"Ch-chase?" The voice that came through the line made his stomach flip, and something electric flashed through him.

Holy shit. It can't really be her.

"Yeah. Aria?" he tried to keep his voice even as he rounded the corner into the hallway, wrapping the cord around the corner. His dad was too damn cheap to buy a cordless.

Asshole.

"Yep. Um, hey." she giggled awkwardly, and his knees almost buckled. "I'm sorry, are you busy? This is weird. I'm sorry,"

"No!" Chase almost yelled; he cleared his throat, "No, this is good. This is good,"

"Okay," Aria replied.

Chase could hear the smile in her voice as she said it. They were silent for a moment, but it wasn't an awkward silence. It was a silence of mutual happiness. The acknowledgement of attraction.

"So, what are you doing tonight, Freckles?" Chase asked finally.

"Oh, so I've been upgraded from Orphan Girl? I mean, I *guess* it's an improvement, though I hate my freckles,"

"What?!" Chase balked. "They're adorable!" he blurted.

Shit. Keep it cool, keep it cool.

"Oh yeah?" Aria said coyly.

"I might be a sucker for freckles, and I won't be shamed,"

"No shame here. I mean, blondes are pretty cute, too," Aria teased, and Chase reddened.

"So, how long have you been in the valley?" Chase asked.

"May. My last school just passed me for the last few weeks of school after..." she cleared her throat, "then Aunt Marnie came and got me."

Chase was quiet a moment, and on your first day, you get called Orphan Girl; that sucks. I'm sorry, I'm an asshole."

"Eh... you weren't the only one," Aria said lightly, her voice more forgiving than Chase deserved.

I'm such an asshole.

"Well, you survived your first day; that's good, right?"

Aria snorted.

She's so cute.

"Barely," she laughed.

From the living room came a groan and the creaking of the couch as his dad found consciousness.

Shit! No no no no no no

Chase's heart rate skyrocketed, and sweat spread across his brow. He hated that his dad made him feel this way, like his body only knew fear in his presence—only felt small and afraid. He had to get off the phone before his dad found him crouching in the hallway on the phone.

"Hey Aria," he whispered, ashamed but still sweating, "I gotta let you go. I'll see you tomorrow, okay?" he lunged around the corner, hanging up before his dad rounded the opposite corner from the living room.

"What are you doing, boy?" he snarled.

"Just making dinner, sir. Meatloaf good?" Chase said stiffly.

I'm so weak.

I hate him.

I wish he'd die.

But he's my dad...

His dad grunted and passed him, turning into his bedroom and collapsing onto the bed. Chase heard him snoring within seconds. He released a breath he didn't realize he'd been holding. He wasn't making fucking meatloaf for that prick. Chase grabbed a bowl of cereal and went to watch TV.

As he sat down, releasing the familiar pit in his stomach, he smiled because she had called.

She had felt it, too.

Chapter Five

Aria

IT turns out the second day is worse than the first. Aria didn't think it was possible, but it was. The only consolation was that she now had Dana and Chase to look forward to. And Jude. Jude had been transferred to geometry after an assessment showed he'd been placed in too low of a math class. Aria was so happy she almost cried when he told her. She was so close to tears. Jude had hugged her and said he hadn't known it was that bad.

When Jude entered the class and saw Chase seated next to Aria, he smiled and happily sat down in front of Aria.

"Hey, kids, how are we doing?" he said playfully. " Is today any better, Aria?"

"No. Today has sucked. I'm like a sideshow attraction." Aria threw her hands up dramatically. "Come see the Orphan Girl of Serenity Springs!" she flopped her hands back down, sighing in exasperation.

The door to the classroom opened again, and in walked Jonah. She hadn't known he'd changed classes, too. Jonah spied them at the back of the room, then his eyes landed on Chase sitting next to her. He cocked his head and approached Chase's desk.

"Can I help you, Jonah?" Chase said, eyebrows raised.

"You're in my seat, Pretty Boy," Jonah challenged.

"Jonah…" Aria started.

"No!" Jonah said, snapping his head toward Aria with such suddenness that she jumped. He stared at her with that intense, dark possessiveness. She told herself it was protection.

"Jonah, sit the hell down," Jude scolded. "It is almost the end of the day, don't pull some shit to get detention," after a moment, Jonah nodded and released a breath as he sat down in front of Chase next to Jude. Jude shot an apologetic glance back at Aria and Chase. Aria looked over at Chase, who smiled at her despite obviously being about to combust from anger. Jonah had that effect on people.

***

FRIDAY came so slowly that Aria thought she might scream. But finally, blessedly, the final bell rang, and she met Jonah and Jude at the front door and walked to her car. Aria's dad had purchased her a car a week before her parents died; sometimes, she thought she could still smell him in the driver's seat. Jude stalked to the car, not saying a word to Jonah or Aria. The jocks, including Chase, spilled out of the gym door. Aria noticed Jude's dark-haired boy from earlier in the week, Miguel, pointing in their direction and laughing. Heads turned in the group, and Aria stopped mid-stride next to her car, cocking her head at them. Miguel and three other guys in the cluster started to shout at them.

"Shit," Jonah said under his breath.

"Aria! Let's go!" Jude pleaded, hurriedly getting into the car.

Jude wasn't his normal happy self; he looked afraid. Aria's heart rate instantly skyrocketed at that. She stared at the guys, trying to understand what was happening, why the twins were panicking, and why they were yelling for her to get in the car. Then it hit her.

Suddenly, the words they screamed came into focus over the buzzing in her ears, ugly words thrown at Jude with venom from someone he had trusted. Words thrown like daggers meant to spill blood from Jude's very soul. Aria suddenly saw red. Her temper had become a living thing after her parents died; the smallest inconvenience would catapult her into a fit of fury. Random people became the targets towards which she would expel the rage. And after she would sob. For what was anger but a shield against sorrow?

Before she knew it, she was inches from Miguel's face screaming at him to shut up, to fuck off, that maybe there was a secret or two she could tell about him.

"Who gave you that hickey, Miguel?" She barked over the crowd.

Miguel shoved her hard backward in desperation to silence her; Aria stumbled back, but she rebounded, coming for him again. Miguel screamed at her, calling her a bitch and telling her to shut up. Aria launched at him, knocking him in the eye before she felt arms around her midsection. The crowd suddenly surged in two directions. One side holding Aria back like a wild animal and the other pushing Miguel away from her. Miguel had blood dripping down his face, but it wasn't enough. Aria wriggled free of her restraints and flew at him again, but before she could make contact, someone had her over their hip.

"PUT ME DOWN!" Aria screamed.

"You need to calm the fuck down!" Chase yelled at her. His voice knocked her back to reality with a jolt of embarrassment. They got to her car, and Chase set her down forcefully. "Are you done?!" he yelled.

"Did you hear what they called him?" She yelled back, still mad but out of the haze of her white-hot rage. Chase put his hands on his hips, hanging his head.

"Yeah… I did," he admitted.

"And?" Aria protested, panting from the adrenaline, "I couldn't see, Chase. Were you laughing or not?" she hissed at him. His head snapped up, and his face flushed with anger.

"OF COURSE NOT! Jude is my friend, and even if he wasn't, I'm not like that! I don't give a fuck what other people do," he pointed at the group of boys across the parking lot, "THAT was fucked up! Understand? NOT okay!"

"Then why am I the one getting hauled across the parking lot?"

"Because you're the one throwing punches, Freckles!" Chase almost laughed.

"Aria," Jude was still hiding in the car, "can we just go, please?" The heartbreak in Jude's eyes ripped Aria open, realizing she hadn't helped the situation or his broken heart by creating a scene and making Miguel bleed. She looked up at Chase, whose eyes reflected that sentiment.

"Okay…" Aria conceded and opened the car door. Jonah and Chase eyed each other for a minute, then Jonah rounded the back of the car and got in as well. Aria rolled down her window, raising her middle finger to the group across the parking lot as she pulled out of the parking lot, leaving Chase standing alone.

***

LATER that night, after begging Jude for an hour to come out of his room to no avail, Jonah and Aria ventured out into the valley's nightlife. The town was small, but the wilderness was vast, which meant infinite places to gather, drink, and make bad choices. This had been one of Aria's favorite things about living here, a person could disappear easily. Jonah and Aria found half the school at a bonfire in the plateaus atop the mountains to the South. They parked Aria's car just off the two-track path and melted into the crowd. Jonah hung close to Aria's side as they made their way through the thick of the crowd. The air smelled of pot, keg beer, and summer freedom. One of the only solaces Aria had found here was the wilderness; the utterly untamed nature of the valley drew her in and welcomed her home. It was comforting to know something else existed that was as wild and angry as she felt on the inside. This area of the Rockies was known for harsh winters, short summers, and natural disasters. Floods from the river, mudslides, avalanches, wildfires, and bear attacks were all common occurrences in the valley, and Aria respected that. Even though people forced themselves onto the land and ripped it apart to build condos, the valley raged against its citizens every year. You had to earn the right to live here.

The sun was slowly setting behind the mountains as Aria helped herself to the keg and wandered around for a bit. Jonah had disappeared with a bleach-blonde girl behind the cars and emerged moments later, counting some cash. Aria didn't know what he dealt, but whatever. It wasn't her business.

"Still mad at me?" a voice said from behind her. Aria turned and saw Chase standing with that adorable, hateable grin.

"UGH!" Aria groaned. "Can't I enjoy one beer before you guys start in?" she teased a little too harshly. Chase held his hands up in surrender, a look of hurt flitting across his face. Aria noticed he seemed more relaxed, rumpled like his shirt. Aria took a deep breath and decided to take it easy on him… for now. "I'm kidding," she said softer. "Are you already drunk? Chase, the sun isn't even down yet," she joked. He seemed to gain his confidence back, stepping closer.

"What can I say? It's been a rough week. Some new girl yelled at me," he said, tipping his cup back into his mouth.

"Well, maybe you deserved it," Aria smiled. She couldn't stop the smile from spreading across her face or the blush from warming her cheeks. Something radiating off of him drew her in like some invisible tether bound him to her.

"Maybe I did, but she has a hell of a temper, too," Chase sipped his beer and dared a step closer to her.

Aria laughed lightly.

"It's a side effect of the red hair," Aria joked as she finally enjoyed her own beer.

"Well, it's cute, too," Chase said, his face blushing slightly.

"So, you DO think I'm cute," Aria teased, feeling the beer warm her from the inside out and loosened her inhibitions.

"I'm pretty sure you know the answer to that, Freckles." He smiled, leaning a little more in her direction. Aria looked around at the party around her.

"So, this is how you party in the mountains?" She smiled, parties back home usually consisted of someone's parents being out of town or dank basements where parents didn't care what happened. She had to admit this was better.

"Yep, and now you do too," Chase grinned.

"It's not too bad, I guess," she teased as she took in the aspen trees and red mountain backdrop to the kegs and tipsy teenagers. She brought her eyes back to Chase, who was intently staring at her.

"Ah," he cleared his throat, catching himself staring. "Well, I'm glad we were able to make such a good first impression."

That smirk was going to be the death of her. She looked away, swigging back the rest of her beer.

"May I fetch you a refill, madam?" Chase chirped in a British accent that made Aria giggle embarrassingly. Her cheeks heated again, but Chase only smiled.

"Shut up," she said, pushing his shoulder.

"That was cute as hell," Chase said as his cheeks reddened as well.

They weaved through the throng and found the kegs; Chase took her cup and filled hers, then his. They fell back into the crowd a bit, touching their cups together and tipping them back.

"So, was it really bad after I left?" Aria said, not able to resist the urge to ask any longer.

"Well…"

Suddenly, the party erupted in chaos as the crowd began surging towards the trees. Aria strained over the crowd only to see red and blue lights emerging into the clearing.

"Shit!" Chase hissed, tossing his cup to the ground. "Come on!" he said in annoyance, grabbing Aria's hand and running toward the trees. Aria took another drink, then tossed the cup to the side as she raced at Chase's side. She scanned the chaotic crowd for Jonah, who she couldn't see.

"I have to find Jonah!" she yelled to Chase as they burst through the edge of the tree line. Chase pulled her to the right, onto the ground, scraping through a thicket of branches. They both crouched, hidden amongst the scrub oaks and trees, swallowed whole by darkness.

"We have to find Jonah," Aria whispered. Chase sighed but stood slightly, peering through the branches.

"Is that him leaving in your car?" Chase pointed; Aria rose next to him, squinting as she followed Chase's gaze to her burgundy sedan pulling down the trail, bobbing up and down as it bounced off the ruts grooved into the earth. Aria sighed. Jonah had told her if the cops came, the first one to the car had to leave and save the stash hidden within the trunk.

Jonah had made it first.

"Shit," Aria sighed.

She and Chase sank back to the ground in silence.

A boy from their chemistry class crashed onto the ground a few feet from Chase and Aria's hiding place; suddenly, a police officer was on top of him, screaming commands. Chase and Aria froze. With all the commotion in the open part of the plateau and the darkness of the woods, they were completely hidden within the foliage; neither the cop nor the kid saw them. The police officer pulled the boy from science class off the ground and pushed him back out into the clearing. Aria watched through the branches as the officers herded her classmates toward the 4-wheel drive cruisers parked near the trailhead. Aria and Chase looked at each other. Chase motioned his head up the hill, and Aria nodded. Her heart was thundering in her ears, but she made herself follow Chase. Slowly, they backed up the hillside, traversing up the hill using the growing shadows as cover. They reached a small trail at the top of the hill that led to a hollow of trees that clung to an outcropping of rock. The roots tangled back around the cliffside in giant chunks, creating a small ledge covered in grass that looked out over the valley of Serenity Springs. Carefully, they made their way onto the rocks netted with an ancient root system. Moss and small weeds covered the small space; Chase and Aria tread carefully, settling into a nook in one of the trees. The night air began to chill, and Aria pulled her hands inside her hoodie for warmth.

"Well… what do we do now?" she asked Chase, who had since sobered.

"Truth or dare?" he teased.

"No," Aria laughed.

"Texas hold 'em?" Chase said again.

"Um… no cards,"

"Then, I guess we wait it out." He looked down at her and noticed she was shivering. He raised his arm to wrap it around her shoulders, and as he did, Aria flinched away for a second. "You're cold, calm down," he snapped defensively, wrapping his arm around her and bringing Aria in next to him.

"Sorry…" Aria mumbled after a few moments of stiff silence, "I don't know why I did that."

"You're guarded; that's okay," Chase said, putting his head back against the tree, sighing heavily, "But just so you know, I'm not that guy. I'm not going to touch you if you don't want me to."

"Okay,"

"AND, for the record, Miguel is a dick, and he deserved the black eye," Chase continued, "And Jonah is a dick for leaving you."

Aria jumped to protest but couldn't because Chase was right. Jonah bailed to protect his drugs. He left her in the middle of fucking nowhere, so HE didn't get in trouble. Her cheeks reddened in anger but not at Chase.

"Fine…." she sighed. "You're right," she said, watching the sun sink completely behind the mountains. She shivered again, and Chase shrugged out of his coat, draping it over her. "Chase, you're going to freeze," she protested.

"Nah, I'm good," he slid his arm around her again, but this time, he put his arms around her waist and pulled her closer to him. "You'll keep me warm," Aria smiled and looked out at the sky as the stars emerged.

"This is my favorite time of day," she said more to herself, "Just when the sun is going down and stars start to take over."

"Yeah, me too. They look like they can go on forever,"

She felt Chase's eyes on her, so she turned to meet his stare and could feel his breath on her face. Warm and still faintly smelling of beer, but she also smelled him, a mixture of earth and aftershave. He breathed carefully like he might scare her away. She smiled as she met his eyes.

"I want to kiss you," Chase breathed.

"Then you probably should," Aria whispered with a laugh, but Chase hesitated.

"Do you feel it? Or am I imagining it?" Chase asked apprehensively.

He didn't have to tell her what he meant; she knew what he was talking about. The pull, that electric warmth when they were close. She was scared to admit it; she was scared it was a trap, but she also wanted nothing more than to fall into his kiss and lose herself in his lips. He was closer to her now, his lips nearly brushed hers, and his proximity warmed her core in a way she wasn't familiar with. Aria took a deep breath and nodded. As if in answer, his lips came closer and touched hers softly yet solidly. His lips were warm and soft, gentle but earnest. Aria leaned into him and returned the kiss, opening her mouth as his free hand came up to cup her cheek. The electric current hummed between them, landing in the pit of Aria's stomach, warming her from within. Chase leaned into her, his lips caressing hers and tongue dancing against hers. His breath quickened, matching Aria's pulse. Aria grabbed fistfuls of the front of his shirt, tugging him closer again. They parted for a moment and stared at one another, both breathless and flushed. Aria pulled him to her again, tangling her arms around his neck, her fingers finding his hair. Chase's arms wrapped around her, one hand coming up to cup the nape of her neck. Aria's world exploded with that electricity, a breathless fervor taking over them both.

Chapter Six

Chase

DAMN.

His only thoughts were of her lips, her body against his, her tongue dancing in his mouth. He wanted to devour her. This was too strong; he needed to stop.

Chase pulled away from her, breathless and fighting every fiber of his being to do so. It was like every cell in his body wanted her. Aria looked up at him through thick, dark lashes, putting her hands on his chest. A small smile dancing on her mouth.

Those lips...

No! Have some self-control, damnit!

Chase softly touched his lips to hers, taking in her scent and her breath. He kept her hands to his chest as he settled them both back into the tree.

"We uh… should maybe try and… relax," he sighed, regret screaming in his brain.

"Yeah, okay," she said, and he was relieved when he didn't see hurt in her eyes.

Aria pulled the discarded coat back up and arranged it over them the best that she could, then, almost shyly, tucked herself into his side. Chase smiled, sliding his arm around her shoulders again.

His heart was thundering in his ears, and his body had not gotten the memo that they'd stopped kissing. He had to calm himself down. He leaned his head back and took a deep breath of the mountain air.

Damn.

Chapter Seven

Aria

ARIA snuggled into Chase's side and looked up at the breathtaking sky. Aria tried to slow her heart rate and even out her breathing, but she was still nearly vibrating. Her skin on fire.

"Tell me about your family," Aria said, her voice quiet in the darkness.

"My mom left when I was 2, my dad is a dick. And that's all there really is." His voice sounded sad.

"I'm sorry," Aria whispered back; Chase squeezed her hand in response.

"I really am sorry I called you Orphan Girl. It was just what people were calling you... I didn't think. I should've thought,"

"It's okay. You were the best part of my first day," Aria said, sounding small to her own ears.

"Good," Chase responded, Aria hearing the smile in his voice.

They were quiet for a moment, and after a few minutes, Aria heard his breathing even out as he slept. She looked up at Chase, noting the color of his eyelashes and the curve of his chin. It suddenly occurred to her that they were in bear country and sleeping outside without a fire. They were mostly shielded, but still, she listened to the sounds of the forest, listening for any snapping twigs or rustling before shutting her own eyes and falling asleep.

Chapter Eight

Miguel

EVERYONE knew.

His father would never look at him the same, and his mom? Oh god, his mom would cry. She would cry and scream. It would break her heart.

Why did he let himself get tangled up with Jude? He'd let himself get distracted and let his guard down. He should've ended it before school had even started.

But… he loved being around Jude. He loved how he felt around him. He loved the way Jude's laugh made him feel, and he loved it when he kissed him. He knew he could never really come out, but he kept going back. Then it was too late. There was no way out now. There was no way to live in a world where he had to go back to hiding. And he couldn't deal with the disappointment in his mom's face…. or the hatred in his father's eyes. They'd disown him. Or send him to one of those camps where they pray for you to be normal. Normal… what the fuck was normal?

Well, it wasn't Miguel.

"Normal" was a hopeless black well of shame.

He stepped up onto the chair and slid the rope over his head.

Let his parents mourn the son they loved and not the abomination he'd be revealed to be.

He couldn't feel like this anymore... he couldn't lie anymore.

I'm disgusting.

A disappointment.

They'd hate him.

Break her heart.

Hide in shame.

Sick

Monster

Going to hell

Just die.

Makeitstopmakeitstopmakeitstopmakeitstopmakeitstop

"I'm sorry," he whispered as the chair rattled to the floor.

Chapter Nine

Aria

WHEN they woke in the early morning hours, Aria was curled into Chase. Her head was on his chest, his head on her hair. His hands were still tucked tightly around her. Aria woke and sat up, looking around hazily, waking Chase in the process.

"Morning," Chase said groggily, looking around while his brain put the pieces of the night before together. He looked down at his arms curled around her waist and looked up at Aria with a grin.

"Um… morning," she said, clearing her throat and tucking her hair into her hood; from beneath her thick hoodie, her stomach growled loudly. They both looked at each other and laughed.

"Well, it looks like we better get down this mountain and get you some food," Chase smiled. Standing, he held his hand out to her, which Aria stared at for a moment, unsure what to do. She didn't want to be locked inside herself forever, with only the twins able to reach her; she had to let someone in eventually. Kisses in the dark were one thing, but taking his hand in the daylight was another.

So, she took his hand.

They made their way back to the trailhead, where the earth still held the scars of all the chaos of the night before, and continued on foot down the hill. Aria was quiet for a long time while Chase chattered about what the mountains were named, what rivers fed into other rivers, what canyons they camped in, anything to eat up the silence between them.

"Why are you being so nice to me?" Aria said so suddenly that Chase stopped in his tracks, giving her a quizzical look, "I just mean… I'm a mess and unpredictable and angry…" her list of her negative qualities trailed off.

"What if I like angry, unpredictable girls?" He smiled.

"You don't even know me," she said quietly, staring down the trail again.

"Well… do you want me to?" Chase asked, matching her stride. Aria was quiet for a moment. Did she want him to know her? Did she want her death-saturated life to seep onto him? Did she want anyone else to hear her screaming from the nightmares of broken glass and blood where she woke up soaked in sweat and crying? Was it fair to ask another person to endure that? She didn't know. But she did know Chase made her feel calm in a way she hadn't felt since before her parents' death. Would it be selfish to tell him yes just to feel that safety?

"I… think so," she answered honestly. "I worry you'll figure out how broken I am and run."

"Nah…." Chase shrugged, "I don't scare easily," Aria was quiet again, chewing on her lip, lost in thought. "Look… it's not like you know me either," Chase said in a serious tone. "Maybe you aren't the only broken one."

Aria let out a breath. She'd never thought of that.

"Okay," she said, smiling over at him. He flashed that adorable smirk and took her hand in his, threading their fingers together. They walked for an hour until they finally came upon a popular marked trailhead with a payphone. Aria called Jude, and the twins headed out to retrieve Chase and Aria from the mountain. The two sat on a boulder as they settled in to wait for the twins.

"So, you guys throw great parties in the Valley," Aria joked sarcastically. Chase smiled.

"Yeah… not our best night," he laughed. In a town this small, the teens were always a collective 'we.' "But a…." Chase stammered, "I had fun… with you,"

"You did?" Aria laughed, "We ran from the cops and hid in the woods, what was your favorite part,"

"After that," Chase said, smiling. Aria giggled involuntarily.

So embarrassing.

"How did you get to the party anyway?" Aria asked.

"Rode with Drew, he was wasted by the time we got there so I'm sure he's in a jail cell waiting for his mom to come get him," Chase huffed with a hint of resentment.

"Well, at least you weren't left," Aria murmured angrily.

They were quiet, while Aria toed a rock with her sneaker awkwardly.

"I think… I think we should hang out again," Aria said quietly.

"Oh yeah?" Chase smiled, "I think we can arrange that." he slipped his hand around hers and looked down at her. For a moment, they simply stared at each other, small smiles playing against their lips. Chase leaned down, and just as his lips touched Aria's, a car horn blared in their ears, making them both jump.

"Hey! None of that on the first date!" Jude yelled mockingly from the passenger window of Aria's car. Jonah sat behind the wheel, simmering in anger. Aria's stomach clenched; Jonah was a lot on a good day, but a jealous Jonah was like a black hole. Sucking everything around him into his angry, dark abyss. Aria slid into the backseat stiffly, eyeing Jonah. Chase slid in after her, close enough that she could feel the heat from his arm on hers.

"You guys have *fun* last night?" Jonah snapped.

"Excuse me?" Aria chirped back, her anger waking up and yawning, ready for a fight.

"I SAID, did you and Pretty Boy here have fun last night?" he snarled.

"Fuck off, Jonah," Chase bit back, "you left us, so that's on you!"

"Her!" Jonah corrected at a yell, "I left HER! You, I could give a fuck about."

"That's your witty retort for why you abandoned your cousin in the mountains!" Chase laughed, "Nice, man..." he shook his head. Jonah's face reddened with rage, but he couldn't find the words, so he threw the car in reverse and spun the car around fast, whipping them all to the side.

"Yo! This is MY car, and I will kick you both out if you're going to drive like that!" Aria yelled seriously from the back seat. No one moved or breathed for a moment. Then Jonah seemed to release a breath, calmly put the car into drive, and pulled the car out onto the gravel road.

"So apparently, I didn't miss much," Jude finally said, smiling wickedly at Aria.

"Nah, it got better afterward," Chase responded, smiling over at Aria.

Jonah sighed heavily from the front seat.

"I think I got one beer down before we had to flee, though," Aria laughed, happily avoiding talking about her and Chase with Jonah right there.

"Was Miguel there?" Jude asked quietly.

"Mig is a bitch! He stayed home!" Chase joked.

"He didn't want to explain his black eye to everyone," Jonah said, reluctantly joining in the shit talk for the sake of Jude.

"Fuck Miguel!" Aria yelled. Jude smiled a small smile.

"Yeah!" Chase yelled, "FUCK MIGUEL!"

"FUCK MIGUEL!" they yelled in unison, laughing as the tires hit the pavement and they reentered town.

***

THAT night, the phone rang. Jude answered, but within seconds, he sank to the floor in gut-wrenching sobs. Aria took the phone, Dana choked out three devastating words:

"Miguel is gone."

***

THE entire school showed up for Miguel's funeral the next week. The entire student body and faculty were given a week off to mourn and a day the next week to attend the memorial and burial. The day felt fitting to lay such a young man to rest; the rain drizzled from darkened skies, and low rumbles of thunder could be heard in the distance. The sound of Miguel's mother's sobs carried over all of it. His father was a giant, stern-faced man who simply draped an arm over his grieving wife's shoulders and stared straight ahead. Jude cried silently next to Aria, who squeezed his hand, so he knew he wasn't alone. Jonah, Aria, and Chase all stood numb as they digested their previous hatred for Miguel versus their grief now. He was a boy, a 16-year-old boy who was so scared to be who he was that he had ended it all. Even though they were just words to make Jude feel better in the moment, they were words that hit differently when said at the feet of a corpse. Jude hadn't spoken much since the phone call. Jude was the last one to hold Miguel's hand or kiss his lips, to utter sweet words in his ear, and when Aria called him out, she had started a countdown. Aria knew it, Jude knew it, Jonah knew it... and Chase knew it.

After the service concluded, Aunt Marnie walked, locked at the elbows with a red-eyed Jude, to her car to attend the luncheon, while Jonah and Aria headed home to feel terrible in peace. Chase caught them just as they got to the car.

"Hey, how's Jude holding up?" Chase asked genuinely.

"You mean after we jinxed Miguel to death... not great," Jonah said coldly. "Only other gay guy in this fucking shithole town, and we fucking killed him," he seemed to scold himself more than Chase. Aria saw the shake in his hands as he pulled a cigarette from his coat pocket and lit it in a cupped hand.

"He hasn't said much, honestly," Aria said as Jonah rolled his eyes as he rounded the car to the passenger side.

"Ignore him," she sighed.

"How are you?" Chase asked, "Because I... feel like shit," Chase's eyes welled with tears, but he sniffed and looked at the sky to hide them. Aria hesitated and then reached out and took his hand. His hands were balled into fists at his side, but he relaxed his grip as her fingers twined between his.

"Yeah… me too," Aria said sadly. "I called him out in front of everyone…. I…" Against her instincts, she pulled herself to Chase's chest and wrapped her arms around his waist- as much for herself as for him. Chase sighed and embraced her gratefully. He sniffed harder and seemed to gulp back a sob. Aria closed her eyes, trying to block the image of blood trickling down Miguel's shocked face. She'd never even stopped to see the edge of fear in his eyes as she implied something that no one knew. Aria sighed sadly. What had she done? After a moment, she let her hands fall away and stepped back from Chase, the rain falling onto her face again.

"Wanna hang out later and be sad together?" Chase sighed, wiping his eyes with an embarrassed chuckle, and nodded. He moved to step away but suddenly turned, leaned down, and kissed her on the forehead. Aria smelled his earth, aftershave smell, and something stirred in her. When he leaned away, Aria wiped his tears away, making him blush and shake his head in a way that was somehow a mesh of embarrassment and laughter.

"Okay, I'll see you later." Aria squeezed his hand one more time, then turned, pulled the car door open, and got behind the wheel.

Chapter Ten

Chase

HE nearly crumbled completely when she wrapped her arms around him, barely containing a sob that caught hard in his throat. Her hair smelled of conditioner and rain. He just wanted to fold into her and release this ball of sadness he'd been holding for days. He felt like he might explode and rip from the inside out. His dad had given him a wide berth and had offered surprisingly sincere condolences before leaving for the night again; bar or work, Chase wasn't sure.

Aria seemed to sense when the lump in his throat subsided enough for him to breathe again because she stepped back, and even though her eyes were ringed with exhaustion, she smiled up at him and wiped an errant tear away. The idea of just being with her later was the light at the end of this shit tunnel of a day.

Embarrassed, he wiped his eyes but couldn't stop the smile that turned up the sides of his lips. He didn't realize how alone he'd been until he felt this. This comfort in someone's presence. Her chaos brought him calm, and all she wanted was calm and safety. As their hands parted, he pulled her to him and pressed his lips lightly to her forehead, lingering a moment, dusting his lips against her skin.

She already felt like home.

Chapter Eleven

Aria

LATER that night, Chase and Aria sat on the edge of their cliff overlooking The Valley, holding hands, wishing they were better people. Aria had snuck a bottle of whisky out of Aunt Marnie's not-so-secret closet stash, and soon, the whiskey began to warm the cold pit in their stomachs. Chase took a long swallow, then set the bottle on the ground in front of them. Aria's car was parked behind them just inside the tree line, low music floating through the open windows. Aria laid back against the ground, looking up at the darkening sky, watching stars appear one by one.

"I was fucking mean to Miguel, man…" Chase slurred suddenly from beside her after a long, quiet moment.

Aria sat up on her elbows and turned to look at him, making her head spin.

"What do you mean?"

"That day at school when you…" Chase paused and looked apologetic.

"It's okay," Aria said quietly. "I hit him."

"Well, after you guys left, I was so pissed. Jude is cool, man. He literally never fucks with anybody, and I… we ALL knew about Miguel, and we didn't care. But when I saw your reaction, I thought… I ripped him apart for being such a prick to Jude, and now…" Chase put his head in his hands, elbows pointing towards the sky. "How did he not know we would've been okay with him if he came out?" Aria scooched closer, tucking herself into the space between his arm and chest, and draped her arm across his lap. After a moment, he let his hands fall from his face and wrap around her shoulders. Aria could feel the tension in his body and the heavy weight of sadness that hung around him.

"You know what I keep thinking?" Chase asked quietly.

"What?"

"That maybe I was the reason he did it," Chase said through a tight throat, the damn of tears cracking open.

Aria tilted her head up towards him, then gently wiped the tear rolling down his cheek with her index finger.

"I think it takes more than one moment to end it… but we may have been the straw that broke the camel's back," Aria admitted. "But Chase, I essentially outed him in front of everyone. It's my fault. Not yours."

Aria turned his face to hers.

"I'm serious. It wasn't your fault,"

"And it wasn't yours," Chase whispered. Aria smiled sadly.

"We both know that isn't true," She laid her head back onto his chest.

"Honestly, I don't know; life, death it all makes no sense," Aria admitted. "Sometimes I think that I shouldn't be here because my parents are gone. What made me 'worthy' of life?'" She sighed heavily, "But here I am… trudging through each day because I've got to live. But there was a while there where I had to choose to be here too, and sometimes people are just done fighting. Done hiding. They've been fighting their demons so long that they just can't fight anymore,"

The sky was rimmed in pink as the last of the daylight left The Valley, a deep, rich blue bleeding into the sky as night crept in. Aria and Chase watched the stars above and the headlights of the cars below. Just as darkness completely took over the town, Aria curled against him and closed her eyes, trying to block out the world and its ugliness.

They woke up in the woods for the second time together, except this time they weren't stranded. Aria woke to find herself snuggled against Chase with her head on his chest, his coat draped over her once more. Chase still snoozed with his arm flopped over his eyes, the sunrise highlighting the golden hue of his hair. Aria studied his face for a while, then sat up on one elbow and leaned over him carefully. She placed her hand on his chest and shook him gently, his arm falling away from his face; his eyes stuttered open, then finally focused in on her. Chase smiled at her as he pushed her hair back from her face, leaning in and kissing him gingerly. She stopped and hovered near him to gauge his reaction; he wasted no time and sat up, taking her face in his hands and kissing her deeply. She moved onto his lap, straddling him and leaning down into him. A groan escaped Chase's mouth, and he brought his hands to cup her butt. Aria pulled her shirt over her head, heat seeming to sear from her skin as his hands slid across her skin. His mouth trailed down her neck to her collarbone, and Aria's core seemed to melt as his lips skimmed the tops of her breasts. Aria needed his skin on hers; she grabbed Chase's shirt and began to tug it over his head, their mouths clashing together again after it was over her head. In a tangle of clothing and limbs, they rolled onto Aria's back, Chase braced above her. Chase kissed her with one hand behind her head to keep it off the ground. He pulled away for a moment and met her eyes, seeming to ask permission, and Aria nodded.

They were sheltered from any prying eyes, but the wilderness saw. It felt their worlds shift as they opened themselves to one another. Aria's world shifted into one where she wasn't alone in the darkness anymore. Suddenly, a door cracked open somewhere inside her, and the lonely being inside crawled toward the incoming light. She wanted to fling the door open and bathe in the sunlight coming from this new experience but also shied away from the blinding light. She'd been alone such a long time…

The sun settled on her skin as Chase pulled on his shirt. Aria tipped her face up to the sunshine, soaking in the warmth, a sigh escaping her. Chase leaned over her from behind, his face upside down to hers, and smiled as he kissed her nose. Aria smiled, the wind catching her hair and tickling it across her shoulders.

And the door inside her opened a few inches more.

***

ARIA pulled her car to a stop at the curb in front of Chase's house. An old black truck sat in the driveway, and Aria felt Chase tense next to her.

"Is it okay you didn't come home?" Aria asked.

"As long as he didn't look in my bedroom," he responded tightly. It's still early, so he's probably still passed out. It is Saturday," Chase said, looking at Aria like it was her fault they didn't sleep in.

"It was cold!" she laughed.

"Yeah, but I kept you warm," he said in a low, overly sexy tone. Aria rolled her eyes and laughed, faking gagging. He leaned over, burying his head into her neck and nuzzling into her playfully, tickling her in the process. Aria laughed and squealed against her will, then pushed him playfully away. Then they were saying goodbye with a kiss. Aria watched him walk to the front door, carefully unlock the deadbolt, and enter the dark house. The door closed behind him, and Aria let out a breath and put her car in gear. Just as she began to pull away, a commotion caught her eye. Chase's front door slammed back open, and Chase was thrown back against the door. An enormous man emerged from the darkness of the home and slapped Chase upside of his head, slamming his head to the right.

Aria saw red.

The white-hot rage exploded inside of her like a rabid animal, shrieking in a feral need to expel itself from her body. She threw her car back into the park, kicked her door open, and sprinted around the front of her car.

"HEY!" Aria screamed, stalking up to the house. "STOP!"

Chase turned, horror washing over his face.

Chapter Twelve

Chase

THE door was barely closed when the beer bottle exploded against the wall next to him, inches from his head. His dad was on him before Chase could even blink, the stench of stale beer pouring off his breath. He was almost eye to eye with his dad now, but he had a good 100 pounds on Chase and no "off" switch with the liquor still in his system. His red-ringed eyes looked like they hadn't seen sleep yet.

He grabbed Chase roughly by the collar and threw him toward the entryway of the house. The door was open a fraction, and it caught on Chase's arm as he crashed back against it, sending it flying open against the wall behind it.

Then, he heard the car door close.

No….

He heard her voice.

No!

Chase wanted to die. Wanted to shrink into himself as his eyes fell upon Aria, storming up the walk to his defense. He'd let this man bully him his entire life, and he still felt small. Still felt like a child caught in the gaze of his father's rage.

His dad's attention turned toward Aria, and panic rose like bile in Chase's throat.

Stay on me, not her.

"Fuck you," Chase spat at his father, every muscle in his body shaking as he said it. His father snapped his head back in his direction.

Yeah, look at me, asshole.

"What did you just say to me, boy?" he roared before slamming his fist into Chase's face, sending his head whipping back into the door with a crack.

Chase's vision went white, and his knees buckled beneath him as the world tilted and dropped out from beneath him. His head felt heavy and like it might split open from within. Chase's shoulders slouched back, and he slid down the door.

Someone… was here…

Who…. was yelling

My head hurts…

I'm gonna puke…

I just need to sleep…

"Chase!" someone yelled.

***

HIS head hurt.

That was the only thought spinning in his brain: how much his head hurt. Someone was talking, but it sounded like he was trying to listen through a fishbowl. Just thinking about opening his eyes made his head swim with nausea.

"Chase…"

No

"Chase…"

Nope…. Nothing good out there

"Should we move him to the couch?" a man's voice asked.

Who the fu….

Chase opened his eyes as hands began to move under his arms. He managed a grunt of protest, and the movement stopped.

"No, put him down. Chase? Chase, can you hear me?" Aria's voice floated through the sludge in his brain, and he pushed through it towards her. "Hey, can you hear me?"

"Watch the blood." Jude's voice suddenly filtered through the haze, and Chase's adrenaline spiked, and his eyes shot open.

NO!

Big mistake… Move slow, Chase.

"Hey, hey, be careful," Aria whispered, putting something cool on the right side of his face.

"What's… what's going on?" Chase rasped, "Jude, why are you here?" Suddenly, his vision cleared, and it wasn't Jude he was looking at. It was Jonah. "Ugh fuck… why are *you* here?" Chase put his hand to his head carefully, hissing when his fingers grazed the back of his head.

"I didn't know what to do after I…" Aria started, but her voice choked.

"Did what?" Chase asked, closing his eyes again. When she didn't answer, Chase lifted his head. "What happened?" A pit was forming in his stomach. Aria looked behind her, and Chase moved to sit up, with Jonah taking his arm to help. "Get the hell off of me," Chase said angrily, shaking off his assistance. He didn't need Jonah pitying him in his own damn home.

Chase sat up against gravity that felt too dense and a spinning head, and when he saw where Aria's eyes looked, he almost threw up. His dad was on the floor in the living room, bloodied head - a rock nearby spattered with blood.

Oh no...

"Aria... What did you do?"

"I..." her eyes were wide and filled with fear, a glassy void of panic, "I just... hit him." she almost sobbed.

"Look, man, she was scared, and he did a number on you," Jonah said, sounding genuinely empathetic, which only increased Chase's blood pressure further.

"Shut. Up. Jonah." Chase growled. Chase lifted himself to a sitting position and took Aria's face in his hands, tears spilling over the edges of her eyes and trickling down her face and over his thumbs. She trembled and almost pulled away at his touch. She was scared of him.

"I'm sorry... he hit you so hard... I couldn't think... I" Aria panted out between sobs.

"I'm not mad, I'm not mad," he said softly over and over again, fighting to keep his eyes open. "It's okay," he stroked his thumb against her cheek, but he had to close his eyes and lean his head back against the wall to stop the spinning. "I just need to know what happened."

"I hit him with a rock," Aria sobbed out.

"Is he alive?" Chase asked tightly, looking up at Jonah.

"Yeah, man," Jonah said quietly, "he's alive," Chase couldn't figure out why Jonah was being so fucking nice. It infuriated him. But he took a deep breath and dropped his head.

"Okay... we need to call Ted," Chase said, his chin hanging down. Ted Garcias was his dad's best friend from high school and had helped Chase before when his dad's drinking and temper had gotten out of control. He kept the foster people away and made sure Chase was taken care of when his dad couldn't… or wouldn't. "His number is in the drawer under the microwave," Chase motioned vaguely toward the kitchen.

"We need to get you off the floor first; I think you have a concussion," Aria sniffed, taking him by the arm before he could protest. Chase gritted his teeth as Jonah took the other arm and helped lift him off the ground. They shuffled around his father's unconscious body and dropped Chase onto the couch. Aria busied around the kitchen and returned with an ice pack. Jonah found the number and dialed it. Chase watched as Jonah waited for the other party to answer. Jonah jumped suddenly and covered the mouthpiece of the cordless phone.

"What the fuck, man! You had me call the COPS?!" Jonah hissed.

"It's not the cops… It's Ted. He'll help, I promise…" Chase said weakly as he laid his head back against the couch, pain burning through his skull. He closed his eyes to the pressure building inside his head. Aria put the icepack against his forehead, and the cold instantly began to relieve some of the pain behind his eyes.

***

"CHASE?" When he opened his eyes again, Ted's concerned face was the first thing he saw.

Did I fall asleep?

"Oh, thank God," Aria said, releasing a sigh of relief. "You passed out, and we couldn't get you to wake up." Aria's eyes were red and wide with fear and the remnants of tears, but somehow, her gray eyes looked even more radiant in the late morning light. Chase reached out and stroked her cheek again.

"Chase!" Ted barked, snapping him out of his stupor. "What day is it?"

I.... can't remember.

"What did you do today?" Ted asked after a lengthy silence.

Chase sifted through the haze in his mind and saw Aria sitting in the sun on the side of the mountain, her bare shoulders soaking in the morning sun. Chase looked at her.

"We... hung out," Chase said, a sly grin spreading across his face as pink crept over Aria's cheeks. He took her hand and smiled his most irresistible smile. "It was the best day ever."

"Okay, easy, kids," Ted interrupted. Jonah stood suddenly and stormed out the front door, slamming it loudly behind him. Chase noticed Aria tense again, a tension she seemed to always carry, but she had forgotten about it and set it down for a moment. When Jonah reacted, she picked it back up again.

What is that about?

"Okay, Casanova," Ted began.

"Who?" Chase joked.

"Shut up, smart ass. What did you do after... um, whatever you two did... what happened after?" Ted asked. Chase rolled his eyes.

"We got dressed," he looked to Aria quickly and smiled, "and then we... we..."

Why can't I remember?

Ted looked at Aria, who took a deep breath.

"We drove down the mountain, and I brought Chase home." She stopped and took another breath. "He came in, and I thought it was fine, but then his dad was just hitting him over and over again and..."

Ted took a breath and wiped a hand down his tan face.

"Goddamnit," Ted whispered, "Okay, then what happened,"

"I lost my temper. I yelled for him to stop, but he wouldn't. I grabbed a rock at some point and hit him in the head, and he fell." Aria's eyes filled with tears again. "He hit you so hard," Aria sniffed, looking at Chase with the saddest eyes he'd ever seen. It broke his heart.

Ted was quiet for a minute.

"When did dipshit Forrester get here?" he asked, Aria bristled at the question but stayed calm and answered.

"I called him after his dad went down, and I couldn't get Chase to wake up."

"You couldn't get Jude down here," Ted complained. In a small town, everybody knew everybody, and most of Serenity Springs preferred Jude to Jonah.

"Ted," Chase said weakly.

"He's a little tied up with grief right now," Aria clipped back, and the connection between the dead teenager and the Forrester twins was made. Ted's eyes softened, and he simply nodded.

"Here's what's going to happen," Ted began, leveling his gaze at Aria. "You were never here. You and Chase went out last night and had too much beer. Chase fell, and you're going to take him to the ER and tell them exactly that. Don't tell them you wrecked the car, or they'll want to do a report; just tell him he fell. Chase, you don't remember shit, so keep doing that," Ted sighed again and began to move to Chase's side and help him to his feet.

"What about my dad?" Chase winced as he stood.

"I figure he won't remember much either from the smell of him. We're going to let him believe he fell and hit his head. I'll make sure to spin that tale to him when he wakes up."

They gathered Chase up, Aria tucking herself under his left arm as Ted led them to the door, picking up the bloodied rock as they passed.

"Ted… my dad…" Chase started. He needed to tell Ted that his dad didn't mean it or that he did, but it wasn't his fault. All the words jumbled in his brain, and he let himself be put into Aria's car.

"I know kid…" Ted said sadly, "I know."

Chapter Thirteen

Aria

AT the hospital, a doctor finally took Chase to a room and planned to keep him overnight for observation. Exhaustion rolled through Aria's body as she pulled into her driveway and turned off the ignition. She saw Aunt Marnie's car in the driveway and couldn't decide if she was happy she was home or not. Aunt Marnie was the only piece of her mother she had left, and sometimes, the resemblance was too much. But Aunt Marnie was also sweet and centered and gave her love unconditionally at a time when that's all she really needed. Aria sighed and opened her car door with great effort, making her way up the front walk.

When she entered the house, the first thing she smelled was bacon, and her mouth immediately began to water; she hadn't eaten anything since the day before, and now her stomach rioted for sustenance. She dropped her keys and bag on the table inside the front door. Aunt Marnie's house was old, with dark woodwork and deep green walls adorned with art and plants hanging from every window. The front room led to the kitchen, which was bathed in warm light and delicious smells. Jonah caught her eye from the table as she came in, and Aunt Marnie turned.

"Aria!" She chirped happily, "There you are! Jonah said your boyfriend got hurt?" Aunt Marnie was short and blonde like Aria's mother, but that was really where the similarities ended. Her Aunt had a wild nature about her that her mother hadn't inherited. But, sometimes, the resemblance was so acute it physically hurt to look at her.

"Boyfriend…" Aria gave Jonah a hard look, but he stared back at her cooly. "Um, yeah. But I think he's going to be okay; they're keeping him for observation."

"Oh good!" she said, pulling out a chair for her. "Sit, I was just making some BFD," Jonah laughed despite himself.

"Aunt Marnie, you can't call it that," Aria laughed as she slid into the chair. "Just call it breakfast for dinner," she chuckled.

"You kids just have such dirty minds!" she tsk-tsked as she plated up some food for Jonah and Aria. She made a third plate with extra bacon and made her way to the back staircase to Jude's room, the stairs creaking as she ascended.

"How's he doing?" Aria asked quietly before shoveling a forkful of eggs into her mouth.

"How do you think?" Jonah responded, shoving an equally aggressive forkful into his mouth.

"What can we do?" Aria asked, picking up a piece of bacon and chewing thoughtfully.

"Well, for starters… not sleep with Chase fucking Gorski the day after the funeral," Jonah said, looking up and staring her right in the eye.

"Fuck you, Jonah, that has nothing to do with this," Aria's face heated, and her pulse quickened; rage wanted to crawl its way out again. Jonah was loyal to a fault, but that toxic possessiveness made Aria want to crawl out of her skin.

"Yeah, but while we're on the subject," Jonah said, stabbing his fork into his eggs again, "You did, didn't you?" The question hung in the air, but the intrusiveness did too. He didn't deserve that information and had no right to ask it.

"Why does it matter IF I did?" Aria asked, taking a tentative bite of her toast.

"Because.... It matters to me," Jonah said quietly. Aria looked up and found his gaze on her in a way that made her want to hide. She wanted to fade into the wall so he couldn't look at her like that.

"Jonah…" She didn't know what to say to him. She loved him; he was part of her life and a small part of the even smaller number of people she had left to lose in this life. He could be sweet, loyal, and honest, but not when he was like this.

Please don't make me choose.

Please don't leave me alone.

Please don't take Aunt Marnie and Jude from me.

Please.

Please.

"Please," Aria whispered as a tear streamed down her face. Her hand visibly shook now, and Jonah saw it. He stared at her for a moment, and then it was like the cloud of jealousy and misplaced emotion cleared, and he was back.

"Okay, it's okay," he said as he sat up and moved to touch her arm, but he hesitated and put his hand back in his lap.

Aunt Marnie returned to the room, a sad sigh escaping her.

"How is he?" Aria asked, wiping away her tears before her aunt could see.

"He's heartbroken, sweetheart," Aunt Marnie said sadly, "I wish I could take it away for him," she stood at the sink a moment, lost in thought, and Aria couldn't help by wonder who she was thinking of right then; her late husband, her sister, her parents, the child she lost… Aunt Marnie had faced so much tragedy and still found love in her heart to open her home to three broken teens simply because she wanted to love. Aria stood and, without thinking, wrapped her arms around her aunt's shoulders, hugging her from behind. Surprised at first, Aunt Marnie squeezed Aria's forearm and leaned her head against hers. "I took him to see the doctor, and he gave him something to calm him… Align or something. I've seen the commercials…" she trailed off.

"I'll go check on him," Aria volunteered, putting her empty plate on the counter and heading up the small back staircase. Just inside the front door, a wide staircase with ornate wooden rails and banister welcomed you up to the second floor; the back staircase was purely utilitarian - and a convenient way to sneak in and out after curfew. Not that Aunt Marnie enforced their curfew; as long as they were safe, she didn't ask questions, which Aria liked.

The small hallway was dim, with light filtering in through the lone window on the opposite end. Dust particles played in the sunbeams, giving the cramped and cluttered hallway a magical feel, though it was anything but. Aria made her way to the second door on the right - directly across from her own - and lightly knocked.

"Jude? Can I come in?" she called. From within, she heard a grunt of approval and entered the dark room.

Jude's room was normally awash in greens and blues, calming colors for his anxiety, but now, no colors could be distinguished from the others. A large blanket hung over the window, and a stale odor hung in the air, stagnant air, and self-loathing. Aria closed the door behind her and stood assessing the scene. Jude was her lifeline; he was that light in this world that everyone needed more of. He was the push to be better and the calm to a panicked situation. It was tragic in a way. Jonah absorbed so much of the darkness they had seen as kids that Jonah had been deprived of light altogether. She and Jonah both needed Jude.

"What?" Jude groaned from under his blankets.

"Just checking in on you," Aria said, pushing a questionably clean sock off his gaming chair and sitting down.

"Jude... I'm so sorry. I'm sorry I made the situation so bad that Miguel..." Aria tapered off. She'd apologized a million times, but it would never be enough. She had taken something from him she could never return.

Jude flipped back his comforter enough to reveal his tear-swollen face.

"It wasn't your fault- or maybe it was all our faults, but it doesn't matter now. He's gone, and I'm sad."

"Can I just be sad with you?" Aria asked. Jude's eyes welled, and he lifted the blanket, making room for Aria, who crawled in and curled up against him. Jude draped the blanket back over them and then reached for the remote to turn on the TV. Some stupid sitcom lit up the room, the volume low but somehow comforting.

"So, I hit Chase's dad in the head with a rock," Aria said after they'd both settled into the show.

"You did what now?" Jude said, surprised.

"Well, that was after Chase and I had sex," Aria joked.

"Wait… how long have I been in this room? Tell me everything immediately!"

"Okay, but then you have to take a shower, deal?" Aria smiled over her shoulder at him.

"We'll see how good the story is. Spill it."

***

ARIA woke to the smell of cigarette smoke. She opened her eyes to see the red ember of a cigarette across her room in the darkness. Jonah sucked on the cigarette, the cherry brightening with his inhale. He was still exhaling the smoke when he asked,

"Do you love him?"

"Maybe," Aria whispered.

Jonah glowered at her from across the room. Tugging the blanket up to her chin, she shifted uncomfortably under his gaze. After a moment, he left her room. Aria sat alone in the darkness, heart racing.

Chapter Fourteen

Dr. Robert Phillips

THESE damn kids were all sad. Sad about their parents not being "cool." Sad about their grades. Sad about whether they like boys or girls. Sad about mean kids. And where do they come when they're sad? To the Doctor! My God! So, I write them prescriptions for their little pills that will help them feel HAPPY. What the fuck is happy anyway? Life isn't all sunshine and rainbows! I have to split half of my life's earnings with a bitter bitch who's upset that I found someone better… and younger! I got the medical degree while she raised two ungrateful children who are, you guessed it, SAD! When I was a kid, I lost half my senior class to a war, but these kids are sad. It's disgusting. The only bright spot in this whole clusterfuck is that for every script I write of that Align shit, I get a nice little kickback that that bitch Connie can't touch, plus I get to stay in luxury hotels while she keeps the shitty house. Then I have this kid in town who has been peddling some samples for me to get them hooked, so they have to come get their next dose. Fucking brilliant man.

Oh my God, my next three appointments are these sad kids…. Jesus Christ, I can't wait to retire.

Chapter Fifteen

Chase

WHEN his dad showed up at the hospital to take him home, Chase sat in a tense silence in the front seat of the truck until his dad finally broke the silence.

"I uh… I'm sorry it took the hospital so long to get a hold of me. I tripped up the front steps and hit the hell outta my head."

He doesn't remember.

Chase suddenly wanted to jump across the cab and attack his father with everything he had. He couldn't even be bothered to remember that he beat the SHIT out of his own son without a second thought. But he also didn't remember Aria hitting him with a rock. Chase's hands shook suddenly from the barely contained rage coursing through him.

"Doc said you can take a few days off school. That's cool, right?" his dad said, trying to sound relaxed and relatable. Chase clenched his teeth and did his best to respond evenly.

"I'd rather go to school," he gritted out. His dad eyed him suspiciously, "I got a girl I wanna see, and tests and stuff… I'm fine,"

"Okay, son." his dad pulled out onto the main road, and they drove the rest of the way in silence.

***

CHASE saw Aria pull into the parking lot, and he was at her parking spot before her car was even in park. She opened the door and stepped up to meet his lips. Chase wrapped his arm around her thin waist, wanting to just smell her and hold her all day until all this ugliness inside of him died. Aria wrapped her arms around his waist as he drank her in.

From behind her, Jonah slammed the car door angrily.

"Aria. Let's go, we're late," he snapped.

Chase scanned the scene and noticed Jude was missing.

"Jude?" he asked.

"He just needs a couple more days. I'm taking some work home for him today," Aria said, grabbing her backpack out of the car and closing the door behind her. "And you have literally never cared about being late ever, for anything," Aria quipped at Jonah.

"Yeah, but I also don't wanna see this shit," he waved his hand vaguely at them both. Chase smiled, taking Aria's hand as they walked towards the front door of the school.

Aria and Chase slid to the side once inside the door, out of the flow of students, and leaned together against the wall.

"Are you sure you should be here? You look terrible," Aria said, putting her hand over the bruise on his face. Her cold hands felt good against his bruised skin, and he put his hand over hers, holding it to his face.

"I wanted to see you," he said, smiling.

"CHASE!!!!" a voice bellowed down the hallway. Aria stiffened and took her hand off Chase's face, but he threaded his fingers through hers before she could take it away completely. John and Drew elbowed their way across the hallway and jostled into Chase. John to his right, throwing his arm heavily over Chase's shoulders, and Drew squeezed between Chase and the wall.

"What the hell happened to you?" John laughed, hitting him on the chest. Drew laughed and then looked over at Aria.

"Well, who do we have here?" he smiled, "Chase, you've been busy. You said you weren't gonna mess with the Orphan Girl."

"Yeah, 'lots of 'baggage' I thought," John sneered.

What.

The.

Fuck.

Not only had Chase not said that, he had explicitly told them no one else better even look in her direction, or he would murder them. Why the hell would they say obviously untrue shit in front of her? Slowly, Chase watched Aria's face drop in embarrassment, her face reddening in anger. She dropped his hand.

"Aria, I…." Chase began.

You sound guilty.

"No, that's not…"

"Go to hell, Chase," Aria said. Then she turned, disappearing down the hall.

Chase spun on Drew, throwing him against the wall, sending the nearby trash can sprawling across the floor.

"What the fuck Drew?!" Chase yelled. John tried to put himself between the two, but Chase pushed him aside like he was nothing.

"Dude, calm down,"

"I never said that. What the hell?" Chase growled.

"We had to!" Drew yelled. Chase stopped trying to push past John.

"What does that mean?" Chase growled.

"Look, bro, she's trouble. Fuck she's here a week, and Miguel is dead; you're blinded by that ass dude."

Chase stood perfectly still for a moment, like a spring stretched completely taught. His friends had betrayed him. The only anchor he had to anything, but anger had been cut away because of these two sons of bitches. Without warning, Chase swung his fist and cracked John across the jaw and then went for Drew. A crowd gathered around them as Chase swung on Drew. Someone pulled them apart, and Chase turned for the doors; he threw the front doors of the school open and left without a second thought or a look at his friends. This day had officially gone to shit, and he was done.

***

CHASE jumped up the porch steps and knocked lightly on the front door. After waiting several minutes, he knocked again, louder this time. Finally, he heard the door unlock, and it swung open.

"What are you doing here?" Jude asked, squinting at the sunlight.

"I just… do you wanna hang out?" Chase asked. Jude cocked an eyebrow, then looked down at his rumpled PJS and shrugged. Jude stepped out of the way, and Chase stepped in. Jude shut the door behind him and motioned to Chase to follow him into the front room. Chase could tell Jude hadn't been out of bed in a long time; he couldn't remember ever seeing him this disheveled.

"So... what's up?" Jude asked, flopping down on the dark green easy chair.

Your cousin.

My dad.

My piece of shit friends.

My guilt...

"I'm sorry. I didn't know he was so far down," Chase said, "I knew he was in the closet, everyone kind of did, but I didn't know he was so fucking lost that he could do this. I was his friend! I should've known." it was like purging the poison.

"To be honest, I didn't either." Jude responded quietly, "We hadn't been seeing each other long; we weren't in love. But it was *something*, something good. It hurt when he turned on me and outed me. I think I am mourning who I thought he was or maybe the possibility of who he could've been. Who WE could've been." Jude sighed, "How do I go back to a school now that everyone knows my biggest secret and thinks I'm the villain in some tragic love story?"

"Well," Chase actually laughed, "That, at least, you don't have to worry about; they're all blaming Aria. You are 100% secure as the heartbroken lover."

"Oh shit," Jude hissed, "How bad is it?"

"Um... pretty fucking bad. And I'm not sure she's going to talk to me again."

"Eh," Jude shrugged, "Just give her a minute." Jude was quiet a moment like he was considering something, "She didn't leave her room the entire first month she was here." he looked at Chase with a pained expression, "When she got here... she cried for days. I didn't know she knew how to smile. But now, she does… because of you, and I don't want that to stop. If she hadn't met you, Jonah would've eventually suffocated her. He still could."

"What's up with him?" Chase asked honestly.

"He's just… messed up, man. Saw too much shit too young," Then Jude noticed Chase's face, "What happened to your face?" Chase sighed heavily.

"That's a longer conversation,"

"I got time," Jude shrugged. Chase smiled.

"Fine, but you gotta shower, not to be rude, but… Wow!" Chase laughed.

Jude smiled and submitted.

"Ya know what? That's fair. Don't go anywhere." Jude headed up the front steps, "Oh! Make pizza rolls!"

Pizza rolls sounded amazing.

Chapter Sixteen

Aria

SHE knew she shouldn't have trusted him. She knew it was all bullshit, the pull of the electricity between them. It was all bullshit.

Aria stalked the halls to the back wing where Jonah's locker was located and found him just as he slammed it closed. He looked up and greeted her with a surprised look.

"Don't you have Chem?"

"Wanna get out of here?" she asked.

"Yep," Jonah said without hesitation. He threw his locker back open and snatched his bag. "What are we avoiding?"

"Chase," Aria ground out the words. Jonah was the last person she needed shit from right now.

"Okay, I'm definitely in now!" Jonah smiled, and despite herself, Aria smiled too. Jonah was who she needed right now. Together, they left school through the back door.

***

WHISTLER Falls was part of a cave system deep in the high country where roads disappeared and aspen trees took over the totality of the landscape. Within the trees was a jutting of rocks that funneled the snow melt down into a crystalline mountain lake. The falls split into two streams, and behind the larger of the twin falls, you could access one of the openings to a system of caves that splintered off into the mountain. Jonah climbed ahead of her up the slick rocks, reaching back to take her hand and help her up to him. The entrance was slick, and her sneakers slipped as she scrambled up into the hole. During the summer, she and the twins had taken flashlights and twine and tried to see how far the caves went, but upon finding a recently used den of a very large animal, they vowed never to trek that far in again. So, she and Jonah settled into the alcove of the cave. Jonah took out his bag of weed and dutifully began rolling a joint.

"So, you gonna tell me what happened?" he said, not looking up.

"Are you going to give me shit about it?" Aria said, chewing her nails.

"Not this time," Jonah said, looking up at her. "I'll make you a deal," he motioned vaguely around them. "This is the cave of no judgment. What is said in the cave shall have no judgment passed upon it," he smiled.

"Okay, deal," Aria sighed, "I think Chase was bullshit,"

"I could've told you that!" Jonah laughed,

"Jonah!" Aria scolded, "You said no judgment."

"Okay, okay, I'm sorry," Jonah said, yielding and returning to his paper and marijuana.

"His friends said Chase said I had too much baggage," she said with sneer. "But I really thought he didn't care… I really thought…" she trailed off as her eyes welled with tears.

Jonah sighed then slid the joint across his tongue, rolled it between his fingers then twisted it a final time. He leaned back, retrieving a lighter from his pocket, and sighed as he flicked the lighter and touched the flame to the end. As he exhaled a plume of smoke, he handed the joint to Aria,

"You're too cool for him anyway."

"That doesn't help me at all," she put the joint to her lips and inhaled.

"I know. I am sorry you got hurt." He reached over, took the joint again, and looked sad. "But I won't say I'm sorry you ditched him."

"What's with you two?" Aria asked, holding in her hit.

"I don't know… Chase has never liked me."

Aria could tell there was something more to the story, but as the weed hit her brain, she decided she didn't care what it was. It was done anyway.

"Now everyone will hate me for Chase and Miguel," she said quietly.

"That was not your fau…" Jonah started.

"Yeah, yeah…" she quipped, "But I sure as hell didn't help things,"

"The Chase shit will die down, and eventually, people will move on from Miguel. Not everyone. You're not alone. Who knows, maybe somebody else already has their eye on you,"

That look. She knew that look in his eye, and she didn't like it. Maybe she was just high, but he watched her with such fervent intensity it made her want to wilt. He stared at her for a long, silent moment that stretched between them.

"I'm hungry. Let's go home," Aria said, standing too quickly and needing to sit down again for a moment. She let the buzz of the pot settle so she could stand. Jonah moved to take her arm, but she tried to turn nonchalantly and move away without being awkward. The thought of his touch made her skin crawl.

But this was Jonah. He loved her and protected her.

Didn't he?

Chapter Seventeen

Chase

"WHAT is he doing here?!" Aria demanded as she entered the front door.

"Aria, hold on. You need to hear him out," Jude stood, holding his hands out in front of him like he was taming a tiger. And Aria might have been one as her face reddened, Chase seeing that rage dancing behind her stormy eyes. Jonah entered after her.

"Oh, hell no!" He almost laughed as he dropped his bag and ran up on Chase, who met him eye to eye, rising from the couch to do so.

"Wo! Jonah, hold on!" Jude yelled, sweat breaking out over his brow.

"What the hell do you mean to hold up J-," Jonah began, but when he turned to look at Jude, he stopped. "Jude, did you shower?"

Jude rolled his eyes.

"Yes… I showered. Can we all calm down now?" Jude looked at Aria, who was still seething by the front door. "Aria, Chase came here to make sure I was okay. He's the only one in this town that's even given a shit, doesn't that count for something?"

Aria seemed to fight the logic, and her mouth tightened.

Please just talk to me

"Jonah, back off. Let him talk," Jude said quietly, and to Chase's utter shock, he did. Jonah backed up and plopped in a chair by the window. But Aria stood like a statue in the doorway. Chase's heart raced, and he began to talk without knowing what he was going to say.

"John and Drew are pricks. They saw you go after…" He looked at Jude apologetically. "Miguel and… they wanted to get me away from you." Chase bit out the last few words. It hurt to say.

"Bullshit," she spat back.

"Aria," Chase began and took a step towards her.

"Ah ah ah pretty boy," Jonah warned.

"And what the fuck are you gonna do, asshole?" Chase snapped at Jonah.

"Protect me," Aria said in a voice like solid steel.

"Fine," Chase said. "You don't believe me? Then let's go."

"Go where?" Aria scoffed.

"John's house," Chase said, stomping towards the door, daring Jonah to make a move.

Just give me a reason fucker

"Come on, you're driving," Chase said, flinging open the screen door, holding it open, and waiting for Aria to make up her mind. Aria looked confusedly at Jude and Jonah.

"Go!" Jude said.

"No!" Jonah barked.

"Shut up! This is not about you!" Jude yelled.

Everyone was quiet, waiting for Jonah to respond to the slight, but he only stood and left the room. Aria blinked and looked at Chase.

"If I go with you, how do I know you won't just humiliate me with your friend?" she asked in a small voice.

I hadn't considered that as a concern.

"Because I wouldn't do that to you. Ever." Chase almost laughed at the ridiculousness of it. "Aria, I just want to be with you. Please come with me," he pleaded.

After a moment, Aria silently walked through the door and down the front steps.

Thank you!

Chapter Eighteen

Aria

ARIA'S hands shook as she followed Chase's direction to John's house. She immediately regretted her decision to come here upon pulling into the driveway. John didn't live far from them, but in a newer subdivision with shiny homes.

She hated shiny things.

Chase opened the car door, walked up the cobblestone path to the front door, and knocked without hesitation. Aria slowly got out and stopped at the beginning of the walkway.

John answered the door in a hoodie and basketball shorts, and Aria almost choked when she saw his eye. It was swollen completely shut and the ugliest shade of reddish purple she'd ever seen.

"What the hell do you want?" John asked gruffly.

"I want you to tell Aria why you said that shit," Chase commanded.

"Hell no. That bitch is crazy!" John laughed. Chase grabbed him by the front of the hoodie and almost lifted him off the ground.

"I don't give a fuck what you think about her, you are going to tell her the truth right goddamn now," Chase snarled.

Aria didn't like him like this. He was too much like Jonah like this.

"Fine!" John yelled, "Chase never said that he wasn't going to mess with you, we made that shit up so you'd leave him alone! I don't want to lose another friend," John said tightly. Chase's temper seemed to cool at that, and he released his grip on him. John pushed him off and smoothed the front of his hoodie. "I'm sorry! Fuck! But I lost a friend, too!" John looked away, embarrassed by the tears welling in his eyes.

"I'm sorry," Aria said genuinely. "I didn't want that to happen."

"I know," John said solemnly, "Look, we're not gonna sing kumbaya or anything. I still don't like you… Just don't…" he trailed off, but the words hung unspoken in the air:

Don't hurt Chase.

"I won't." Aria couldn't breathe around the lump in her throat. Her heart was still racing, and she didn't know what to believe. She'd hurt so many people with one action, like a ripple across a lake. She couldn't be here anymore. Aria turned and started for the car again. She heard Chase say something rushed to John, and then he was sliding into the passenger seat again. Aria didn't start the car. She couldn't.

"I hurt so many people," she finally said aloud.

"Aria, it isn't your fault," Chase said, putting his hand over hers, and God, it felt good to feel his touch. Suddenly, tears were pouring from her eyes down her cheeks, her head falling into her hands. She felt Chase's hand on her back as sobs wracked her body.

"I'm sorry," she coughed out amongst the tears.

"I know. We all are," Chase said softly.

Once the tears had seemed to subside, Aria started the car and put it in gear. She didn't know where they went from here, but she had to start with something, so she drove with Chase.

***

THE nightmare was different this time. She was in the road staring at the carnage of her parent's car crash. The blue two-door on its hood, broken glass everywhere, her mother's open eyes... And Miguel, laying amongst the wreckage, blue and purple with an angry red rope burn around his neck.

"No," Aria said.

But the image didn't fade; suddenly, she was standing next to Miguel, his blood touching her sneakers. Her father's twisted frame creaked against the dented metal of the car.

"Arrrrrriiiiiiiaaaaa" Her mother's voice called.

"No," Aria said again, struggling to find the escape to consciousness, but the dream was suffocating her; she was drowning in guilt and grief and anger and couldn't see the door anymore. She couldn't find her way out. She gasped for breath and screamed for someone to help her. Get her out of here, find her, save her!

"ARIA!" Jonah's voice yelled.

I hear him!

Aria threw herself awake, sitting up still gasping for breath, tearing at her throat like someone was choking her.

"Aria," Jonah's face came into view. He held her face in his hands, and she crumpled against him. She threw her arms around her cousin and sobbed for all the hurt she felt and all the hurt she had caused. She didn't know how to breathe with the weight of it all.

"Hey, you're okay. You're safe," Jonah said quietly, enveloping her in a hug.

"No, I'm not," she cried miserably, "I am not okay."

Chapter Nineteen

Chase

WHEN Jonah's voice came through the phone, Chase almost hung up, but then he listened. Then he was out the door, running the seven blocks to her house.

Her room was dark, but he felt his way to her bed. As his eyes adjusted to the light, he saw her. She was curled in a ball, sobbing into her knees in the middle of her bed; Chase's heart split into a million tiny pieces at the sight. He looked back at the door where Jonah stood quietly. Chase could see the jealousy in his eyes, but he also saw the raw concern for Aria painted across his face. Chase took a deep breath and got on the bed, scooping Aria into his arms; he brought her to his chest. Aria curled into him and began sobbing harder.

I didn't think a person could be this sad.

Chase glanced at the doorway and Jonah had disappeared.

"Shhh," Chase said, stroking her hair.

"NO!" Aria yelled, "You need to get away from me! I can't!" She cried harder, and her words jumbled into just her screaming how she couldn't do it again. She pushed against him and writhed in his arms, Chase held fast and rode out the storm with her. He cried with her and for her. Is this what the twins had seen all summer? Is this how she'd spent her first weeks here? Paralyzed by grief and fear of losing someone else?

Miguel's death and her guilt had triggered it all over again, and Chase wanted to rip his heart out of his chest to replace her broken one.

"I'm sorry," Aria mumbled miserably into his chest when the worst of it had passed.

"Don't apologize," Chase whispered.

"Why are you here?" she asked sadly. "You should hate me,"

"Well, I don't." He said matter of factly. "I'm here because I need you to be okay. So, I will wait it out with you."

"What if I'm like this forever?" Aria sniffed.

"Then forever it is Freckles," Chase said as Aria slid her arms around his waist and squeezed him back. His heart unclenched as her skin warmed against him. He pulled her closer and tucked her head under his chin.

Forever it is.

Chapter Twenty

Garrett

GARRETT walked along the cold sidewalks of Denver, steam puffing from his lips as he exhaled. He was tired. He thought of his shitty twin-sized bed longingly but pushed on; he had one more stop to make. He'd been collecting samples of a new depression drug from the shadier doctors in; he had studied the chemical compounds online, and he was fascinated.

Garrett was a smart kid, so smart that he earned a scholarship to a gifted school and graduated early, earning a place at MIT… where he got caught making meth in the basement of the dorms. His case didn't go unnoticed, and one night, he was approached by Carlos, who gave him a lot of money to do it again. And again. And again. But now he was on to something even better. If he could break down the Align to its base components and mix it with a microdose of LSD, it would be better than ecstasy. The party kids would love it.

Garrett turned the corner and saw the ridiculously new Corvette parked along the curb. This particular doctor was an unimaginable douchebag, and he had to suppress his laugh when the window rolled down, revealing a dark head of hair where last week there had definitely been a silver one. This guy was pathetic.

"Where's the cash?" The doc griped.

"Here, man, take it," Garrett quipped, tossing the cash into his lap and then holding his hand out expectantly. The doctor inspected the money, then shoved a brown paper grocery bag into his hands. "Nice hair doc."

"Piss off, shithead," he threw the car into gear and peeled out; Garrett stepped away and laughed as he watched the car speed down the street.

"What a douche,"

Chapter Twenty-One

Aria

CHASE had gotten suspended for giving John the blackeye, and his dad, in turn, had given him a matching one. Aria had to fight the urge to take a rock to him again, but Chase had been adamant he was fine. Aria knew his dad worked today, so during second hour, she had Jude and Dana cover for her as she slipped out the side door and ran to her car. When she got to Chase's house, she'd parked down the road, making sure the big black truck was absent from the driveway. Aria made her way around the back of the house and knocked on the back door. She heard scrambling inside, and then the door flew open to reveal a sleepy-eyed, hair-tossed Chase, and heat lit in Aria's core.

"Hey, Freckles," he grinned. Aria put her hand on his chest and pushed him back as she entered the house and closed the door behind her. Chase didn't take his eyes off of her, the purple bruise on his left eye made his blue eyes seem brighter. Aria put her hand to his head, lightly touching the black eye with her thumb. Chase took her hand, putting it to his cheek, leaning into her touch. Her heart raced, and her skin flushed as he closed his eyes and relaxed into her hand.

When he opened his eyes again, Aria stepped closer, bringing her mouth to his gently.

"Are you sure you're okay?" Aria whispered, parting.

"You're here… I'm amazing," Chase said, taking her by the chin and bringing her lips back to his.

This time, Aria devoured him. All the sadness and anxiety of the last few days came out in a fury of kisses and the desperate need for touch. Moving down the hallway to Chase's room Aria let her flannel fall off her shoulders to the floor, a tank top underneath. Chase ripped his shirt over his head as they nearly fell through the doorway into the bedroom. Chase slammed the door closed behind them as Aria fell backward on the bed and kicked her shoes to the side. Chase leaned over her and just stared at her; she stared back, wanting nothing but to exist in these moments. When they could both hide from everything dark in the world. Aria reached up and ran her hands through his sleep-mussed hair and decided it was her favorite Chase Look. She pulled him to her, and together, they hid from the world.

After, they lay in Chase's bed holding hands hidden under the sheets.

"Wanna go to homecoming with me?" Chase asked quietly.

"Yeah… I don't want to end up with pig's blood on me, thanks," Aria joked darkly.

"I'm serious. It's still a month away. Things will calm down," Chase reassured her.

"Chase…" Aria began in a way that said she'd go with him to hell and back, but not to a school dance when he sat up on his elbows and begged with his eyes. HUGE blue pools of sadness begging her to be his date. "Okay, that isn't fair," she laughed. "You're entirely too adorable for that not to work."

"Does that mean you'll go with me?" Chase smiled.

"Fine. Chase Gorski I will go to homecoming with you," Aria laughed as Chase smiled broadly and leaned down and kissed her.

"Thank you. It's going to be fine, I promise," Chase said against her cheek.

You can't promise that.

***

IT'D been a long month, but she'd made it. Everyone had mostly stopped whispering about her in the halls and class. Dana had tried to tell her to ignore them, but when Dana overheard a pair of preps (as she called them) talking about Aria, Dana had lost her mind and ended up with detention. Aria mainly hid amongst the twins and Chase, who seemed to be a buffer between her and Miguel's friends. John and Drew wouldn't even look at her, which she thought may have been worse than the whispering. Being invisible was its own kind of hell.

Homecoming was tonight, and Aria was a ball of nerves. The idea of walking into the dance and every single pair of eyes falling on her made her sick to her stomach. Aunt Marnie had taken her and the twins shopping for the dance, and Aria had found a form-fitting black spaghetti-strap dress and shoes at the first consignment shop, and the twins got some suit jackets at the second and called it good.

It must be nice being a guy.

Aunt Marnie curled Aria's hair with old steam curlers and then twisted it up in a soft updo. Aria stared at herself in the mirror and wished her mother was there. Aunt Marnie seemed to sense her thoughts because she kissed her cheek and smiled.

"You look just like your mother did on our prom night," she said, her voice choking.

"Thank you, Aunt Marnie," Aria whispered, tears filling her eyes.

"Hey," Jonah said, stepping into the bedroom doorway. He stopped for a minute, blinking at Aria.

"Jonah, don't be rude," Aunt Marnie chided.

"I wasn't. I... You look beautiful," Jonah smiled, then kissed Aunt Marnie on the cheek. "We have to go though,"

"Fine, fine. Wait, let me take some pictures before you kids leave," Jude groaned loudly from the hallway, but they all stood smiling on the front porch for her moments later.

Dana was meeting them at the door so they could all walk in together. Aria knew it was for her benefit, but Dana had insisted it was because she didn't have a date and thought everyone would talk about her. In truth, several guys had asked Dana, but she'd said no to all of them. Her gaze seemed to linger on Jonah as they met her outside the school.

"Well, look at you," she said to him. "You clean up good, Jonah," she said, smiling at him.

What is happening?

Jonah seemed just as taken aback but quickly recovered.

"Someone has to show these slobs how to dress," he smiled, offering his arm to her. Dana accepted with a flirty grin.

Chase slipped his hand into Aria's.

"We got this," he said, looking down at her and giving her that grin of his.

"If you say so," Aria sighed heavily, trying to bolster her courage. Chase leaned down and kissed her.

"Okay, let's go. Fifth wheel here," Jude joked, pushing them both through the door.

There was no record scratching silence when they entered the gym. In fact, no one seemed to notice she and Chase. Jonah and Dana were currently attracting way more attention as they swept off to the dance floor.

"When did that happen?" Chase asked.

"I have no idea," Aria laughed.

"Well, whatever gets him to quit obsessing over you," Chase grumbled.

"Chase!" Aria hissed.

"Okay, sorry," He laughed, holding up his hands in defeat. "Let's dance," He pulled her lightly, and she fell against him, wrapping herself around his arm, hoping it protected her.

Aria's heart raced as she wrapped her arms around Chase's neck, and his hands slid around her waist; they swayed slowly to the music. She felt a hand slowly sinking to her butt, and she shot him a playful look. Aria dropped one hand and grabbed his ass and squeezed back.

"Oh, it is nice, though," she teased.

"Okay, young lady," Chase laughed, putting her arm around his neck again. He leaned down and put his forehead to hers, and it was like they were the only two in the room.

Aria closed her eyes and imagined them alone, dancing among the balloons and streamers, with no one to watch or judge or whisper about them. It was only the two of them, alone in the world of new love and a forever promise. She smelled his earth and aftershave scent with a hint of cologne that stirred her. As they danced, Chase moved his head down, and she felt the whisper of his lips on hers

"Forever Freckles," his breath carried his words to the corner of her lips, and as he slid his lips lightly over her mouth, she breathed,

"Promise?"

His answer was a kiss so sweet that Aria wanted to cry. He slid his hand up to the nape of her neck and drew her closer to him but pulled away before they sank any deeper into the moment. Aria put her head against Chase's chest, and between the music and his heartbeat, she'd found her new favorite sound. The steady *thump thump thump* of Chase.

Please don't let me break him.

Chapter Twenty-Two

Chase

CHASE was happy.

He dropped Aria at her door, kissing her again, looking into her rainstorm eyes, and never wanting to look away.

He said goodnight and went home.

The next three days were the worst of his life.

Chapter Twenty-Three

Aria

JONAH had been busier than usual for whomever it was he worked for in Denver; they demanded he bring another person in case someone were to jump him and try to steal the shipment, and since Aria was bored, she tagged along. Though what she would do in the unlikely event they were robbed, she wasn't sure. Maybe there would be a rock nearby… she laughed darkly to herself.

They pulled into the parking lot of a shady apartment complex, and Aria immediately regretted coming.

"Just stay by me, okay?" Jonah whispered as they started up the steps. The apartment door was open, and a group of intimidating men hovered just outside the door.

"Sup, Jonah?" One guy with a huge beard said, "Who is this?" The guy sneered, stepping in front of Aria, splitting them up. Jonah spun on the guy who outweighed him by at least 100 pounds without a hint of fear.

"Back the fuck up, Dom! She ain't here for that!" Jonah growled up at him. To Aria's surprise, the man backed off. Jonah pushed his hair back from his face, a nervous habit Aria had noticed. "C'mon, Aria," he took her by the upper arm and pushed them into the apartment.

The interior was dim even in the light of the afternoon, the coffee table was covered in pot pipes and seeds, razor blades and a hash rig.

"Jonah, sup my man!" a dark-haired man said from the stove. He was Latino in his late 40's; he wore normal khakis and a polo shirt while happily stirring something that smelled amazing on the stove. Jonah greeted him and they did some handshake that Aria didn't try and copy.

"So, who is the girl?" Carlos asked.

"This is my… cousin? Sister? Aria" Jonah had lightened up considerably being away from the group outside.

"Sister cousin? What the fuck you into man?" Carlos laughed, "I'm kidding, I remember you telling me about her" he turned his attention to Aria, "I am very sorry about your parents mija, You both have had so much tragedy for being so young," Aria smiled and thanked him but her eyes wandered to the pan on the stove as her stomach growled.

"Sorry," she laughed, wrapping her arms around her stomach, "He wouldn't stop to eat on the way here." Aria laughed.

"Well, Jonah knows not to be late," Carlos said seriously, "Come, sit down and eat,"

"No, that's okay," Aria began, but before she could finish, Carlos was ushering her to the table and plating her up rice and beans and some type of chicken. Before she could stop herself, she was shoveling the food into her mouth and moaning as the flavors hit her tongue. "This is delicious!" she said to Carlos, who clapped happily and then excused himself and Jonah to do business. Aria hungrily scooped the meal into her mouth, happy for an excuse to turn a blind eye to their dealings.

Carlos and Jonah came back out a few minutes later, Jonah holding a backpack. Aria took her cue, politely finishing her meal then neatly placing her plate in the sink. She did NOT want to be rude in this man's house.

"Bump before you go?" Carlos said, motioning to the mirror on the table with several thin white lines of powder waiting.

"Um," Aria started.

"Nah, she doesn't partake," Jonah tried to say lightly.

"I insist," Carols growled. "It is a house rule," He handed a rolled-up dollar bill to her, and the dangerous look in his eyes told her if she refused, she'd be killed for being a narc. She looked around the room, suddenly aware of how outnumbered she and Jonah were... and she was the only girl in the room. Nodding in agreement, she tied her hair back behind her neck and took the rolled-up bill, and tucked it inside the rim of her nostril, pinching the other nostril closed and sniffed.

Pain pinched at her sinuses behind her eyes but that was quickly erased by a wave of numbed bliss. It was feeling everything at once but also feeling nothing. She smiled and motioned to move the rolled-up bill to her other nostril to take on another line, but Carlos actually stopped her.

"Mija, let's stay on the bunny slope, huh?" Aria cocked her eyebrow, "Ugh, flatlanders... you do too much, you will overdose and die,"

"Oh gotcha... Okay," Aria said as her throat went numb and another wave rushed through her as she sniffed back whatever was left in her nostrils. Carlos motioned for her to wipe her nose, and she giggled. Giggled! Chase and cocaine had that effect on her apparently.

Her body felt awake and ready and numb but fuzzy.

"Okay, we gotta go, come on, Aria," Jonah pushed her toward the door, grabbing the bag of his inventory from the floor.

"Wait!" Aria spun, "Can I buy some to take with me?" Carlos smiled and opened and metal box on the table took out a small round white ball and walked over to her, putting it in her hand.

"It's on me this time. Enjoy, mija," Carlos smiled at Jude, "She's going to be fun!" he smiled, slapping Jonah on the back.

The ride home felt like a blurred flight; Aria talked to Jonah about Carlos and how nice he was, about Chase and how much she really liked him and really felt he could be the thing she needed to pull herself out of her hole. But she also talked about Jonah and Jude and Aunt Marnie and how she loved them and was so lucky to have these brothers just given to her when she was at her lowest.

She felt amazing.

Aria loved this feeling.

She never wanted it to end.

She forgot about her parents and that hollow feeling in her soul.

She forgot about Chase and not breaking his heart.

Luckily, the coke was numbing that too.

In what seemed like 30 minutes, they pulled off the highway from the 3-hour drive. They drove straight home, but when they pulled into the driveway, Jonah got nervous.

"Don't tell Jude about the coke," he seemed to think for a moment, "You know you could sell it, make some easy cash,"

Something twisted in Aria, the part that had awakened at the blessed numbing of the pain, and the trauma suddenly didn't seem so traumatic. This thing smiled and made Aria close her fist around the eight ball of cocaine.

"Jonah, what's up with you?" Aria whined, "why are you brooding,"

"I am NOT brooding," Jonah scoffed, then released a laugh, his shoulders relaxing as he did. "Okay, I'm slightly broody, but I don't want you getting into this shit," Aria rolled her eyes and scoffed right back at him.

"I am so freaking sick of boys telling me what not to do so I won't get hurt like I'm made of fucking porcelain. Like I might break! I'M ALREADY BROKEN JONAH! Let me worry about what I do, okay?"

Jonah nodded after a moment, and they lapsed into a weird silence until Aria suddenly needed music and needed to find the perfect song.

"Can we do more?" Aria asked like an excited kid, then she had a thought, "Chase… is going to be pissed…oh my god, we can't tell him either. We're supposed to hang out later".

Jonah grunted, but Aria was already talking again; it was like a stream of words dripping constantly through a numb mouth and throat.

"I think I might love him, Jonah. I should call him. Wait! Can we do some more? What are we going to do now?"

Jonah seemed to consider something, then smiled.

"I have an idea…"

Chapter Twenty-Four

Chase

ARIA didn't answer her phone that night.

Aria wasn't at school on Monday.

Or the next day.

Or the next….

***

DANA hadn't seen Aria, and Jonah hadn't texted her since the dance.

Chase called Jude, but he hadn't seen her or Jonah in two days.

Fucking Jonah.

On the third night, he finally spotted Aria's car parked at the rental cabins near the river notorious for drugs; in fact, Jonah sold a lot here.

I am going to kill him.

Jonah answered the door, Chase pushing past him immediately spotting Aria on the couch. She was dark-eyed and wired.

"Chase?" Aria smiled tiredly.

Her pupils are fucking huge.

I gotta get her out of here.

"What's she on?" Chase asked Jonah tightly.

"A few things," Jonah giggled. The motherfucker giggled.

Chase took a steadying breath and scooped Aria up like she weighed nothing into his arms.

"Nuh uh, Pretty Boy, you aren't taking her with you!" Jonah said, straightening like he was going to stop him. Then, he promptly fell sideways into the wall.

"Yeah. I am." Chase corrected and left.

***

JUDE helped Chase get her in bed, and after finally convincing her it was time to sleep and tucking her in, she closed her eyes. Chase and Jude quietly stepped into the hallway.

"What is going on, Jude?" Chase hissed.

"I don't know. She was better, but she went on a run with Jonah, and that's the last I heard from them,"

"Oh my god," Chase groaned rubbing his hands down his face. He was exhausted and pissed off. "Fuck, this girl might break me," then his stomach dropped as he heard the creak of a door. He spun to see Aria standing in the doorway, stormy eyes wide and angry.

"So, it was bullshit?" She rasped.

"No, Aria, that's not..." Chase and Jude both started, but she slammed the door in both of their faces.

I cannot catch a break.

Chapter Twenty-Five

Aria

LINDSEY Fitzgerald's house was a massive 8-bedroom mansion cut into the south edge of Church Canyon. It was Saturday evening, Aria and the twins walked up giant polished stone steps through an oak entryway. The foyer was all shiny stone and huge log pillars. Aria wanted to ask if she should take her shoes off, but since Kyle Landry was currently vomiting on the same shiny floor, she figured she was good. She found an assortment of cheap liquor bottles on the kitchen counter and mixed something resembling a Long Island iced tea as she perused others in attendance. Scott Whatshisname handed her a joint, she heard the word "laced" but didn't care. Then she felt that numb, that beautiful white numbness of coke twined within the smoke of the weed. She turned to see Chase walking across the hallway. stopping when he saw her. Joint in hand and skin buzzing from the cocaine within it, her eyes locked with his.

He'd said she was going to break him. And she wasn't sure if she was mad at him for saying it or hurt that he was right. She was too broken.

Fuck him.

Aria took another hit of the joint and angrily took a shot of something close by and flipped him off as she left the room. She spied Dana mingling with a group of theater kids in the front room, second living room? Either way, she went to join Dana, who squealed when she saw her.

"There you are! Where's Jonah?" Dana asked obviously a couple of drinks in already.

"Do you like him, Dana?" Aria asked, but Dana only shrugged coyly.

"He's here somewhere, come on…" Aria laughed, throwing one last heated glance over her shoulder at Chase.

Chapter Twenty-Six

Chase

ARIA'S here.

> *Get your shit together, Chase!*
> *She is spiraling…*
> *Is it my problem?*
> *Yeah… it is.*

Chase watched Aria from afar and saw the way her walk got droopier; her voice got louder, and her reactions got slower. She was easy to spot in the giant orange hoodie she'd drawn on in Chem class. He'd doodled on it too that day. She'd laughed at his bad drawing but proclaimed it her favorite. He shook his head.

Chase had to talk to Aria tonight; Ted had pulled some strings and got him a spot at a police academy in Denver so he could finish high school and be free from his dad. But he left soon. Too soon. Ted had gotten the okay two days ago; he was running out of time.

Goddamnit Chase

Chase had been so deep in thought he hadn't noticed Sophie Jenkins rounding the corner and almost collided with her. She called him an asshole and pushed past him.

And then Aria was gone.

Damn that girl!
This is stupid.

Why am I doing this?

Chase swiped a beer from a nearby table and chugged it greedily. He didn't need to play babysitter. He was done chasing her when she ran at the first sign of concern from him. He spotted Aria outside with a cigarette in her hand and crossed his arms.

No. I'm not going out there.

She can calm down and talk to me. She took off on me. Everything was fine, then SHE ghosted me.

He took another swig of beer, and even though he fought every step, he began marching towards her.

I'm so weak.

She saw him approach and held up a hand.

"No, I can't. I can't focus on this," she motioned between them, "right now,"

"Aria, you are super fucked up; let me take you home," Chase reached for her, but she snatched her hand back and shook her head.

"I'll just cry," she mumbled and wandered into the house.

Okay. I'm out. I tried.

He stayed where he was and took another long swig of his beer.

"You better fix that shit Chase; I told her you weren't an asshole," Dana said, emerging from the darkness, Jonah ducking away from the same shadows.

"Yeah, yeah, yeah," Chase groaned. "I know,"

***

THE party had started to reach the point of the evening where people paired off and disappeared into unknown rooms to mess around, but here Chase was chasing Aria! His resolve to not babysit had lasted all of five minutes when he rationalized he was protecting her. All he wanted to do was protect her. The ever-present thorn in his side, the eternal pain in his ass, Aria, the girl he would love forever.

Two bedroom doors led to embarrassing reveals, and curse words spit in his direction. So at the third door, Chase paused and almost turned away. But at the last second, he pushed it open anyway.

Jonah was on the bed with a girl. Chase started to apologize again and slink back into the hallway when the color of the girl's hoodie caught Chase's attention. And the permanent marker on the sleeve…

Aria has a hoodie just like that… she was wearing a hoodie just like that…

Then he saw the girl's head lob to the side, unconscious and unaware.

Aria

I'm going to kill him.

Jonah's lips were pressed to Aria's, and he dragged his lips across her jawline in a desperate kind of way that made Chase's stomach turn. One of Jonah's hands cupped her breast, then moved to the waist of her jeans, fingers tucking beneath them. Chase snapped out of his stupor.

"What the HELL?!" Chase roared.

He's on her.

Jonah jumped off of Aria at the sight of Chase and began to stammer about how it wasn't what it looked like. Chase saw red. His vision tunneled, and the logical part of his brain shut off; all he could see was Jonah's lips on Aria's, her limp body lying on the bed as he groped her. Jonah had something twisted up in his brain, and Chase was about to untangle it.

Touched her.

"It's not what it looks like…" Jonah started, but Chase couldn't hear him over the blood thundering in his ears. He started across the room, picking Jonah up off the ground and throwing him against the wall, a loud thud echoing in the room.

GROPED HER

"What the fuck else would it be?!" Chase screamed, throwing him against the wall again; a picture fell from the wall, hitting Jonah's shoulder as it fell.

"I LOVE HER!" Jonah pleaded.

"Wrong answer!" Chase threw a fist at his face, then grabbed Jonah by the collar, lifting him off his feet again and finally slamming Jonah down to the ground. Chase punched him again and again. Chase felt no pain as his fists collided with Jonah's face, a satisfying release of hatred bloomed through him each time. It was all he could do to make himself stop.

Stop.

I need to stop.

Chase pulled himself off of Jonah.

She wouldn't want me to do this.

Not wanting to relent but knowing he needed to, he stopped himself. His chest heaved, and his knuckles bled, his entire body quaked with rage. He wanted to rip Jonah apart, eviscerate him, tear every limb from his body and

Stop

Don't be Dad!

He took a deep, angry breath and turned back to the bed.

Aria was still unconscious on the bed, still panting. Chase went over and smoothed her hair back from her face as he listened to her shallow breaths. He couldn't tell if Jonah had drugged her or if she had done this to herself, and in the end, Chase guessed it didn't matter.

Her jeans are unbuttoned…

RAGE

Calm… she's not safe yet.

Glancing over his shoulder at Jonah as he began to stir, Chase picked Aria up. Careful of his bloodied knuckles, he cradled her against him.

"Please…" Jonah coughed.

"Shut up!" Chase barked, turning back towards him.

"Please don't tell her," Jonah begged.

"Are you fu…. I'm telling her!" Chase balked.

The audacity of this motherfucker

"She's already hanging on by a thread… what do you think this will do?" Jonah smiled, "Jude and I are all she has left… You're dumb-ass friends told her you didn't want her, and now that you said she'd break you…. You'll never convince her otherwise. You can't take us away from her… you can't take ME away from her!"

Chase wanted to scream. He knew logically that Jonah was wrong, that it wasn't Chase taking away her only family. It was Jonah ruining that family by trying to take something Aria hadn't offered. But Chase also knew that Aria wasn't logical; she was all emotion and willpower, and she would make this her fault, and she'd sink. Chase screamed a curse word at the heavens and then turned for the door.

Chase knew she was struggling and couldn't push her off that last ledge…. He wouldn't tell her.

Chapter Twenty-Seven

Garrett

GARRETT hadn't left his apartment in days. He knew he stunk, but he didn't care. He'd nearly perfected his concoction, and after two days, he couldn't walk away. He got obsessive about things sometimes. That's how the meth incident happened. He didn't even do drugs, but he loved the chemical components. He was intrigued by the way the drugs interacted with different parts of the brain and nervous system. It was fascinating how different concoctions activated different receptors. He'd been working for weeks on this batch, and finally, he was going to try it out!

He left the vial in the kitchen and went to finally shower and sleep on day 4, satisfied with his final product. He'd heard about a party in one of the newer loft clubs downtown and planned to find some subjects for his first drug trial.

The Cliff was the new hot spot in town, and Garrett hated it. The clubs and bars downtown were all the same; shitty old factories repurposed as elite clubs for rich assholes and their asshole kids with fake IDs. The industrial look was in, and the exposed beams of the ceiling looked down upon sleek gray walls and metallic tables scattered about one long space with a raised dance floor in the center of the massive room. Lights flashed and Garrett had to shield his eyes when the strobe lights spattered at his vision. He already felt the headache starting behind his eyes from the sporadic light effects. Reaching into his pocket, he grabbed his migraine medicine tearing open the single service packaging and popping the pill, swallowing it dry. He figured this would happen; strobe lights always triggered his migraines, so he came prepared.

He found the bar sprawled along the back wall, all black iron, and reflective metals. He ordered a beer; it was a non-threatening choice when approaching college girls. He had to be basic enough to pass for their age yet mysterious enough that they'd trust him enough to buy drugs from him. Garrett knew he was conventionally good-looking, tall with sandy hair and hazel eyes, so if approached, they wouldn't immediately turn him away. It was all about getting them to talk to him… once he got them talking and worked his charm on them, then he had them.

The first set of coeds he approached was a group of three, definitely not 21 - whoever made the fake IDs in Denver either made them impeccably well or no one actually cared. Either way, it worked out for him.

"Hey ladies, I'd like to introduce you to my new friend… Alice."

One to two drops later, the word spread fast on who had the stuff, making the girls roll like Molly with a hint of delusions like LSD. Alice worked the room that night as she spread through the crowd. One by one, coeds dropped the liquid into their mouths; it was amazing how eager they all were to try a substance totally unknown to them; it could have been his spit for all they knew. Thank God he was ethical. And that Alice was pure and beautiful and made them all smile. Euphoria swept the room, and the few left out of the loop were engulfed by the wanting hands and bodies writhing to be freed.

Garrett watched their movements, sometimes there was a twitch or an erratic arm spasm that Garrett didn't like - he jotted it down in his notebook and took another swig of his beer. A girl who was already dancing with Alice stumbled to the bar next to him, dragging a sober-ish boy in a gross yellow hoodie with her. She was sweating profusely, but Garrett zeroed in on a single bead of sweat rolling down her temple... it was blue. Almost iridescent. Glancing around, he saw similar blue shimmers on everyone's cheeks and foreheads, leaking through their shirts at the armpits like spilled ink. Everywhere between strands of hair and streaked down cheeks, the blue hue of Alice. Garrett smiled and turned back to the girl.

"We need another hit!" She yelled over the music.

"All right, same price," Garret moved for his pocket and withdrew the vial, and undid the stopper. One or two drops is all you need," he indicated to the guy as the girl stuffed cash in Garrett's pocket.

"Nah, dude, I'm paying to get high!" the guy snatched the dropper and squeezed the entirety of the contents into his mouth.

"Wo!" Garret said in surprise, grabbing the dropper back from the man who was cheering and walking away, soon to be lost in the crowd. He hoped the guy had drank a lot to dilute the mixture, but an overdose of Alice would probably produce effects similar to overdosing on any party drug. There were risks with drugs, and the buyer assumed the risk. Garrett counted the money that had been shoved into his pocket and returned to scanning the crowd.

Suddenly, someone screamed.

Chapter Twenty-Eight

Aria

EVERYTHING hurt.

It hurt to think.

It hurt to breathe.

Her lips cracked when she parted them to vomit.

Tears streamed down her cheeks as she threw up again, and someone wiped her face and held her hair back. Once she'd expelled everything in her system, she curled up on her side, and someone put a cool rag on the back of her neck.

"Thank you," she whispered before falling asleep again.

The next time Aria opened her eyes, there was less pain and less vomit. She looked around, and it took her a minute to understand where she was… Was she in Chase's room?

"Chase?" Aria whispered, trying to sit up, but the world began to spin again.

"I'm here, just lay back. Here," Chase said, entering the room. Aria felt a straw touch her lips, and she took a drink; she could've slurped the entire glass, but Chase pulled it away before she made herself sick again.

"How did I get here? Did I drive?" Aria asked, worried.

"No….I drove, I found you…" Chase cleared his throat, "passed out in a bedroom upstairs at Lindsey's house,"

Aria watched his face and knew there was something he wasn't telling her. Her head began to throb, and she brought her palms to her eyes trying to push the pain back.

"Do you have any Tylenol or something?" Aria asked, cradling her head in her hands.

"Yeah, here." and handed her two Tylenol from a bottle on his bedside table.

There was a long tense silence that made Aria want to scream. He hated her. She knew that. He didn't want her. What more was there to say?

"Aria… You disappeared. Where were you?" Chase asked cautiously.

"I was with Jonah at some drug dealer's house in Denver then…. Everywhere." Aria said sluggishly. When Chase didn't respond or laugh, Aria sighed and continued, "I went off grid with some coke, okay? We partied,"

Chase tensed.

"Did…." he seemed to be choosing his words carefully.

"Okay… did anything weird happen?" he finally said.

"I mean… the whole thing was weird, Chase." She laughed, a new wave of pain in her head, shattering her thoughts. "Weird, like how?"

"Did anybody touch you?" he spat.

"No! Jesus, I was with Jonah!"

"Yeah…" Chase scoffed, wiping his hands down his face. Then Aria noticed his hands, bloodied and ripped at the knuckles.

"Are YOU okay?" she asked, reaching towards him.

"Yeah… I'm fine," He said stepping back from her.

"Just get some rest, we're good here for a couple hours," Chase said stiffly, then left her alone in his room. As her head settled back into the pillow, she fell into a dreamless sleep.

As soon as Aria was able, they snuck out the back door, weaving through backyards. They ducked out of sight and came out two houses down from where Chase had parked Aria's car. They drove quietly through town; Aria could feel something was off about Chase. Anxiety rippled off of him like a mirage off of hot pavement. Hearing Chase say she'd eventually break him sent Aria into a tailspin, and now, on the other side of a bender, she thought she might have overreacted. And that she was in the wrong.

Chase pulled Aria's car into her usual spot in front of Aunt Marnie's house and put the car park but made no move to exit the vehicle.

"Um… can I come back later and get your car back to you? I have to… be somewhere," Chase said, not meeting her eyes. Aria knew he was lying but her head hurt too much to figure out what he was lying about or why.

"Fine," Aria mumbled, then got out of the car and made her way up the front steps.

When she entered the house, she slipped her shoes off, leaning around the corner to peek into the kitchen when her eyes caught the sight of blood and purple flesh. Jonah's face was awash with bruising and dried blood.

"What the hell happened to you?!" Aria yelled as she ran to the kitchen table where he was seated.

"Got in the way of some dude's fist last night," Jonah said sardonically.

"Who?!" Aria demanded.

Jonah stared at her as if pondering something, then shook his head.

"Doesn't matter,"

"Jonah!" Aria demanded.

"Drop it, Aria!" he snapped, standing so quickly his chair nearly tipped over behind him. Then he stormed from the room, leaving Aria alone.

***

ARIA showered and changed out of her vomit-stained shirt and sat in the old, worn-out chair by the window. Her room was small, but hers. Aunt Marnie made sure to paint it a shade Aria had liked and hung lights and pictures of her mom and dad on every wall.

Aria couldn't get the picture of Chase's bruised and bloody knuckles out of her head. his stiff demeanor that morning and then Jonah's mangled face… Suddenly, Aria knew.

An hour later, Jude drove Aunt Marnie's hatchback slowly down Chase's road, hoping Aria would change her mind, but her body vibrated from rage.

"You don't know if…" Jude tried.

"I know!" She said through clenched teeth.

They pulled up in front of Chase's house, and before the car was even stopped, Aria's feet were on the ground and stomping to Chase's front door. She tried to knock, but her arm slammed over and over again into the wooden front door. Chase answered, and Aria almost hit him in the chest.

"WHY?!" Aria screamed. Chase already knew what she was talking about.

"Okay, hold up, you need to know…" Chase began, but Aria was on a runaway train of fury. She couldn't think straight; her cheeks pulsed hot, and her heart hammered in her chest. All rational thought had escaped her.

"I KNOW CHASE!" she screamed! "I saw what you did!" She pushed her way inside and looked around hastily for her car keys which she found on her third lap around the living room. She was panting from the adrenaline but made her way back out of the house before she began smashing shit that wasn't hers.

"Aria, wait!" Chase yelled, following her out the door. He tried to take her by the hand, but she spun on him and slapped him across the face.

"Do NOT touch me," she hissed.

They stared at each other, stunned for a moment, but Aria's rage was in control now. The sound of her hand hitting his face had taken it down a notch. Ashamed but still enraged, she turned and stomped towards the car again.

Chase stood stunned for a moment longer but then began to pursue her again.

"Aria, please,"

"NO!" Aria had reached her car and flung open the door, throwing herself into the driver's seat. Before she could close the door, Chase put himself between the door and the car.

"Please, Aria," Chase pleaded; Aria paused, "I'm leaving in two weeks for this police academy Ted got me into, and I…"

"Good," Aria growled, pushing Chase backward, slamming the car door. She pulled away in a haze of smoking tires and anger.

Chapter Twenty-Nine

Chase

CHASE watched her pull away. She didn't care that he was leaving.

Jude lingered behind Chase, silent.

"He deserved it," Chase said not turning to face Jude.

"Yeah, I bet he did… too bad she won't listen to you now," Jude said, turning and leaving Chase alone in the street.

Chapter Thirty

Garrett

AS the crowd parted, Garrett watched, horrified as the boy in the yellow hoodie sunk his teeth into another man's nose. The music and screams muted the grisly noises of crushed cartilage and snapped skin. As the skin parted the face, blood gushed from the wound, drowning the man in his own blood. The guy in the yellow hoodie dropped his victim to the floor, standing as he surveyed the stunned crowd around him, seeming to size up those around him. His face twitched and his arms jerked at odd angles, Alice's side effects becoming too much for his nervous system. Garrett hastily jotted some notes, then stowed his pad and tried to get closer. The man in the yellow hoodie was still assessing the crowd, twitching his head left and right again like an animal waiting to pounce. He jumped from the DJ platform above, seizing a woman by the neck, sinking his fingers into her jugular, blood streaming down in wet ribbons on the stage. The club burst into chaos, and Garrett was knocked away towards the door. Desperately he fought the surge of the crowd to see what happened next. The woman's scream strangled out after a moment, and Garrett looked back long enough to see her body fly down from the second story with a sickening *thunk* on the first floor. Someone hit the yellow hoodie guy with a chair, but he was unphased. Three men rushed him and took him to the ground, and as Garrett was pushed through the door back into the night air, he saw the yellow hoodie-wearing immortal rise again as he threw the three men off of him as if they weighed nothing. Then he rushed, teeth barred at another man…

Interesting, he thought.

PART TWO

2 years later

"Good evening this is Dan Evans with WRTM news with a report on a new street drug called Alice. No, not the fairy tale character who fell down the rabbit's hole but a dangerous chemical compound that has already claimed 14 young lives. Alice began her murder spree nearly 2 years ago with what would be dubbed The Cliff Massacre, where one man eviscerated dozens of people before being shot by police officers; one officer was among the victims. Originally formulated for the treatment of depression by RTO labs in Denver, Alycytraline or Align as it was marketed, was supposed to save lives but now… it's taking them. After being illegally transported out of RTO, street-level chemists formulated Alice by combining Alycytraline with LSD and some variations containing a drug called "krocodile" thus giving birth to Alice. This drug promises a smooth high with little to no lasting effects or hangovers in low doses. However, if dosages are too high, it can be known to cause decreased activity in the frontal lobe, causing the patient to exhibit feral animalistic behaviors. A 27-year-old woman in Seattle clawed the face off of her husband and consumed some of his body. Officials also say a 19-year-old man in Nashville went on a killing spree, taking the lives of 5 innocent people. Similar stories are popping up in cities and small towns throughout the United States. Authorities say they are watching known drug operations but are, so far, perplexed as to how Alice is spreading so quickly. Police and DEA are asking anyone with any information to please contact them at the number on your screen."

2001

Chapter Thirty-One

Aria

ARIA groaned when she heard her phone vibrate against the wood of her side table. She was nestled in her bed with a book, a messy bun on top of her head, wanting no contact with the outside world on this gloomy evening. She ignored the call and lazily turned the page of her book. When the phone vibrated again she sighed and set the book on the bed as she rolled to grab her phone. She slid back into blankets and looked at the screen, her heart dropping to her stomach. Chase's name lit the screen.

Chase is calling…

Aria bolted upright in bed, her book falling to the floor and her hair flopping into her face. She hadn't heard from Chase in years. She didn't know what happened between him and Jonah years ago, but she knew she hadn't handled it right, and… Jonah probably deserved it. She'd abandoned him, and she had never forgiven herself for it. Aria had been swallowed up by the sadness for a year and a half after Chase left. She barely graduated, and if it hadn't been for Jude and Aunt Marnie, she didn't think she would have. They pushed her through the darkest parts where alcohol and cocaine were all that had motivated her, Jonah fed that urge as often as he could. She was controllable that way. Jonah was an ever-present figure, and his darkness seeped into every part of her life now. But where Jonah was darkness and secrets, Jude was light and happiness. She took the good with the bad. This was the family she had.

KNOCK KNOCK KNOCK

Aria's head shot up, she quickly untangled herself from the blankets, fixing her hair as she made her way out of the bedroom and into her small living room. She padded across the carpet in her fuzzy socks and peeked through the peephole. She exhaled sharply, turning the deadbolt and throwing open the door.

Chase stood on the stoop, rain pouring down on him, drenching his clothes.

Aria stared at him silently, her phone still clutched in her hand.

He hadn't changed. He looked older and had more muscles than she remembered, but he was still the same blue-eyed boy from that first day of school. He was her first, and she had hurt him so badly.

"Chase I..." Aria began, but Chase held up his hand.

"I don't care about anything that happened before. I tried... I tried to forget you," He sighed heavily and took a step through the doorway, "I couldn't,"

"Me either," Aria whispered, "I'm so sorry, I should never have... I'm sorry,"

"Me too," Chase whispered softly, kindly. "Can I stay?"

Aria nodded, and Chase paused only momentarily, then scooped her up into his arms, Aria jumping into his arms to meet his lips. Her body sang as they collided, like it had finally found the song that made it dance. His lips felt familiar, and his body felt like home.

Chapter Thirty-Two

Chase

LATER, Chase curled against her naked back, breathing in her scent as her warm skin rested against his. He never wanted to let go.

"Chase?" Aria said quietly in the darkness, her voice like music to his soul.

"I'm so sorry," she said her voice choking up, tears lacing her words. "I don't even know why I was mad anymore… I HIT you! And then I just let you leave," She sniffled next to him, and he felt her shift as she wiped tears away from her face. "I was terrible, and I am so sorry,"

"It doesn't matter anymore," Chase said into her hair as he tightened his grip around her. "None of it matters anymore. I'm home,"

Chapter Thirty-Three

Aria

WHEN Aria awoke the next morning, she almost expected it all to be a dream, but there he was, asleep in her bed. His blonde hair fell across his brow, his mouth slack in sleep. He was the most beautiful thing she'd ever seen, and suddenly she knew she couldn't be without him again. The inky black pit in her stomach was gone now that he was here; she could breathe with him next to her again, and God, his scent filled her with a sense of safety she hadn't felt in years. She raked her fingers through his hair, feeling the silken strands slide between her fingers. His eyes fluttered open and focused on her. That sexy smirk spreading across his face, and Aria melted. She slid closer as he slid his arm around her waist.

"I really missed you," Aria admitted. If she wanted things to be different, then she needed to BE different. And that meant letting Chase in and letting him see the dark places. The places that didn't seem so scary now that he was home.

"Miss isn't a big enough word… I was always going to come back to you," Chase said in a husky morning voice that heated Aria's core. He pressed a kiss to her forehead and settled his head on hers.

"I didn't realize how lonely I was until I saw you standing there," She murmured against his bare chest.

"I thought about calling you once I got to school but…:" he trailed off.

"It's probably better you didn't. I had a hard time after you left, it was rough. I slept a lot. And cried a lot. Was mad a lot. I don't think you would've liked the Aria you talked to if you had called,"

"I was scared. I'm not going to lie, you broke my heart, and I couldn't hear that tone in your voice again," Chase said quietly.

"What tone?"

"The indifference. That hurt more than anything," he responded.

"I'm sorry," she said again miserably, "I was full of shit too because I cared so freaking much," Aria laughed. "I was so mad though… It swallowed me up for a while,"

"So, you were happy to see me?" Chase teased.

Aria laughed and dramatically sighed.

"A little," she giggled, tucking herself in against him tighter. Her arms stroking the skin on his back, "Don't leave me again," she said quietly.

"I won't," he said plainly. No jokes or sarcasm, just the truth in his voice that he would never leave her again.

"Promise?" Aria asked shakily.

"Promise Freckles,"

2 weeks later

Aria woke with a start as a peel of thunder ripped through the sky outside, then an arm tightened reassuringly around her waist, and she remembered who lay next to her. She settled back against his chest, tugging the blankets up around them. Chase nestled his chin onto her shoulder and lightly kissed her skin. Aria tilted her head back into him and arched her back as he moved her hair and brushed more kisses up her neck. Her pulse quickened, and heat rose in her chest. His hands slid up her front, finding her bare breasts, and Aria sucked in a breath suppressing a moan. She ground against him as his teeth skated across her shoulder. Aria turned in his arms and met his lips with hers. Hungry and hot, her hands raked over his back, letting her nails lightly scrape up his spine; he shivered in delight. Chase tugged a handful of her hair at the nape of her neck, tilting her head back so she could trail kisses up her throat, and Aria's center turned molten.

Then there was pounding on the front door.

Chase and Aria froze.

No. Not now.

They'd been blissfully alone for over a week, pretending there was no one else in the world, locking themselves in Aria's apartment for two days. Aria skipped her art classes all week and Chase took shortened shifts. Chase took Aria to his new house, that Ted had helped him find, and they proceeded to christen every room. They did the same at Aria's. Apart from the sex, they'd talked. Talked about everything they'd done wrong and all that had happened when they'd been apart. How Chase survived and even thrived in the police academy, and how Aria discovered a love for art while fighting her anger and sadness. She'd started mindlessly doodling while she hid in her room, staring out the windows at the mountains. Before she knew it, she had a full portfolio and was majoring in graphic design at the local college.

They didn't talk about Jonah, they pretended he didn't exist. That was a discussion for another time.

Now the world had caught up with them.

Another round of thuds came from the door, then they both heard Jude yelling for Aria to open the door.

"I am going to kill them," Aria grumbled in frustration as their lips fell apart. Chase groaned, trying to pull her lips back to his, but the thudding intensified. "UGH!" Aria grunted as she rolled off the bed, pulling begrudgingly from Chase's grip. She hurriedly pulled on some pants and a shirt.

"Don't go anywhere," she said, leaning down to kiss him again before exiting the room and closing the door behind her.

Aria threw her hair back into another messy bun, trying to smooth it down, then she looked through the peephole out of habit, only to see another eye staring back at her.

"Goddamnit, Jude!" She yelled as she jumped back in surprise and threw open the door, "Why do you do that!? All I see is a horrifyingly huge eye!"

"I like to keep you on your toes," Jude said as he and Jonah stepped in out of the rain and shed their soaked outer layers dropping them on the chair next to the door. The valley had been drenched with rain for weeks, and the constant moisture was a whole new frustration as she watched the water drip onto her floor.

"What the hell are you guys doing here? It's 3 am! You need to go," Aria whispered.

"Why are you whispering?" Jonah whispered back seriously. Aria tried not to let her eyes twitch toward the bedroom, but they moved on their own, and Jonah knew.

"Do you have a suitor here?" He said with a dark glee.

Once they all graduated, Aunt Marnie had told them all to stay as long as they needed to get on their feet, but Aria had been gone within weeks of leaving high school. She loved Aunt Marnie and Jude, but on the nights when Jonah "went dark" as she called it, it was suffocating. Jonah's control issues were going to slowly kill her.

After Chase, any boy who showed interest in Aria was promptly threatened, bullied, bribed, or otherwise been persuaded to end things with her. Not that there were many after Chase left. She'd basically become the town pariah, leaving her alone with no one but Jonah and Jude. But in the rare moments where she'd meet someone from another town who didn't know about the Killer Orphan Girl, Jonah would manage to scare them off.

And now he thought he smelled fresh meat.

"Jonah, don't!" Aria snapped, grabbing for his arm. He shrugged out of her reach, but she charged after him, taking him hard by the arm this time and pulling him toward the front door.

"What's wrong with you? Don't you want your dear *brothers* to meet him," he cooed at her sickly. She hated him when he was like this when he got that sadistic glint in his eye, and suddenly nothing got through to him. Like when she'd dared to date a classmate from her oil painting class, and Jonah had refused to eat until she dumped him, she'd screamed and pleaded until she'd lost her voice, but in the end, Jonah won.

Jude shifted uncomfortably behind them now.

"Jonah, let's just go, it's fine," Jude tried to placate, sighing heavily.

"NO!" Jonah snapped, spinning on his brother, breaking his cool facade momentarily. "I want to know who our dear Aria has deemed worthy of her affection,"

"Stop it," Aria said through gritted teeth and tears in her eyes. Jonah stared back at her darkly for a moment, jealousy rolling off of him.

"What's the matter? Are you embarrassed?" Jonah cooed.

"Fuck you," she whispered, a tear slipping down her cheek.

A soft click came from behind Jonah as Chase opened the bedroom door. Jonah turned and stiffened. Chase stood in the doorway in only his jeans, hair tousled, and chiseled abdomen on display. Concern laced his face as his eyes met hers.

"Everything okay?" Chase said, looking at Jonah with a razor-sharp stare.

Everything was silent for a moment, and when it was clear Jonah wasn't going to react, Chase looked past Jonah and smiled, "Hey, Jude,".

"Hey, Chase," Jude said in shock, smiling at the revelation. "THIS is the guy you've been seeing?" Jude said to Aria, who was still tense next to Jonah.

"Well, I love it," Jude said, clapping his hands in front of him. He looked at Jonah and saw the seething way he breathed and tried to taper down his enthusiasm, "Oh damn...sorry," Jude laughed.

Chase looked at Aria again and seemed to track the tear down her cheek, his jaw tightening as he angrily shrugged on his T-shirt. Aria had released her grip on Jonah, but he didn't move; she could feel the rage vibrating off of him. Behind them,

Jude walked over and plopped on the couch like the room wasn't a powder keg of tension and testosterone, kicking his feet up just to be extra. Chase shoved his feet into his shoes, leaving them unlaced, stepping into the living room, and snatching his coat off a nearby chair.

"I gotta go," he said with a bite to his words, staring daggers into Jonah.

"No, Chase..." Aria said, stepping around Jonah and taking Chase by the hand. Desperation welled in her belly, so she followed him to the door, she couldn't lose him again, and it already felt like he was pulling away. She could feel his anger and it made her panicky in a way only Jonah's obsession did.

"It's okay, I have to work in a couple of hours anyway," he said, kissing her on the forehead, her heart slowing some. "I'll text you later," he said gently, looking down at her. He gave her a small smile, then he flipped his hood up over his head and headed into the deluge.

Chapter Thirty-Four

Chase

CHASE couldn't stop his hands from shaking. He balled them into fists and shoved them into his pockets as the rain soaked through his hood into his hair and down his neck.

That motherfucker. The way he talked to her. Had he heard fear in her voice? Seen a tear on her cheek?

Son of a bitch!

He started down the walkway to the parking lot, the rain soaking him through, his jaw clenched with tightly controlled rage.

He hated Jonah. He wanted him so fucking far away from Aria that she'd forget he existed. They'd avoided talking about him in any capacity since he'd gotten back, but Chase had known it couldn't stay that way. They were family, and he was the toxic anchor bringing Aria and Jude down with him.

FUCK!

Why did he sign up for this again?

He couldn't share her with him. Wouldn't.

Chapter Thirty-Five

Aria

JONAH was silent as the door closed.

"When did Chase get back?" he said in a barely audible whisper.

"A while ago, bro," Jude said from the couch, "he's a cop now; that's why he left before the end of Senior year. He got into some academy…" Jude trailed off when Jonah's eyes burned daggers into him.

Aria made her way to the kitchen, taking a sweater off the back of the couch and pulling it on over her head.

"You guys want some food?" Aria asked, sighing, trying to change the energy in the apartment.

"Heck yeah! I'm starving," Jude said, turning on the TV and the gaming console, he looked over at his brother and rolled his eyes. "Jonah, sit down,"

Instead, Jonah spun and looked at Aria, following her into the small, open kitchenette.

"So… Chase?" Jonah scoffed.

"Yes. Chase." Aria said solidly. "And you aren't going to mess with it! You don't get to ruin this,"

"Oh, so I ruin everything?" Jonah feigned offense. Aria spun angrily to meet him. He wouldn't win this one.

"That's not what I sai-" Aria started.

"What have I ruined? I'm your FAMILY!" Jonah hissed at her. "We are all you have!"

"That doesn't mean you can be a dick!" Aria snapped, heat flushing her cheeks as her temper began to boil over. Less than thirty minutes ago, she had been naked in bed with Chase, his hands roving over her skin, and now here she was having the same old argument with Jonah.

"Oh, so I do ruin everything because I'm a dick,"

"Oh my god," Aria whispered, looking up at the ceiling in exasperation, "Not what I said! Stop!" she screamed.

"ENOUGH!" Jude yelled. Jude had far more tolerance for Jonah than Aria, but only because he wasn't the object of his obsession, "Jonah, you are possessive of her, and it's freaking weird if we're being honest, and you need to stop. Aria, that was a surprising turn of events, but I, for one, am a total fan of the 'come back tour of Chase and Aria 2001.'" He gave his brother another pointed expression, then returned to his seat on the couch and started the video game. Eventually, Jonah released his breath, stalking over to the chair and angrily rolling a joint, stuffing his bag of weed dramatically back into his jacket pocket after he was done.

As the joint burned, the tension slowly seeped out of the room. When it was just the three of them, the world could be perfect, but adding anyone else disturbed the peace. But Aria couldn't live on that alone, she needed more.

She needed Chase.

"What are you guys even doing here?" Aria asked once she poured herself a bowl of cereal and sat down next to Jude.

"I gotta meet Garrett in Denver, and your place is closer to the highway," Jonah said, lighting the joint and inhaling deeply.

"Ew, Garrett? Isn't he that skeezy meth cook?" Aria scowled in disgust.

"Dude he's gross but brilliant. He's made meth that was honestly a work of art. I was up for days," Jonah said, hitting the joint.

Jude and Aria side-eyed him, and he shrugged.

"What? It was objectively good meth."

"Aunt Marnie's place is like two miles away from the highway; why are you really here," Aria said, still feeling Chase's lips on her bare skin.

"We missed you," Jude crooned. "Plus, you have snacks,"

Jude died in the game, and Aria motioned for the controller, handing him her cereal bowl in a very practiced manner. This was their normal. Sitting side by side and moving more in sync than the two actual twins. Jude took some bites of Aria's cereal while she maneuvered the controller. Jonah kept to himself in the old easy chair, smoking his joint. Aria had found the chair at the consignment shop; it had hideous orange flowers against a purple velvet backdrop, and she had had to have it.

"HA HA! Suck it!" Aria laughed, lifting her controller in the air triumphantly. Sticking her tongue out at Jude and laughing devilishly.

"This game is glitching! I didn't get the code right!" Jude protested. They passed the controller back and forth as they always did, but tonight, it was forced. Both looked sideways to see if Jonah was still awake. Finally, Jonah dozed in the chair, and Jude whispered.

"So, Chase, huh?" Jude said suggestively, raising his eyebrows excitedly at her. Aria's cheeks reddened, and she smiled.

"Yes, Chase," Aria grinned over at him, "Always Chase,"

They were silent again then Jude motioned his head towards his brother.

"He's getting worse," Jude whispered to her as Jonah began snoring from the chair.

"I know," Aria said.

Aria had known Jonah was in love with her for a long time. But it was a toxic possessive kind of love born from a traumatic childhood. She knew her cousin wasn't evil, he was ill. He needed help. The trauma of losing his parents had made something break in him. Aunt Marnie loved her boys, and Aria too, but whatever Jonah saw before coming to Aria's family had changed him. He had protected Jude from it and that act had to come from someplace good in him. Some place in his soul that loved his brother enough to see or do whatever it was so that Jude didn't have to. There was good in him, Aria had seen it. In small moments where he covered her head with his bag in the rain, or that he always made sure her car had gas, and always took her trash out, which he knew she hated doing, ignoring her tears when it was all too much as an orphaned teen. It was in there somewhere. The question was: was he too far gone?

After Miguel died, Jonah punished himself in his own ways, chasing a thing he could never have, and he devoted himself to that so thoroughly that it eroded their relationship.

She loved her brothers; he and Jude were all she had, and together, that was her family.

"What time is the run?" Aria asked, wrapping a blanket around herself and stretching out across Jude.

"Get your nasty feet off of me!" Jude said, shoving her legs off of him. He hated feet, and it delighted Aria to no end to torture him as often as possible, she wiggled her toes at him again, then she curled her legs beneath her, satisfied for now, "we need to leave at 6 am," he looked at his watch, "which is in an hour," he groaned. "He said we're bringing back something 'crazy,'" Jude said, making air quotes with his hands.

"What do you think it is?" Aria asked, concerned. She knew Jonah ran coke, shrooms, crack, heroin, and even LSD and ketamine for the guys out of Denver; what else was there?

Oh god.

"You don't think it's a person, do you?" Aria said, bolting upright.

"Jesus, Aria! No!" Jude said, looking stunned at her response. "It's just probably some pills or something; he gets excited over pharmaceuticals," but there was worry in his voice. "Want any treats while we're away?" he changed the subject, clearing his throat. Jude dabbled in the illegal wares his brother sold because 'life was for living' but never overused it, he had an irrational fear of being incapacitated and not being able to save himself if an emergency were to arise. He also never wanted to be so inebriated he peed himself, that would have been a fate worse than death for Jude.

"So…. Have you been out on any dates lately?" Aria asked after they had settled back into passing the controller back and forth between rounds.

"Aria, you know there are no new men in this dating pool. How were *you* doing out there before Chase came back?" Jude shot back at her.

"Terrible… bought so many vibrators," Aria laughed.

"Exactly! So don't judge, missy. Also, what'd you get?" he grinned.

"I dunno, some pretty pink set of 6 I saw on TV super late at night. They came in a cute case!" She explained.

"Oh, nice. I love a full set," he said, taking a drink of his soda.

Aria grunted in frustration at the game then handed the controller back to Jude.

"Anyway, you know as well as I do that my temper and moral failings were not the only obstacles in the way of my love life," she looked at Jonah who was still passed out in the chair. Head drooped to his chest, his now short hair hidden under a black cap, long fingers curled over the arms of the chair. His legs were splayed out in front of him emphasizing his long, slender stature. His dark eyelashes were so thick they cast shadows on his under eye. Even in sleep he seemed to be holding on so tightly to some unseen thing. Squeezing the life out of whatever it was, even in his dreams.

"Yeah… I know. I'm sorry," Jude said quietly. "It's for the best anyway…" he trailed off, pausing the game.

"Why?" she asked, exasperated; she knew where this was going. Where it always went. Miguel. Jude had never moved on. He never wanted to hurt someone like that again even though it hadn't been Jude who had done the hurting. "Jude, that wasn't your fault! We all… we all suck. Me most of all." She sighed. "Despite how we felt about him that day,

NONE of us wanted him to die. None of us wanted him to hurt himself." Aria had told herself that every night for years, and eventually, she started to believe it. She sighed again, "I know it doesn't make it any easier, but at least you didn't punch him the day he did it. That particular asshole award is only for me," Aria snatched the controller from Jude and unpaused the game, and they lapsed back into their comfortable silence.

"I think you've paid enough for that, don't you?" Jude said finally.

"I could say the same to you," she said, concentrating on the game and hitting the buttons in the proper combination to rip out the spine of her opponent.

"OH! I'M AMAZING! LOOK!" Aria exclaimed, throwing the controller on the couch and pointing in Jude's face. Jude squinted at the screen and saw his long-standing high score shattered by Aria, who was still doing a celebration dance in the middle of her small living room. Jonah raised his head suddenly.

"What happened?" he asked shaking his head to clear the sleep.

"I kicked his shitty score to the CURB! BOOM!" Aria said, exploding with animation.

"Ohhhhh shit! Nice!" Jonah reached out and high-fived Aria, who returned the gesture, "That's my girl! That's how we do!" he celebrated as well. "What time is it?"

"5:30 something," Jude replied, pouting over the score.

"Okay, here," she tossed the controller to Jude, "I need a snack after that victory and some caffeine since I've been up all night." She headed for the kitchen and opened the fridge, retrieving a container of yogurt. Jonah stood and stretched, then slowly ventured over to her, leaning, back against the counter next to Aria.

"What?" she said flatly, feeling his eyes on her.

"Chase? Really?" Jonah began, Aria sighed heavily, but he pushed on, "He LEFT you,"

Aria slammed her spoon on the counter, yogurt splattering on the surface.

"I need you to be okay with this." She willed her voice to be like stone, she wouldn't budge on this. "Jonah…. Please. I need you to just let this go and let me be happy."

Jonah rolled his eyes.

"But Chase?" Jonah pushed.

"Oh, give me a break, Jonah! The only girl you dated of worth was Dana and you fucked that up for both of us!"

"Fair enough," Jonah said, "But It's more than me just not liking him," Jonah slid closer down the counter towards her.

"Then what? Because we can't fight about this every time I…"

Before Aria could finish her sentence, Jonah pulled her to him and pressed his lips to hers. Hungry and desperate. Aria was frozen, a sick pit of ice landing in her stomach. She tried to pull away, but Jonah held her hard against him. He forced her mouth open, his tongue darting into her mouth in a disgusting invasion. She could taste the stale weed on his breath. Aria pushed off his chest, trying in vain to break his grip on her and get his lips off of her. But she couldn't pry his mouth from hers, nausea bubbled up her throat, and she coughed against his mouth.

Suddenly Jonah was ripped off of her, revealing Chase, fury written across his face. Chase had Jonah by the back of his hoodie in one hand and a box of donuts in the free hand as Jude took Aria protectively by the shoulders.

Aria barely registered that Chase had come back before work. He had brought her donuts.

"You son of a bitch" Chase growled, tossing the box of pastries aside and spinning Jonah towards him, gripping him by the front of his shirt. He brought Jonah close to his face and snarled something Aria couldn't make out before throwing Jonah against the small kitchen table behind them, his upper body flopping across it. Chase collected him off the table and threw him again, across the small space against the opposite wall.

"Wo, wo wo wo!" Jude said, putting himself between his brother and Chase, holding his hands out in front of him like he was trying to stop an angry bull. Jonah was crumpled on the floor gasping for breath, trying desperately to stand.

"Chase, no!" Aria screamed. He was radiating anger and stood looming over Jonah, with Jude being the only thing keeping him at bay. Aria wanted Chase with all she had but she couldn't lose the only family she had left either. Jonah was sick, and he needed them to protect him from himself. But Aria could still feel the memory of Jonah's kiss on her lips, and it turned her stomach.

Still, she couldn't turn her back on Jonah.

"Are you kidding me?" Chase said over his shoulder to Aria, "He does this shit AGAIN, and I'm supposed to just let this fucker walk outta here?" Then Chase's face changed, he dropped Jonah and literally wiped his hands together.

"Fine. fuck it. I'm done." Chase started for the door.

"Chase, man…" Jude started.

"Chase, please," Aria began.

"Fuck you, Jude! Fuck you, Jonah, and fuck you, Aria! You all deserve each other!" Chase said as he pointed at them with each word. Then turned and stormed for the door.

"Chase..." Aria yelled again just as the door slammed shut. She exhaled sharply; her first reaction was always anger; adrenaline flooded her veins, her cheeks flushed, and she couldn't think straight. Chase was right. Indifference did hurt.

"Get out," she whispered,

"Wait... hold up..." Jonah started defensively, stuttering to his feet.

"GET OUT!" She screamed. She stormed across the room and threw open her door, pointing furiously outside. Jonah walked to the door as if he should be the one who was wronged, but Jude stopped and whispered.

"Sorry Aria" then he followed his brother out into the rain.

Aria shut the door but didn't move.

"Again," she whispered, "Chase had said again,"

Chapter Thirty-Six

Chase

RAGE.

That's all Chase felt.

When he opened the door to Aria's apartment, it had taken him a breath to understand what he was seeing. Jonah had Aria gripped against his chest, lips pressed against hers as Aria visibly struggled and gagged against him. All he could see was that night in Lindsey Fitzgerald's bedroom, Jonah looming over her, and his vision went red. He'd crawled back to this shit mountain town to throw himself at the feet of a girl who couldn't separate herself from her psychotic sibling! Why couldn't she see it? He couldn't be with her and know this predator would always be lurking, vindicated by a secret Chase chose to keep. The thought made him suffocate.

2 weeks! We made it two goddamn weeks without him fucking it up.

At this rate, he'd wreck his truck trying to drive in the rain while this angry, he had to calm himself down.

He spied a side street; turning down the small road, he pulled and parked. He put his head back against the headrest, sighing heavily. He closed his eyes and tried to slow his breathing. His temper was trying to get the better of him, but he always made himself imagine his father, red-faced and screaming at him. Or punching him over and over while he screamed in rage. Chase would never be him, so he took deep, shaky breaths. He tapped each finger to his thumb one at a time over and over again, focusing on the pattern and repetition, and slowly, his anger subsided.

It was a great two weeks, though, he thought miserably.

He took another steadying breath.

Despite it all, he still loved her. He still felt that pull to her that he couldn't ignore When she'd opened the door, it was like everything had all snapped back into place, and the dark well inside him had disappeared. And when he'd kissed her, it was like his first drop of water after weeks in a desert. He'd relished every moment they'd been together, hidden from the world beneath a set of sheets. But even now, he didn't think he'd fully appreciated her touch. Her skin. Her smell. He hadn't soaked in enough of her.

All he wanted was her.

Why was it so hard?

Over the police scanner on his dash came reports of mudslides taking out part of the highway on the West side of town and structural damage to the roadway. Every year, the mountains would burn from the dry hot conditions, full forests burning to the ground in a matter of days. Then the rain would finally return only to lose entire hillsides that would crumble down upon the town. The cemetery had been taken out when Chase was in elementary school, and the only fast-food place in town had been taken out a year ago. Currently, there was flooding in South Canyon and officials were concerned about the bridge. It was years overdue for repair, and with the rising waters, they worried it wouldn't withstand the storm, so they were calling in all uniformed officers to help manage the situation.

To hell with it.

Chase put his truck in gear, swinging it around back onto the main road, and headed for the station.

Chapter Thirty-Seven

Garrett

Somewhere in Denver

GARRETT fidgeted with his car keys, trying to keep his impatience at bay. Jonah was always late. He hated doing business with him, but he was the IN to the valley and the other mountain towns ripe with rich people who wanted to spend money on their mountain vacations. Many times that meant drugs. But Jonah creeped Garrett out, he had this deadness in the eye that made Garrett's stomach twist. But he had no choice. This vial of Alice was hot in his pocket, and he knew the cops had been circling him like a vulture scoping out a corpse for at least 6 months.

After the shit at the nightclub, Garrett almost quit cooking altogether. He'd gone home, packed his essentials, and abandoned his apartment for a month or two. After watching the place for a couple of days and seeing no movement, he went and retrieved the rest of his "lab." He'd moved six more times in the two years since the night at The Cliff. And still, the cops always seemed to be right behind him. Low-level narcs would float his name to cut a deal, and soon, he'd be moving again. It was a pain in the ass, and it pissed him off. He liked to lay low and cook in peace. He liked the science of drugs and what it did to people - it was *Science*. But he also knew the law didn't share his particular opinion on this, so he waited. Soon he saw the familiar gray van turn into the Walmart parking lot. He could see Jude in the passenger seat and relaxed a little, Jude wasn't weird like his brother. Jude was laid back and covered for Jonah's awkwardness and…. Darkness? Garrett didn't know what it was about the kid.

They parked next to Garrett, driver side to driver side, and Garrett sighed as he rolled down the windows. The parking lot was busy, and it made Garrett nervous, his eyes scanning the cars.

"Garrett!" Jonah called in a weird sing-song voice.

"Shut the fuck up," he hissed, "Jesus Christ, do you have no chill? You're loud as hell!"

"Hey, Garrett," Jude said from the passenger seat.

"Sup Jude," Garrett grumbled as he took the vial out of the case next to him, he reached his hand out the window and held out the vial to Jonah, "This is Alice," He smiled. "One or two drops, under the tongue or put it in a carrier liquid."

Jonah took the vial, squinting his eyes as if inspecting it. Then he smiled. He tossed a wad of cash into Garrett's lap.

Garrett juggled it a moment, then slid it back into the case he'd pulled Alice from.

Jonah didn't deserve Alice.

Garrett sighed.

"Be careful with her," Garrett warned then put his car in drive, leaving Denver behind him.

"Goodbye, Alice,"

Chapter Thirty-Eight

Chase

"GORSKI!" Lieutenant Ted Garcias yelled, snapping Chase out of his stupor; he flipped his phone face down on the desk quickly, concealing the screen.

"Hey, we've got mudslides up Miners Trail; I'm sending Parada and Saunders up there with the two newbies. You, me, and Stokes are going to be manning this shit show, Kennedy and Farrow are back there doing admin and bookings, but they can't do shit else, so I need you on your toes, got it?" Ted said.

"Yes, sir," Chase nodded.

"They're booking two right now, but one should be out within the hour; hopefully, it's a quiet night downtown. He looked toward Chase's phone disapprovingly but grumbled, "Just call her son,"

Chase sighed and nodded; Ted patted his hand on the desk in front of Chase, then turned and left him to his thoughts.

Ted had aged while Chase was away. His dark beard and hair had faded to gray in more areas than not; hard lines wore into his forehead and at the corners of his eyes. Chase hadn't even seen his dad since being back and Ted had simply shaken his head when Chase asked if he should go see him. Every time he'd called home from school; it'd gone to the answering machine. After a while, that was full, and he had given up.

Fuck him.

Chase sighed and turned his phone back over, looking at Aria's picture for a moment longer. She was laughing that laugh of hers, her head tilted back and mouth open. Not trying to hide her joy but feeling whatever it was 100%. And that's what Chase loved about her. She was like a live wire that awakened every sense in you without even trying. The picture was dark; he'd taken it after they'd been together the first night, a sheet was draped over her shoulders, and blush colored her freckled cheeks. Before he could stop it, the vision of that piece of shit's hands on her waist and his lips on hers filled him with rage. Then he saw him leaning over her in that bedroom so many years ago, his hand poised to take something that she hadn't agreed to. Why hadn't Chase told her? The Forrester twins were all she had left, but she needed to know what he was and what he had tried to do.

I should call her.

Instead, he set the phone face down again. It was going to be a long night.

***

TEN hours later, Chase sat at the front desk, mindlessly typing out paperwork for the trainees. He rubbed the exhaustion out of his eyes and took another drink of his soda. He was stretching when Deputy Stokes swung open the door with Jonah in custody. Jonah glared at him as he passed by the desks, Jude following closely behind them but not in cuffs like his brother. Chase cussed under his breath. He knew what Jonah was being arrested for and grabbed his phone to call Aria. When she answered she sounded hopeful, expectant. His stomach dropped at her voice, a mixture of butterflies and bombs, but Chase took a breath. He wasn't sure what he wanted to say to her about their relationship yet, but he had to let her know Jonah was being booked.

"Yeah… uh hey," Chase put on his official voice, "We have Jonah down here being booked, he's gonna need bail money," he sounded stiff and cold to his own ears.

Aria was silent for a moment.

"Okay," she matched his business tone perfectly.

Damnit.

"I'll be right down," then she hung up.

Chase stared at her picture again. How did he fall in love with someone so complicated?

She did warn me.

He put his phone away again and rubbed his face with his hands hoping it would clear his head. Suddenly, Jude appeared at the desk again.

"Did you call her?" Jude asked in a panicked tone.

"Yeah," Chase croaked at him, "she's on her way,"

Chase schooled his features and focused on the paperwork in front of him, but when Jude didn't move, he said. "Is there something else?"

"Come on, man, don't talk to me like we don't know each other," Jude said.

"I'm just trying to stay impartial here, okay?" Chase said, shrugging.

"Because if you haven't noticed, I love Aria, I like you but Jonah… can go fuck himself. But I'm also a cop, and Jonah was just arrested for what? Distribution?" Chase asked, clicking keys on his computer to see if the information had been entered yet.

Jude looked down, confirming Chase's suspicion.

"I thought so! Now I had to call my… I don't even know, my girlfriend maybe, to bail this piece of shit out of jail," Chase said, throwing his hands up in exasperation. "And after what he did… What else do you want from me? I didn't kick the shit out of him like I wanted to…" Chase sat back, crossing his arms angrily. "For HER. And for you, damnit."

Chase simmered in his anger while Jude stood awkwardly in front of him.

"He… he's just confused," Jude said quietly, "He gets stuck on stuff sometimes,"

"Yeah, well, I don't care," Chase snapped. "He's been stuck on HER for years,"

"So have you," Jude said flatly, Chase flinched. "I'm just saying… Don't punish Aria," Jude said softly in that way that annoyed Chase because he knew Jude was right.

Chase sighed in defeat and put his head back in his hands.

"Why did I come back here," Chase moaned.

"Because you love her," Jude said matter of factly. "Don't let Jonah turn you into him,"

Chase dropped his hands from his face and digested what Jude had said.

"That was low, Jude, but…" Chase said slowly, "But… You're right,"

"Yep," Jude agreed as he left Chase alone in the front lobby.

Chase was holding on so tight because HE needed her to be his light, to be his life raft. But what if she needed a life raft? What if she was the one who needed to be saved? He remembered her crying in his arms in high school; he'd been her safe place, but then he'd left. Jonah had absorbed that role, and Chase would be no better than Jonah if he began suffocating her to make himself feel whole. But he couldn't get the memory of Jonah's hands on her out of his mind either. He wanted to talk to her and make sure she knew why he was so dangerous.

As if on cue, the front doors swung open, and Aria entered, sheltered under an umbrella. She struggled momentarily to close the umbrella while keeping it outside, the door propped open slightly with her butt. Chase smiled; Aria was superstitious, so she'd stand there all day and wrestle with that thing or abandon it outside before she came inside with it open and angered whatever gods cared about umbrellas.

She's so goddamn cute.

And it was like his heart thawed, all the anger melting away.

Chase stood and rounded the front desk, slowly approaching Aria. Watching the dimple that appeared on her cheek when she was concentrating and envying the water that dripped down her back.

In the years Chase was gone, he'd dated a Rebecca, a Heather, a Jessica, an Amanda, a Lindsey, and a Claire but his heart always came back to Aria. Even when Amanda had professed her love and spent the night with him, he stared into the darkness after wishing the girl curled into his side was Aria. He tried to forget her, tried to find someone to fill the hole she left with his criminal justice classes or the academy or alcohol.

But she was always there, this gaping hole in his soul that only Aria could fill. So, he had come home to her. And for a moment, it had been everything he'd needed.

I need her.

Aria was bent over, red hair wet and dripping down her face, frustration creasing her forehead. Just as she was about to break it over her knee, Chase reached out and took the umbrella from her. Aria let go but didn't move; Chase leaned down and clicked the release button, collapsing the umbrella on itself. He stepped back, allowing Aria room to step into the mezzanine, and let the door close behind her. Awkwardly, he offered her back the umbrella. Aria didn't look up at him; she was dodging his eyes, which meant she was trying not to cry. She guarded her emotions well, and the few clues Chase had learned about her inner workings he kept safe. They were like partial codes to the lock that was Aria.

"I'm sorry for what I said and that I didn't call," Chase said. "And… I didn't mean it…"

"Okay, whatever… What did Jonah do?" Aria mumbled angrily.

"He kissed you, Aria," Chase hissed.

"I know, Chase! I meant today! What did Jonah do TODAY?" Aria snapped.

I mean, it technically was today.

Nope… don't say that.

"Distribution, but we have to talk about this," Chase said, desperate to right this and just be with her. He knew he had made a mistake as soon as he saw her walk through the door. He knew she wasn't at fault, just a victim of all the shitty things that had happened to her in her life living under the gaze of a psychopath.

"I wanted to! You're the one who stormed off okay?" Aria retorted, "You said 'fuck you, Aria. Fuck it, I'm done.' and you left! I didn't do anything wrong!" she ground out. Chase could hear the lump in her throat. Her face was flushed with embarrassment or anger, Chase couldn't tell which.

"I know. I'm sorry. I am, but now things can't just go back to how they were with you two. He's made it really clear what he wants from you, and I'll be damned if he's going to be having sleepovers and shit again," Chase's voice was like steel.

"You don't get to decide that!" Aria snapped, and then she took a deep breath. "But, I know," then she whispered sadly. "He changed everything,"

Chase was shocked at that. And then he saw the tears.

She finally sees it.

I'm watching her heart break… again….

"I tried to talk to him, but he won't listen," She wiped a tear away angrily, "Everyone leaves, right? I'm going to lose him and Jude because Jonah can't have me. Because what he and I have isn't enough for him. And I'm going to lose you because of Jonah!" Aria's eyes were dark, and Chase embraced her. She leaned into him but didn't return the embrace.

"I was mad and jealous, and I was dick… I'm sorry," Chase said, his chin on her head.

And I wasted donuts.

The truth was he knew he'd never know Aria as well as Jonah and Jude. At 17, the three of them lived together, they were bound by the trauma of loss, and Aria was one tragedy away from total collapse by the age of 18. Jonah had seen her through all of that, they were legally siblings. And now, Jonah had twisted it all up in his head, and Aria was the one hurting. Chase bit back the rage building in him, he wanted to snap Jonah's neck for causing her to wet his shirt with her tears.

Finally, Aria reached her small arms around his waist and lightly squeezed him back. When she let him in, it was like standing in the sunlight; when she froze him out, it was like being alone on the moon. They had to find a middle ground that didn't strand him. Or her. Aria pulled away slowly and took a deep breath, all signs of grief erased.

"So, what did he get picked up for?" Aria asked.

"Distribution," Chase sighed. Aria wouldn't abandon him, "It's not good. He had enough in that car to get a felony. He's in deep shit," Chase answered honestly, walking towards the desk.

"Where's Jude? Are they charging him?" Aria asked, following him.

"Aria… everyone knows it's not Jude. And even if they didn't, Jonah took all the blame," Chase hated admitting that to her now. It made him seem like a decent guy. But that was one thing Aria and Jonah did have in common: their love for Jude. They'd both throw themselves into traffic to save him a single hurt. They'd seen what collapse looked like in Jude, and everyone, including Chase, hated it.

Chase rounded the desk and clicked into the computer.

"What's his bail?" Aria asked.

Chase focused on the computer screen but frowned when he realized the booking file wasn't up yet.

"It doesn't say yet, but it's not going to be cheap," Chase looked back to her.

"I can dip into my college money," Aria said hesitantly.

"Aria, no!" Chase started, "Don't use your college money. We'll call the bail bondsman, Hal is a decent-ish guy,"

Aria met his eyes; her gray eyes opened like wells in front of him. Like the sky before a storm. He could look at them forever. "Chase, I don't know what is wrong with him, but I'm going to help if I can. Then… I'll deal with the next step later. I promise. But… I won't use my school money,"

"Okay, good. I'll call Hal and…"

Suddenly screams ripped through the station.

Chapter Thirty-Nine

Aria

CHASE and Aria raced across the lobby to the booking doors. Chase threw up his arm, pushing her behind him, unholstering his gun. Aria was immediately offended and then realized this was maybe one of those times she should just trust Chase. He was an armed police officer in the station; she was an unarmed citizen; this was his area of expertise, after all. Chase raised his weapon and pushed the door open, sweeping it over the room as did his eyes.

The booking room was a rectangular, beige monstrosity with rows of backless benches down the middle of the room. Cubicles lined the back wall along with the mugshot wall to the right. Across the room from them, barred cells lined the wall - one of which stood open, an officer kneeling within. The room was silent and smelled of coffee and something metallic.

I know that smell, Aria thought. But she couldn't place it.

Her heart was racing and thundering in her ears, but she followed close behind Chase as he surveyed the room. The door closed behind them, causing Aria to jump and tuck herself further behind Chase, clutching the back of his shirt in her shaking hands. Jude was against the wall ahead of them, horror painting his face a sickly green. Jonah was standing at a weird angle, still handcuffed to the last bench. Both were staring towards the cubicle in the back. Aria followed their gaze, heart hammering in her chest. In the silence of the room, she heard a wet ripping sound. An unnatural squelching noise crawled into her ears and down her spine, raising the hairs on the back of her neck. Something wasn't right.

"Stokes? Ted?" Chase said anxiously as they made their way deeper into the room towards Jonah and Jude. Aria saw Chase bite his lip and knew he was afraid, which didn't help slow her own heart rate.

"He killed her…" Jude whispered.

"What?" Chase barked, "Where's Garcias? Stokes?!" his voice rose in fear, and anxiety rolled off of him. Aria had never seen him like this; Chase was the calm one… what was happening?

Then she saw the blood.

"Chase…" she gasped.

From under the cubicle walls seeped a deep crimson puddle, spreading across the tiled floor. Someone moved from behind the walls of the cubicle, their steps sounding sticky in the ever-expanding pool of blood. As they watched in horror, Ted stood from behind the divider, gore dripping from his mouth and chin. His uniform was caked in blood, soaking his chest and forearms. Black/blue liquid dripped down the sides of his face, running down his neck and forehead. Ted's eyes were wide and blank as he took in the room as if he'd never seen it before.

"Holy shit," Chase whispered in horror.

"Oh my god," Aria breathed as he took in the sight of Chase's friend drenched in blood.

"Stay behind me," Chase whispered frantically to Aria.

Turning his attention back to Ted, Chase relaxed his tone, softening his face. Feigning the air of calm.

"Ted, what happened?"

"Just took care of something," Ted said in a gravelly voice Aria didn't recognize. Ted's eyes twitched around, and he seemed to sniff the air around him.

"Yeah?" Chase's voice shook slightly, "You all right?"

Aria heard the quiver in his voice, and her stomach clenched. Chase was scared, which made her terrified.

"Yep," Ted leaned down and retrieved something from the floor, then raised it up for them all to see.

A face.

Not a head. A FACE. It looked like plastic or wax. Aria's brain couldn't comprehend what it really was, it couldn't be real. But even as she watched the horrifying scene, she heard the blood drip to the floor. The edges of the skin were jagged and red, light sneaking in through the holes where eyes and nostrils used to be. Ted's hands and forearms were utterly covered in blood, shiny and sticky. Ted held it up over his face like a mask and smiled.

"See. I got it," Ted grinned manically.

Aria felt bile rise in her throat, and her vision swam at the edges.

Then she remembered Jonah and Jude.

"Chase, the handcuff keys," Aria whispered next to him. Chase was frozen at the site of his sergeant, his friend, feral and grotesque. "Chase!" Aria hissed.

Seeming to finally hear her, he kept his eye on Ted and took his left hand off his pistol, unclipping the keys from his belt and handing them with a shaky hand to Aria.

"Jude," Aria motioned quietly to Jude to Jonah. Jude looked at her with wide terrified eyes, shaking his head. He pressed himself against the wall behind him as if trying to be swallowed up whole to escape the horror around them.

Help me!

Aria mouthed at her cousin as the keys shook in her hand. Reluctantly, Jude peeled himself off the wall and joined her. To get to Jonah, they'd have to walk towards Ted and the carnage, though still across the room, the space felt excruciatingly small. The heavy aroma of blood closed in on them, it seeemed to choke off all the air. Chase angled himself between them and Ted, walking with them up the row of benches. They moved slowly, trying not to draw Ted's attention. Aria's heart was hammering in her chest, and she fought the nausea threatening to choke her breathing in through her nose. The air was acrid with the stench of death, and Aria struggled to find an untainted breath.

"Hey," Ted said, noticing Jude and Aria, who froze in fear, "What's your girlfriend doing back here?"

"She's just going to post bail for her cousin then we're going to go. We gotta clean up this mess," Chase said calmly, desperately trying to distract him.

As they neared Jonah, two more bodies came into view. A woman's mangled corpse stared back at her. Her face was destroyed, a huge chunk of her cheek a void of mangled flesh. Teeth marks marred the skin around the hole, and Aria gagged. The other body was a rookie Aria knew; she'd met him once when she and Chase had met for lunch, and he'd seemed kind and funny. He was now twisted and broken on the linoleum; head arched back at an unnatural angle. But it was his eye that stopped Aria in her tracks…. One eye was missing completely. A sunken cavity where a green eye should've been. Jude nudged her, and she began to move again, forcing her quaking body to move. Chase stole a glance at them and Ted smiled.

"I always wondered how she'd taste," Ted grumbled, something boiled behind his eyes. Like someone longing to be free saying *Look at me! Look at me!*

That wasn't Ted anymore.

Aria froze.

Next to her, Jude went rigid.

"Get him uncuffed and get to the cellblock door," Chase said through clenched teeth, "Ted, don't move!" he yelled. "Hands up!"

Aria ran to the bench flipping through the keys, fighting the tremble in her hands. Jude was next to her and soon he was shuffling through the other keys on the ring. After what seemed like an eternity, Aria spied the small handcuff key and pressed it into the cuff on Jonah's left wrist. When the cuff released, the three released a breath.

"Come on, come on, come on," Jonah was whispering urgently, head whipping between Ted and Chase

"I'm trying," Aria sobbed, hands trembling.

"Give them here," Jude said quickly, taking the ring and unlocking Jonah's other cuff.

Ted regarded Chase for a moment, then bent over and picked up his service pistol, which had become unholstered at some point. Blood dripped from the barrel.

"No! Ted put it down. Ted, freeze, damnit!" Chase yelled as Ted stood and took a step towards Aria and the twins.

As the cuffs fell to the floor, Jonah flew to his feet. Jude took the keys and ran to the cell block door, a barred door that opened to a cement hallway leading to the back exit. To his right was the line of cells. From his periphery Jude caught a movement and jumped as an arm clawed through the bars at him, snagging his shirt.

"Aria!" Jude screamed.

Aria and Jonah ran to Jude and pulled at him desperately, trying to pry him from the vice-like grip. Jonah wrestled with the hand closed around Jude's shirt and pushed back each finger one by one. Finally, the grip released, and all of them fell away from the cell. Aria's heart froze when she saw the other body. Within the cell lay what appeared to be another man, ripped apart like a bear had been locked in the cell with him. Her eye caught glimpses of torn skin, ripped hair, blood, bone… and then she noticed Stokes. His head twitched back and forth at them, blue-black droplets rolled down his face, but it was insignificant compared to the shear amount of blood that covered the cell. His uniform was sopping in the other man's blood while a wide puddle spread from the pieces of the corpse. Stokes seemed to see Jonah, and recognition twinkled in his eye.

"I know you," and then rushed the bars of the cage like a feral animal. Jonah jumped back, evading his grasp. He tripped over his skidding feet and fell to the ground landing in another grisly puddle that seeped from yet another cell. Jonah scrambled to his feet, blood soaking his back and butt. Jonah slipped again as he swiped desperately at his hands, trying to rid himself of the blood covering them

Stokes' arm slashed madly out at them. The door was open, not four feet from him, but it was like he couldn't see it. Like he didn't have the critical thinking skills to find it. He'd been reduced to a base animal. Jude tried again for the door, keys jingling as Aria screamed for him to hurry.

"I'm trying!" Jude sobbed.

Then a gunshot rang out.

Chapter Forty

Chase

"DON'T make me do this Ted, please" Chase begged. Ted cocked his head at Chase like a confused animal, his movements were jerky and twitchy. Blood and some black shit covered him.

This is TED. The kindest man I've ever met. What the fuck is happening?

Ted jerked forward suddenly, running toward Chase… and he squeezed the trigger.

No.

The world went silent and slowed - just blurred colors and Ted's eyes.

Ted hit the ground. The twins and Aria covered their ears as the shot echoed off the block walls of the station.

"Chase!" Aria screamed; her voice muffled by the ringing in his ears.

Chase turned to see Stokes coming from behind them from a cell.

"Stokes! Freeze!" Chase screamed but he couldn't raise his gun without pointing it at Aria and the Foresters.

Stokes reached for Aria, and Chase screamed her name.

Chapter Forty-One

Aria

A blood-drenched hand gripped her shoulder, spinning wildly her feet slipped on the blood-slick floor, landing on her back, air rushing from her lungs. She tried to crawl away but couldn't move fast enough or get enough oxygen. Stokes seemed to suddenly see the open cell door and lurched towards the opening. Aria screamed and kicked the door closed, sending Stokes flailing backward against the outer wall. Chase ran up and slammed the door closed, motioning for the keys from Jude, who tossed them without question. Chase locked the cell stepping back, watching Stokes rise to his feet again. His movements were jerky and disjointed, spittle hanging from his bloody mouth.

"Back door!" Chase yelled.

Aria was on her feet as Chase found the key for the lock to the back door. Stokes slammed against the cell again, reaching wildly for any of them. Aria heard the lock click, and they all spilled into the back hallway, closing the door tightly behind them. The hallway was silent, except for their ragged breaths. Watching the room through the bars of the door.

Then Ted groaned, guttural and raw.

"No…" Chase whispered.

"But you shot him…" Jude whispered.

From across the room, Ted slowly rose. His cheek was ripped from his nose to his jaw. Muscle and tendons gaped at them as he cocked his head to the left, studying the group. Bloody scraps of flesh moving with every jolt. He stood statue-still, yet somehow unsteady. Then, he ran full speed at the iron door, slamming his body against the metal door again and again. Bones cracking and snapping with every blow. It was like he was nothing but a meat puppet being whipped around by some sick puppet master. Over and over again, he rammed his body against the bars, blood pouring from the hole in his face and spattering through the door.

"What's wrong with him?" Aria shrieked; she felt Jonah shift uncomfortably to her right. She looked up at him and recognized the look of guilt plastered across his face, "What did you do?" she asked coldly.

Then a hinge began to groan.

"Shit," Aria gasped. Chase scrambled to a crouch and trained his weapon at Ted.

"Back door, behind us," Chase whispered.

"Back up," Aria barked at the twins, who did as they were told. They moved as a group down the cellblock to the emergency exit.

"I wanna taste her…. I wannnnnnnnnaaaaa taaaassssste hhhheerrrrrrrrrr" Ted began to sing. "Alice wants to taste her,"

"What the fuck?!" Aria cried, fear sliding down her veins like a frost.

"Just get outside," Chase yelled. They all turned and ran, bursting through the back door to the sounds of alarms. Chase slammed the door behind them, and they all stood in the sudden quiet.

They all stood shocked and silent.

"What the fuck, what the fuck, what the fuck," Chase said over and over again, suddenly still braced against the door.

Jonah leaned against the brick building, panting, and Jude was on the ground with his elbows on his knees, head in his hands. Aria stood to the right of the door and glared at Jonah, then suddenly she stalked towards him, heat flashing through her, shoving him violently against the building.

"Wo, wo, wo!" Chase yelled, pulling Aria back to him.

"What did you do?!" Aria screamed at her cousin.

"What do you mean?" Chase ground out, "What does she mean?" he roared, turning to Jonah.

"Jonah?" Jude questioned, "What does she mean?"

Jonah coughed and straightened, trying to stand taller than Chase.

"I had to ditch it," he said plainly.

"Ditch what…" Jude said in horror.

"What are you talking about?" Aria demanded.

"Alice…" Jonah said.

"Alice….!" Aria stilled, and she felt her adrenaline pumping and her face reddening again, rage pushing at her edges. She knew what that shit was and what it did. The urban rumor mill had claimed everything was laced with her, causing people to bite faces off or worse under her influence.

"Shit," Chase whispered.

"ALICE?!" Aria yelled again.

Ted had said Alice wanted to taste her.

"It's fine…. In small doses," Jonah said apathetically.

"What does it do in large doses?" Chase asked.

"I guess that," he shrugged, motioning vaguely at the jail.

"Jonah!" Aria snapped, "What. Did. You. Do?"

"I put it in the coffee maker," he sniffed casually, "They brewed a pot. This shit is supposed to be cut, like one to two drops is enough to get high but…"

"How much did you have?" Chase asked quietly.

"4 ounces and I…"

"You poured all of it in," Jude finished for him in dread, putting his head in his hands.

Suddenly from what felt like all around them, a deep rumble rolled through the mountains. The sound reverberated through them even though the ground beneath feet wasn't moving. Cracks and snaps echoed down the valley, and suddenly, the lights on the exterior of the building went out, backup lights stuttering to life.

"You guys…" Jude gasped.

They looked out across the mountain range that curved around and boxed them in the South and East. In the high country above the tree line the entire earth began to move. Rock into liquid. Like some mythical monster pushing its way down the valley towards the river. The mudslide slid down the mountain ranges on two sides as the entire world shifted beneath them. Power poles were swallowed by the tide, one after the other, down the entire ridgeline, wires snapping away from their other halves. Behind them, the high country looked the same, moving in an almost surreal state. Cascading down the horizon, meeting finally with the sludge from the other ridge and spilling down the mountain, and stopping somewhere downtown they couldn't see. Rockslides were common here, but this was huge. This was two mountain faces sloughing away like it was shedding old skin. Rivers of sediments pushed West and followed the natural flow of the land downward to the river, taking everything in its path with it.

"Please tell me this isn't happening," Jude whimpered.

From inside the station, they heard guttural screams and banging against the bars.

"Jude, help me," Chase motioned to a nearby dumpster and together they pushed it in front of the back door of the station.

Aria was trembling everywhere, her ears still ringing from the gunshot in the enclosed space she struggled to catch a breath. Jonah had poisoned an entire police station. A massive mudslide had just moved the entire earth and probably obliterated some of the town and here they were hiding in an alley behind the police station. No weapons or survival gear.

"We need to get to a squad car," Chase said, tucking his pistol back into the holster "I don't have a radio on me, and we need help,"

Thank God he's here.

"Okay, let's go," Aria agreed, frantically grabbing for him. She needed to feel his touch right now. He was the only thing tethering her to sanity and safety, so she clung to his arm as if her life depended on it… and it quite possibly could.

Chase looked down at her hand clinging to his and she saw the corners of his lips twitch up. He still loved her. She hadn't lost him yet.

"Stay together," Chase whispered back to the twins.

Aria motioned Jude and Jonah to follow them. Chase eyed Jonah as he passed, and Aria hoped he fought the very apparent urge to shoot him.

Carefully they made their way around the corner of the building to the back parking lot and spotted three cruisers. In the mountains, most of the vehicles were four-wheel drive, but the force always had a couple of sedans in its fleet. They split up, Chase made his way to the driver-side door of the first cruiser, but it didn't open. Aria and Jude yanked anxiously on the handle of the second, and both cursed when it also didn't open. Jonah and Chase reached the last cruiser at the same time both grabbing the handle and freezing, locking eyes. A silent tension suddenly built between the two. Chase stood tall, looking down on Jonah who was just an inch or two shorter.

"Are you kidding me right now?!" Aria hissed angrily, pushing them both apart, "This is a stupid fucking time to do this! Get your shit together!" She looked from Jonah to Chase and back again, "BOTH of you!"

Jonah held his hands up and backed away from the door, Chase pulled the handle, and they all released a breath when the door opened. Chase slid into the driver's seat and found the keys in the ignition.

"You were JUST lecturing me about leaving my keys in the car," Aria scoffed as she went around the car and crawled into the passenger seat. Chase grabbed the handset of the radio and pressed the button.

"Station to patrol, station to patrol…"

Nothing

"This is Officer Gorski; Serenity PD needs backup!! Officers..." Chase looked at Jonah and sighed, "Officer down. Civilian casualties. Requesting immediate assistance,"

Aria held her breath and reached over and clutched Chase's arm anxiously, needing his grounding touch again.

"Patrol to station. That's a negative, Officer Gorski. The mudslide cut out... all roads.... Impassible... trapped.... Our team can't get down.... road.... Ranger station... call.... Emergency protocol... eva.... Sh...." the static took over, and then the radio went quiet.

"Did he just say we're trapped?" Jude yelled.

"What about Ted and Stokes?" Chase asked.

"They should be stuck, right?" Jude asked anxiously.

"I don't know for how long, but we can't subdue them. I SHOT Ted... And he just kept fucking coming!" Chase gripped the steering wheel, hiding the shake in his hands. Aria watched him closely, then softened her grip on his arm and covered his hand with hers.

"I'm sorry about Ted," Aria said quietly. "Let's head through town and check out the highway; maybe we can get through." Aria offered. Chase took a breath and nodded, blinking back a tear.

"You alright there, Boy Scout?" Jonah mocked from the back seat. Before Aria had a chance to think, she rounded on Jonah and smacked him across the face. The car erupted into chaos. Jonah was yelling at Aria; Jude was yelling at Jonah. Suddenly, Chase slammed his hand on the horn, startling them all into silence. Chase turned slowly back to Jonah, who sat behind him; Aria watched wide-eyed, sure that Chase was going to break his nose.

"Get out," Chase growled.

Jonah stared at him in surprise.

"Excuse me?" Jonah said incredulously.

"You want to be an asshole, do it on your own time, I am the only thing keeping you alive right now, and that's only because I respect these two. Keep your mouth shut or you're gone," Chase glared.

Jonah clenched his jaw; Aria could tell he was warring with himself. Eyes flitting to her then back to Chase. He wanted to get out, to prove a point, but Jonah also knew his survival depended on staying with the group.

"You're in charge, officer," Jonah spat.

Aria released a breath.

"Good," Chase grunted as he turned around, putting the car in motion.

Chapter Forty-Two

Chase

THEY drove silently through town. Aria stiff next to Chase, chewing on her lip.

"The highway crew will be out… we're not trapped," Chase said more to himself than to anyone.

I shot Ted.

Fucking Ted… he was my friend…

"That cop ripped that guy's face off," Jude whispered in the quiet car, "right in front of us,"

"What happened in there?" Aria asked, turning around to face Jude.

"He was still drinking the coffee, and it was like he just had an idea, he dug his nails into that lady's forehead and literally peeled it off," Jude said in horror.

"'I've always wanted to do that'" Jonah said,

They all turned to him in disgust.

"Jonah! What the hell?" Aria gasped.

"No! That's what he said after," he said defensively. "That's what Garcias said… after he did it,"

"Jesus Christ, Jonah, this is a mess…." Aria sighed.

"I didn't mean to," he whelped.

"You poured it in the fucking coffee maker Jonah!" Jude said in exasperation.

"You never MEAN to do anything," Chase muttered.

Ted didn't deserve this.

"Nah man, I meant to kiss Aria," Jonah shot back.

Chase instantly saw red. His vision tunneling, he slammed on the breaks, throwing the car into park. He turned, nearly leaping at Jonah over the back of the seat. Pain flared in his fist as it connected with Jonah's face slamming it into the window next to him.

"Yeah, what else did you mean to do motherfucker?" Chase yelled as he threw wild punches over the back of the seat.

Ted didn't have to die.

"ENOUGH!" Aria screamed.

Chase froze, heart hammering.

Everyone silenced immediately.

"We can't do this right now! Jonah, you fucked up and kissed me. You will never do it again... understand? And for the remainder of this particular emergency, you will NOT talk to me as anything other than your friend and sibling. You will ALSO treat Chase with respect and gratitude for not leaving you cuffed to that bench" She turned to Chase, "You attacking Jonah every five seconds isn't going to get us through this either. We need you right now... I need you to be you. So, drop this macho bullshit, or I'll leave you both on the side of the road. We will deal with this," she motioned between them, "after we get through this, okay?"

She's right.

Get your shit together.

"Okay, Freckles," Chase said, sitting back down into his seat.

"Okay?" Aria asked Jonah louder.

"Yeah... Okay, you're right," he said begrudgingly.

"Good," Aria huffed.

God, I love her.

After a moment, Chase put the car in gear, pressing the gas, and slowly they drove towards downtown. Serenity Springs was split in two by the Colorado River and the main highway through the state. Across the width of those was a 4-lane car overpass with a newly renovated bridge, all leading to the north side of downtown. As they neared the 4-lane bridge that crossed into the next section of town, Aria gasped, and Chase's stomach sank.

The bridge and the entire north side of town were gone.

There was nothing but a field of rubble that spilled into the river, raging whitecaps roiled with sediment and red muddy water. Skeletal remains of buildings poked from the ruin, electric cables sparked into the open air, and water pipes drained down the hillside. Chase stopped the car near the end of the road. The four could only gape at the destruction across the water. They opened the car doors and as one walked towards the collapsed edge of the bridge.

Oh. My. God.

Half the town is gone.

Jonah and Jude ran to the edge of the broken roadway and began to scream.

Aunt Marnie. She lived in West Serenity Springs. Her section of town downriver was completely gone. Thick, muddy slides had swept trees and homes over one another. Full neighborhoods were buried beneath a veritable mountain of sludge and debris.

Aria joined them and fell to her knees, sobbing as Jonah held Jude, who was buckled over, screaming her name. In all the tragedy those three had seen, and it had been a lot, their one constant was always Aunt Marnie. Steadfast and sweet. Her home had welcomed three kids from broken worlds and had loved them. Chase had always felt welcome in her home, and on the nights his dad drank too much to control himself, he'd wished he was a Forrester. Maybe that was one reason why Chase hated Jonah so much. Jonah had Aunt Marnie and didn't even appreciate it. Half the teens knew Aunt Marnie, and all called her as such, even Jude and Jonah, despite living with her since they were young. Not mom. But it had worked for their little family, and she had loved them. Had loved Aria. Chase sighed sadly and knelt next to Aria, wrapping his arm around her; she crumpled into him.

"No! No no no no NO!" Jude was screaming.

Chase's eyes followed the river and saw the devastation extended far into the west section of town downriver. Boulders and dirt and cement chunks sloped into the Colorado River, clouding the water. The highway was gone. Half the town was gone.

From across the river, movement caught their eye.

"Person!" Chase yelled as a mud-covered man stumbled from the wreckage. He stumbled forward slightly as blood began cascading down the man's face. His knees buckled, and he fell to the ground, unmoving.

"Chase call somebody," Aria whispered through sobs.

Jude wailed again, and Jonah coughed out a sob.

"Okay," Chase whispered, blinking back tears at the scene. The heartbreak and utter destruction were overwhelming.

Chase got to his feet and returned to the patrol car, ducking in and grabbing the radio.

"Gorski to Patrol… West Serenity is gone. Multiple casualties. Requesting assistance," Chase said into the radio. There was nothing but static for several seconds.

"Negative Gorski. Patrol is stranded… State troopers have been alerted and are en route but won't be there till first light," The static clouded transmission again, and Chase sighed.

Shit

"Tomorrow morning?" Jude choked.

They were trapped in the valley with two homicidal cops until morning.

"Yeah…" Chase said resigned.

What are we going to do?

"Chase?" A voice called from the side street leading away from downtown.

"Drew?" Chase yelled back. "Is that you?" He hadn't seen Drew since leaving for the academy, but he would know that face anywhere.

Slowly others emerged from the shelter of the buildings. Murmurs of confusion and worry, all eyes looked to Chase.

Shit!

Chase stiffened, suddenly aware of everyone's expectations.

He glanced over his shoulder back at Aria and the twins, who were making their way back to the car.

"It's okay, they need help," Aria said, holding Jude's hand tightly. "You got this,"

Okay, I got this.

Chase nodded and held his hands up to the growing crowd.

Chapter Forty-Three

Aria

AUNT Marnie was gone.

Every lunch, every dinner, every time Aunt Marnie wanted her to come to breakfast but Aria skipped, suddenly raced through her head. Every time she was too busy to answer the phone when Aunt Marnie called suddenly tattooed itself on her heart. She gasped at the pain. Aunt Marnie was their safe place. Where she and the twins had fallen when their worlds had crumpled in upon them. Aria stopped and leaned in, embracing Jonah and Jude.

"What did you kids do to the real police officers?" Suzanne Raymond snipped; she was an old biddy who lived alone and called the cops on kids for being on her grass. And she was always calling the cops on Aria and the twins… some of those calls were, perhaps, warranted, like when they graffitied her mailbox, but still…

"'Excuse me?" Aria demanded, anger approaching easily on the heels of sadness, a safe mask to hide behind. "Are you kidding me?" she pulled away from the twins stalking towards the crowd.

Chase held out his hand to her.

"They're just scared," Chase said softly, "It's okay, I got this,"

Aria nodded tightly. She turned to see Jonah and Jude hugging, both with tears rolling down their cheeks. Aunt Marnie was the only mother they'd really had, Aria, at least, had had 16 years with her parents. They'd lost the only loving parent they'd ever known. Aria's eyes welled with tears as she curled into the driver's seat of the patrol car. Leaning against the back of the seat, she choked back sobs, not able to bear the pain in her cousins' eyes.

Glass in the road… a crumpled car…

She pushed the heels of her hands into her eyes, wanting to shove the image from her memory. She wanted to rip the image from her brain, so she never had to relive it.

"Aria?"

Aria's eyes flew open, wiping the tears from her face as she did.

"Hey, Dana," Aria said, sniffing.

"What's going on?" Dana asked, and as she asked, she seemed to remember something and looked out over the river. "Aunt Marnie?"

Aria simply shook her head as more tears gathered in her eyes.

Aria and Dana hadn't spoken in years. She was the only friend Aria had in her last few months of high school, but as prom crept up, Dana grew increasingly distant from Aria. Dana and Jonah were dating, so the four of them had gotten ready for prom at Aunt Marnie's house. Jude and Aria attended the dance together- the Heartbroken Lover and the Killer. Aria had wanted to bring fake blood for a fun prank, but Dana had talked sense into her at the last minute. Jonah and Dana made a beautiful couple, both with their raven hair and tall, slender stature, and as they danced, Aria saw a glimpse of a future where she didn't choke under Jonah's gaze. Then Dana was storming for the door, tears pouring down her beautiful face. When Aria chased her into the parking lot Dana turned on her.

"What happened?" Aria had asked, "Are you ok…"

"No! I'm NOT Okay, Aria!" Dana had cried.

"What did he do?" Aria had demanded.

"It's what he won't do," Dana met her eyes, "He will never look at me the way he looks at you,"

Aria had only looked at her sadly, not knowing how to react or what to say. Dana nodded as if affirming her suspicions. Dana had left Aria standing in the parking lot, crying. And that was it. The last person outside of her home that cared about her was gone.

Back in the street, as Chase talked to the panicked citizens, Dana looked at her with none of the coldness, just fear and questions. Jude and Jonah had retreated to the other side of the car, backs to the crowd, huddled together, still reeling.

"I know you aren't going to bullshit me… what's happening?" Dana asked her pointedly. Aria stared at Dana a moment, then waved her down to her level.

"We just watched two police officers literally rip a person apart," Aria said, "There are two cops locked in the police station…."

"What?!" Dana exclaimed, horror coating her beautiful features.

"Shhhhhhhh!" Aria chastised, "Jonah got busted this afternoon and had some Alice on him, and he poured it into the coffee maker… they went insane, Dana… they killed… They ripped this woman's face off…" Aria shook as she spoke, wiping her face with her hands.

"Jonah…" Dana said like it was the answer to the riddle.

"Jonah," Aria agreed. "It was a super concentrated amount or something, and he poured it all in," she cleared her throat and turned over her shoulder. Jonah and Jude were still on the other side of the car and as far as Aria could tell, they couldn't hear her. "And THEN this," she waved her hand toward the other side of the river, "happened, and now…" she choked on a sob.

"Jesus Christ, Aria," Dana sighed, "how fucked are we?"

Aria snorted, "Pretty fucked," she chuckled a bit through the tears.

Dana straightened and looked around at the ruin across the river and the unhappy crowd to their left. Sighing heavily, wiping her hands down her face in exasperation.

"Aria I-" Without warning, Dana's head exploded in a crimson red splash against Aria and the squad car. Aria stayed perfectly still as chunks of her former friend fell off of her arms, chest, and face. The world went silent. The only sound in the world was the blood dripping from Aria's chin, a drip-drop sound every time it hit the ground. The high-pitched echo of the gunshot rang in her ears, but all she could hear was the drip drop of the blood. Dana was crumpled on the ground at Aria's feet. She was talking to her seconds ago, and now… she was a husk on the pavement.

Then the crowd broke loose, splitting into a frenzy of scared, panicked people. Chase was swept away by the tide pushing him into the side streets as Aria was frozen in the front seat of the cruiser. The crowd plowed against the car, and suddenly, Aria was grabbed by Paul Fitzsimmons, who threw Aria out of the car and onto the pavement. Her knees landed on Dana. Aria gagged and crawled off her friend's body, turning back towards the car, and watched as Paul fumbled to turn the ignition. Just as the engine roared to life the back window of the squad car exploded. Glass showered down upon them. Aria covered her head and then stared in horror at Paul. Blood poured from a gaping hole in the left side of his skull, the layers of muscle and bone on display made Aria wretch. Paul's jaw muscle released, his mouth falling open in a silent scream before he crumpled out of the car onto the pavement in front of Aria.

Aria gaped at the slaughter at her feet. Two lives over in a blood-drenched second. Aria shook herself out of her haze as another gunshot echoed off the buildings. Staying low and stifling her sobs, Aria crawled to the front bumper, out of the line of sight.

Where were the twins?

Back against the bumper, Aria fought the hysteria bubbling up in her. Dana's brain…. Paul's jaw… Dana's blood…. Her blood… Her breath came in fast gulps as she tried to wipe the blood from her hands. Another gunshot, but this time, the pavement exploded next to her.

"Chase!" Aria screamed, "CHASE!"

Chapter Forty-Four

Chase

CHASE couldn't fight against the crowd and was pushed into a side street. Finally, he freed himself and got low and around the corner of the building, looking for the source of the shots. Then he saw them. Ted and Stokes walked boldly down the middle of Main Street, rifles in hand. Chase cursed as he remembered the gun locker. They both carried rifles and had shotguns slung over each shoulder. Ted was reloading after taking out the window of the squad car. He fired randomly into the mass of people running away. Suzanne and her snide comments hit the ground, then another as Stokes began firing. Aria was on the ground on the front side of the car, screaming as the cement exploded around her. Suddenly, Jude and Jonah ducked around the front of the squad car grabbing Aria and pulling her to them. When the three of them were safely shielded by the bumper, Chase looked back to Ted and Stokes, who were both reloading.

Get the fuck out of there!

Aria locked eyes with Chase as he screamed for them to run.

I love you.

He turned from Aria and opened fire, screaming for Ted and Stokes to look at him.

Chapter Forty-Five

Aria

ARIA screamed for Chase but was suddenly dragged across the pavement and then backward down a rough embankment toward the river. Jude gripping her tightly by the arms, they stumbled along the edge of the remaining pavement. Aria couldn't stop shaking, her hands were sticky with her friend's blood. Flashes of Dana on her first day of school here, welcoming and complimenting her Goodwill clothing. Her laugh. Her smile.

Her blood.

Jude was in Aria's face, but she couldn't hear him over the ringing in her ears and her heartbeat pulsing in her temples. Suddenly, she was up again; Jonah basically carrying her now. They went down another shallow embankment and cold water was suddenly being splashed on her face and hands. The cold shook her from her haze, and she gasped as if waking from a dream.

"Aria?" Jonah said, concerned.

"Is she hit?" Jude asked.

"Can you hear me? Are you okay?" Jonah asked again.

Aria stared at him for a long time, then nodded slowly.

"Hey, can you move? Are you hurt?" Jude said, shoving Jonah aside and surveying Aria's body himself, "Is this your blood or…" Jude stopped and met Aria's eyes. He couldn't say her name.

Dana. Dana was gone.

"I'm okay," she told the twins and herself out loud.

She had to be okay. There were no other options, move forward or die.

"We need to get off the streets," Her voice was hoarse, "Chase's place is that way; we can wait there for him," She flicked her eyes to Jonah, but he didn't protest. He was pale, frightened, and panting.

"Are you guys okay?" she asked. Both were silent. Jude's eyes were wide with panic, and Jonah kept his head up and eyes constantly surveying their surroundings. "Okay, come on. Stay close, okay?" Aria focused on the steps ahead of her, not thinking about Dana or Paul Fitzsimmons or Chase or bloody clothes, she just watched the pavement right in front of her. One step at a time.

They climbed the incline back onto the street, they ran low to the ground to the next alley. Chase's house was up two blocks and over one. The street was at a steep incline up the mountain, and they'd be visible from the street below if they went straight up, so they stuck to the alleyways and backyards. They climbed the street by hopping retaining walls between small homes that were once owned by the mining company and used to house their employees. Small square houses with small square yards lined most of the streets up the hillside. When they reached the end of the alley, the open expanse of the road downhill loomed to their right. They peered around the corner of the building; the street sloped down into the main intersection downtown, revealing Chase's now abandoned patrol car. Aria looked away, her stomach churning at the scene. They saw no one, and after a collective deep breath, they sprinted across the road, diving behind a fence on the other side. Gunfire ripped through the air, echoing off the mountains and buildings.

"It's not close," Jonah whispered.

Jude exhaled next to her in relief.

Aria looked up and saw a tiny pair of eyes peeking around a curtain in one of the houses. Anxious and afraid. Aria put her finger to her lips - Shhhhhh- and mouthed the word "HIDE" and waved the little boy away. The boy nodded and disappeared from view, the curtain falling back into place. Aria motioned with her head for the twins to follow her. Chase's house was the third one down, a small one-bedroom row house that had new paint and a newer roof. Chase loved his little house. Aria crawled up the steps, sliding a potted plant over, revealing a key. She unlocked the door shakily as two more loud gunshots erupted in the direction of downtown, and Aria jumped up. Suddenly willing to sprint back down the mountain and make sure Chase was safe.

"Aria…." Jude eased, "He'll be all right. It's Chase,"

She swallowed hard around the lump in her throat.

Aria turned the knob pushing, the door open, the twins crawling in behind her. Quickly, they closed and locked the door; Aria exhaled, falling back against the door.

They were in Chase's kitchen. It was small with a short counter and a block of cabinets to the left and a small area for a table to the right. The appliances took up the rest of the left wall. The living room opened off the kitchen with a back door to the right, next to the stairs and basement access. He'd put so much time and love into this little house, and Aria wanted nothing but to crawl into his (certainly) made bed and hide away from all this ugliness. She looked down at herself, taking in the gore.

"Does he have a gun here?" Jude asked.

"Um, I think he has a hunting rifle in the basement," Aria said, suddenly feeling desperate to get out of the sticky blood-stained clothing. "I'm going to wash off… I'm going to wash," Aria said thickly, the twins both nodded as she crawled across the kitchen and up the narrow staircase.

The second story consisted of a bedroom and a small bathroom with vaulted ceilings. Chase had to practically bend over in the shower, but it fit Aria perfectly. She closed the door at the top of the steps and locked it. She stripped off the bloody clothes, peeling them away from herself like a second skin. As she kicked off her shoe, she saw a small piece of flesh clinging to her laces by a cluster of long ebony hair.

She immediately ran to the toilet to vomit.

She'd dealt with death but never worn it. She peeled the rest of the clothing off and then stepped into the shower. She turned the knob, and water sputtered out of the showerhead, and soon it was blissfully warm. Thick streams of crimson streamed down her legs and swirled around her feet and down the drain. Aria turned it hotter until it scalded her skin. She wanted to burn the death off of her epidermis.

Finally, the water ran clear.

She finished up quickly, wrapping a fresh towel around her midsection while she went into Chase's bedroom. She grabbed a t-shirt and a pair of basketball shorts and tied them tight around her thin waist. Chase's bedroom was bare bones, a mattress on a metal frame, one side table with a lamp, and one dresser. No messes, no piles, clean lines, and emptiness. She opened his top drawer and found all of his clothing folded perfectly, she laughed to herself. Aria and Chase couldn't be any more different, but that is why they worked… most of the time.

From outside somewhere, gunshots ricocheted off a building, and Aria dove to the ground. They were getting closer. Outside, the evening sky deepened to night, and Aria resisted the urge to flick on the lamp by Chase's bed.

"Aria!" Jude whispered up the stairs, "Did you hear that?"

"Yes, Jude, I heard that," she hissed back sarcastically.

Aria twisted her hair up on top of her head and then padded down the steps. Jonah and Jude were sitting on the floor in the small area between the kitchen and living room - the only area not visible from a window. Aria crouched down, her knees rattling beneath her.

"Did you try the phones?"

Both twins nodded.

Jude opened his mouth to say something but stopped when a faint *tap-tap* caught their attention.

"Did you hear that?" Aria whispered. Jonah nodded, standing, then as if thinking twice, he snatched a knife out of the block on the counter. He took a couple of steps across the kitchen, carefully pushing the curtains away from the tiny window on the top of the door and released a sigh. He unlocked the door, and Chase slipped in. Chase relocked the door, then leaned back against the door, panting. He opened his eyes and found Aria. He crossed the kitchen grabbing Aria and pulling her tightly to his chest.

He was okay. He was okay. He was okay.

He was shaking under her touch.

"I couldn't get to you," Chase kissed the top of her head, "I'm sorry,"

"I know, it's okay. I was worried about you," Aria mumbled. "Are you okay?"

"I'm fine. Let me see, are you okay? You were covered in blood," Chase said, stepping back and assessing her.

"It was…" Her throat caught as the image of the chunk of bloody flesh upstairs flashed in her mind, "It wasn't my blood,"

"Okay," he said quietly, he pulled her to him again. "I love you,"

"Hell of a time to say that for the first time," Aria laughed as he released her.

"We have to get out of here," Chase said to the twins as he opened the cupboard under the sink. Chase grabbed a small duffle bag and threw it to Jude.

"They were following me and are going block by block, they're fucking fast!" Chase said, "It's like they're tracking me… their eyes aren't right either,"

"There are people hiding everywhere, we need to find a basement or something and hide out until help can get here," Aria said.

Another shot rang out, but this time, it sounded like it was right outside. Aria's heart was racing as she dove to the floor, Chase and the twins dropping at the same time. Chase motioned for them to go towards the basement. Jude was closest and reached up, turning the handle until they heard the *click* and slowly, he pulled open the door. The old hinges grounded together but didn't squeak, together they crawled down the cement steps into the old utilitarian basement. An old metal work bench sat on one side, and a cellar-style door led up and out on the other side. Chase pointed towards the gun safe in the interior corner, whispering the combination to Aria. as he rushed across the basement and pushed the cellar door open just enough to look out. They all winced as the old hinges screamed in protest. They all held their breath, and that noise carried. Suddenly, a door was kicked in on the house to the left, and a woman screamed. Chase carefully closed the cellar door again, and Aria spun the dial with shaky, sweat-slicked hands until the safe clicked open. Inside, she found two shotguns, a rifle, and a smaller case, which she handed to Chase. Chase opened the smaller metal case revealing two pistols, one a revolver and one automatic pistol.

Aria reached in, handing back the shotgun to Jude, then hesitated as she made to hand the rifle to Jonah. His hand closed around the barrel, but for a second, Aria couldn't let go. His lips against hers and his hands desperately pulling her towards him flashed through her mind, making her heart falter, and she paused. Hurt flitted across his face, and Aria released the gun.

Shots rang out from the house next door; they all jumped and swore at the close proximity. Aria slapped her hands over her mouth, hoping the sound of the gunfire had covered their screams. Chase took the automatic pistol, giving Aria the revolver, and after a moment's thought, he also handed her the other shotgun. Aria inspected the gun. Her dad had taught her to shoot when she was nine, so she knew how to use one. She smiled to herself; this scenario is probably not what he would have ever imagined when he taught her.

Chase started shoving boxes of ammo in his pockets and tossed one to Jude and to Jonah, much to Aria's shock. He handed Aria a box, and as her hand touched his, he held it for a moment, looking her in the eye. Aria read fifty emotions in Chase's sky-blue eyes before he leaned forward and kissed her. He looked terrified. Like he was saying goodbye. He took a deep breath, releasing his grip on the box, and turning back to the twins.

"Okay, we get out of here and head straight out to the road and back down into town. If we can get to Drew's bar, we can hide downstairs; he has a walk-in freezer and a wine cellar which should provide some protection," Chase said as he checked both his guns.

"Unless they burn it down," Jude said, horrified.

"Why would you say that?" Aria snapped, and then she saw Jude's eyes fixated on the small cellar window. They followed his gaze through the small pane and gasped at the dark plume of smoke rising from the direction of downtown.

"Oh no…" Chase gasped.

Aria had no love for Drew after high school, but this was too much. No one deserved this.

Upstairs the front door suddenly smashed open. There was a crash followed by the clatter of a chair being tossed. They all stared at the ceiling listening to the footsteps above, slow, and deliberate. They followed the heavy steps across the ceiling, holding their breath collectively praying.

"Go!" Chase whispered, waving them all toward the cellar door. The footsteps reached the far side of the house just as Jude pushed the cellar door open with a sickening rusty squeal. There was a crash from the kitchen and footsteps speeding toward the basement door at the top of the steps.

"Shit! GO!" Aria yelled, pushing the twins toward the door.

They crawled up the steps then sprinted out across the small yard.

BRAAAAAAP

Shots cut up the grass and air around them as they ran for the next retaining wall, wood splintering off the fence as shots ricocheted off of it and splitting the group. Dirt and splinters spat back at Aria as she, Jude, and Chase slid around the fence at the corner, Jude's shotgun skittering away from them across the pavement. Chase stopped, dropping to a knee, turned, and aimed at Stokes, who stalked across the yard towards them from the side of the house. He must have gone around while Ted went in, they're lucky they made it across the yard at all. Aria covered her ears and watched Chase fire the handgun, catching Stokes in the shoulder and setting him off balance momentarily, but he recovered quickly, swinging his own weapon up and spraying an arc of bullets wildly in their direction. Chase ducked back behind the fence, draping himself over Aria. Once the barrage ceased, Chase motioned for her and Jude to follow the wall to the next yard. Aria scrambled across the ground after Jude, looking back to make sure Chase was still there. She couldn't lose him now. Jonah had taken cover behind the brick house across the street from them. Bullets chipped at the house above him as another spray of bullets peppered the air around them, and Aria suppressed a scream. It was like being hunted. And that's exactly what it was, they were being hunted.

How had they found them so fast? Could they smell them?

Aria wondered how much human was left in them at this point.

"I'm going to try and draw his attention; I want you two to head over the next retaining wall and hide…" Chase began when the brick above Jonah exploded again across the narrow road from them.

"Jonah!" Jude and Aria screamed; as the dust settled, Jonah rose from the debris, eyes wide as they landed on her and Jude.

"RUN!" Aria and Jude screamed, and without hesitation, Jonah tore from sight.

Aria looked panicked at Chase again.

"Do not leave me again," She ordered.

"I'll be right behind you, I promise," he said tightly.

"Chase!" She hissed.

"You have to go," He turned, sighing.

"No! Chase! NO! Chase! Come on!" Aria screamed, panic climbing its way up her esophagus.

She clawed at Chase's arm as Jude tried to wrestle her to him. Jude had her by the waist, but she kicked at him, wrenching free, when Chase finally grabbed her by the front of the shirt and pulled her into a kiss. Soft and sweet against the chaos around them.

"Go," he whispered as they parted.

"No, I…" She began, but he suddenly shoved her towards Jude so hard she couldn't hold on to his arm anymore.

"Go Jude!!" He roared as he turned and fired two rounds into his backyard.

"No! Chase!" Aria screamed, desperate to make him come with them, but Jude had her in a bear hug, and she couldn't get free.

"Jude! Goddamnit make her go!" Chase yelled as he stood and turned, shooting at Stokes again. "GO!"

Jude lifted Aria off the ground as if she weighed nothing and pulled her with him.

"Jude, no! He's gonna die! He's gonna die! He's gonna die!" Aria screamed, feeling panic lace her words and reason leave her mind. Jude threw himself behind the next house. Propping Aria against the building and taking her face in his hands.

"He's not going to die, and I need you to get your shit together!" Jude whispered harshly. "I love you, but we gotta do this, okay?"

Aria nodded, knowing he was right. That same fear of someone she loved dying again gripped her so hard that she had forgotten where she was, who she was, and what was happening around her. All she could see was death and feel the heart-crushing pain. She took a deep breath focusing on Jude's breath and his hands on her face.

Aria nodded.

More gunshots.

But she and Jude were already running down the hill towards downtown.

Chapter Forty-Six

Chase

CHASE backed up the road, taking potshots at Ted and Stokes, trying to keep their attention on him so the twins and Aria could get away. He knew he had a good hit to the shoulder on Stokes, which should have at least slowed him down, but he barely stumbled from the shot. Ted was closing in on him, though, and the grenade in his hand made Chase's gut twist.

We had grenades at the station?

"Ted…" Chase croaked, not wanting to shoot him again. Ted was sweating and panting, his mangled face a mess of blood and skin. The wound was deep, a gaping mess of flesh with flashes of teeth through the meat of his cheek. His sweat was translucent like oil in a puddle of water; it stuck to his hair and face, soaking through the shirt of his uniform.

What the hell?

To his left, Stokes, also coated in blood and oily sweat, trained his rifle on Chase, and he knew he had to take one of them out of the equation. He lowered his aim and shot Ted in the knee.

Shit

Ted's knee shattered and bent backward at the wrong angles, causing him to stumble and then fall to the side. Ted roared and screamed but was already attempting to put the pieces of this mangled leg back together.

Just stay down… please.

Then he turned to Stokes and screamed.

"Hey! Follow me fucker!" Chase said, waving his arms over his head.

Stokes cocked his head and twitched towards him, stalking towards Chase. He tucked his gun in the holster, turned, and then ran up the road. His feet pounded against the pavement as he rounded the corner of the next building into the alley and spun to make sure Stokes was still in pursuit. A second later, Stokes emerged around the building, and Chase turned to take off again but tumbled over a collection of garbage cans, landing on the concrete, his spine cracking hard against the ground. The air exited his lungs, and he gulped for air as he desperately tried to free a weapon.

Shit.

A door to Chase's right suddenly opened into the alley, and a man holding an iron skillet like a bat emerged from the building and looked down at Chase and then over at Stokes, the anger dripping away from his face and shock replacing it. The large man was easily 300 pounds and donned a dirty white apron stained with grease and food remnants. His stubbly face was contorted in confusion, then it exploded in a gory mass of flesh and blood.

No….

Chase couldn't breathe.

He couldn't hear anything around him.

The man's body fell in slow motion next to Chase as crimson fluid rained down on him.

Chase turned back to Stokes, who had already trained a gun on him.

Chase closed his eyes and thought of Aria. Her strawberry blonde hair blowing in the breeze, her smile… God, her smile…

"Chase!" A voice screamed from behind him, Stokes' head jerked up. Stokes took his attention off of Chase for a second but just long enough for Chase to catch him off guard. He scrambled to his feet and tackled him at the waist, sending them both flying backward onto the pavement. Chase's shoulder slammed into the cement as Stokes went down, Chase felt it dislodge immediately. Stokes rolled to his side, howling like a wild animal, but Chase was already up and running down the alley toward the voice. A familiar face peeked from around the next building. It was Abby Reynolds; a girl he knew from the diner he ate at most nights. She waved him around the corner of the building and into a nearby door leading above whatever business this building housed. Abby swiftly locked the deadbolt behind them, then ran up the narrow staircase to the small apartment upstairs. When Chase crested the top of the steps, sweating and gasping for breath, he saw a room filled with terrified people.

"We just ran here after the shooting downtown," Abby said, surveying her small home and the people in it. Her blonde hair was a tangle on the top of her head, and freckles dotted her face and arms. She had always been cute, but now her pale face was stricken with fear. He looked around the room again. Abby must have just collected people off the street as she ran. Kids were cuddled against their mom near the covered windows, an elderly woman still clutching her grocery bag was stuffed into a chair near the blank TV, an older couple was holding each other in the kitchen sobbing.

"You did awesome, Abby," he smiled, wincing at the pain in his shoulder.

A lady wearing scrubs that Chase recognized from the ER eyed his shoulder and approached him.

"Gorski, let's set that," She said professionally, "I have a feeling we may need you,"

Chase nodded, knowing this was going to hurt like a bitch.

"Can we use your bed? He needs to lay down so I can set it,"

"Yeah, totally, over here," Abby said, chewing nervously on her lips. They stepped around a couple, trying to get their cell phone to work. Abby opened a door to reveal a small bedroom, neat and simple. There was a small wrought iron frame against a pale pink wall with soft accents.

Chase felt too dirty to be in here.

"It's perfect. Thanks, Abby," Chase said. "Keep an eye out that front window, okay?" Chase warned.

These people are all terrified. What the fuck am I going to do?

God, my shoulder hurts

I want to sleep forever.

"I'm sorry… I don't remember your name," Chase said as he sat down on the bed.

"Erica," She smiled, helping him lie back, "Lay on your back so your arm can hang off the side," Erica instructed. Chase held his arm steady as he situated himself, but when he released it to Erica, pain shot through him, and he gritted his teeth.

Oh fuck!

She straightened his arm and swung it down, then straight out from his abdomen, bumping into the wall behind her. She cursed under her breath and then looked at Chase. "This is going to hurt."

Of course, it is.

"I'm going to count to three," Erica warned.

Chase nodded.

"One,"

He could feel every nerve in his arm, all of them alight like fire with pain.

"Two,"

Just fucking do it!

POP!

Erica shoved his arm up and in at the same time and popped the joint back together.

Chase screamed fuck seven times, then laid back against the bed, panting as Erica draped his arm carefully over his chest.

"Don't move, I'm going to grab something to make you a split." She started to walk away, then stopped, "Also, there are kids out there, dude, watch your mouth," and then she disappeared through the door.

"Sorry, kids," Chase yelled weakly without moving, still trying to catch his breath.

Erica returned with a ripped towel, a frozen bag of peas, and ibuprofen, which Chase swallowed dry.

"Come on, Gorski! Sit up," she urged.

I hate you.

Chase groaned as he sat up, feeling like he was carrying thousand-pound weights on his shoulders. He swung his legs over the side of the bed and let Erica manhandle him as she made him a brace. She threaded one corner of the towel between his arm and his chest and around his neck. Then she brought the other corner up and pulled it tight to secure his arm across his chest.

"Best I can do for now," she said, adjusting the ends to cover his fingers and tying another knot at the base of his elbow. She pulled on it again, pain shooting down Chase's arm.

"Shit!" Chase hissed.

"Oh, don't be a baby," she chided. Her face softened as she brought him a glass of water, "you're going to be fine," she said.

Is she not afraid?

"Yeah, yeah, yeah," he snapped.

From the front of the apartment, Abby was whispering urgently for everyone to be quiet and to stay down. She appeared at the door, fear stark across her face.

"One of them is right outside," she said, trembling, tears filling her eyes.

How the fuck did they find me? Are they tracking us?

From down the steps came a vicious pounding sound against the door. Persistent and heavy.

The kids began to cry, and one of the women yelped.

Abby looked at Chase in panic.

Okay. Here we go.

Chase stood despite his protesting muscles and nerves. He wanted nothing more than to lay back down in that bed and sleep forever, but these people were scared and needed help.

I got this.

"Okay I need everyone to go to the bedroom and lock the door, barricade the door with the bed or whatever furniture is in there. I'm going to lead him away…. Stay here until its safe," Chase rasped.

Everyone moved quickly and relatively quietly into the bedroom; before closing the door, Abby smiled sadly at Chase.

"Thank you," she mouthed.

Chase nodded then she shut the door. He kicked the couch in front of the bedroom door, then reloaded his gun awkwardly with the last of his bullets. He sighed heavily. His body hurt, and his muscles screamed for rest, but he stood and started down the narrow staircase. He stopped a few steps up so he could get the right angle on the door. His plan wasn't great; he'd jump feet first into the door, hopefully knocking Stokes away, giving Chase time to sprint away from the building. He glanced back up the staircase as the door to the bedroom closed, he listened to the scraping of a large piece of furniture being pushed across the wood floor in front of the door.

Good… they should be safe.

I hope Aria is okay.

Here I come motherfucker.

With one last heavy sigh, Chase gathered every ounce of courage he had, then vaulted himself toward the door feet first, bracing his wounded arm against his chest.

Chase slammed into the top of the door, jarring every vertebrae in his spine together but splintering the wood in the middle. He felt the shard of wood scrape along his calf as his feet connected with Stokes, who was standing on the other side. The hinges held, and Chase was whipped to the side as the door cracked against the frame. Both men falling into a heap on the cement in a tangle of wooden shards. Chase stumbled to his feet.

Holy shit, I didn't die.

Unholstering his gun and spinning clumsily, he found Stokes rising slowly and moving toward the apartment doorway. Panicked, Chase screamed and waved his hands, like trying to get the attention of a rabid animal. Stokes paid him little attention and began tripping over the jagged pieces of wood that remained of the door stumbling in vain over the wreckage like he didn't understand how to avoid it. Chase grabbed a nearby chunk of concrete and tossed it at Stokes' back, hitting him in the shoulder blade, but Stokes barely reacted. Chase cursed, then raised his gun shakily. He aimed for Stoke's back and squeezed the trigger causing Stokes to stumble forward from the force of the bullet. Finally, Stokes turned his eyes, focusing on Chase.

That's it. Come this way…

Stokes snarled as Chase stepped backward off the curb and into the street, preparing himself to run and lead the deranged man away. But instead of stepping down onto the asphalt, Chase's ankle rolled, and he tumbled backward into the street, his fatigued muscles unable to right him. Stokes sneered and charged, his eyes wide and pupils huge. Chase dragged himself backward with his one good arm, desperate to put distance between him and Stokes. From Chase's right an engine revved as a sedan roared up the street towards Chase. He swung his gaze back to Stokes, but just as Stokes reached Chase, the car squealed up the curb and plowed into Stokes, sending him flying. Chase stared in disbelief as the driver-side door flew open.

"Get in, dude!" Jonah yelled, a panicked edge to his voice.

Chase didn't hesitate.

He stumbled to his feet, throwing open the back door of the car and diving into the back seat. Jonah reversed, swung the car around, and angled it back down the hill towards town. Jonah turned to Chase, "Did you see what way Aria and my brother went?"

Before Chase could answer, Stokes appeared against the driver's side window, slamming blood and ragged flesh against the glass. Jonah and Chase both screamed.

"GO! GO! GO!" Chase screamed. Jonah stomped on the gas, whipping the car to the right down the hill; Stokes tumbled off the side of the car to the ground, skidding across the pavement. Chase watched him fade through the rear window, holding his breath.

Then the twitching figure in the road stood. Chase just turned and settled back into the seat.

They don't stop.

They drove in silence for a block, both breathing heavily and ragged.

Chase adjusted his splint, securing his arm against his chest, then laid his head back against the headrest, attempting to catch his breath. Jonah flew down the road into downtown, desperately scanning the streets for Jude and Aria. Chase sat up and surveyed Jonah for a moment before speaking.

"Why'd you save me?" Chase asked in a hoarse voice, Jonah's eyes flicked to Chase in the rearview mirror.

"I'm not an asshole," he retorted.

"No, you definitely are, but… it'd be a lot easier for you if I were gone," Chase said. "She'd never know if…," Chase just trailed off.

Jonah was quiet for a moment.

"Aria doesn't love me," Jonah snapped, "Now shut up and look for her and my brother,"

"Where'd you get this car?" Chase asked, suddenly realizing that this wasn't Jonah's vehicle.

"The keys were in it," Jonah mumbled, "You gonna arrest me, officer?" Jonah challenged.

"Nope..." Chase responded with a hint of a smile.

Jonah nodded once then turned onto Main Street towards Aria's house.

Chapter Forty-Seven

Aria

ARIA and Jude slid along the back of a building, hidden amongst the deep shadows created by the buildings around them. They stayed low and nearly crawled when they reached the alley that backed up to Aria's apartment. They pushed past a small bush and shimmied the window open. Ducking through, they both toppled inside, landing on Aria's bedroom floor. Aria quickly jumped up and closed the window, locking it and drawing the shades. Jude ran to the front room double checking the deadbolt on the front door. Aria started throwing open kitchen drawers in search of a knife or a weapon of any kind. Jude found the small baseball bat Aria had hidden by the front door and gripped it with white knuckles, sweat speckling his forehead and upper lip. Drew's bar was just a couple blocks away, and the smell of a burning structure filled the air.

"I hope Jonah made it somewhere safe," Jude whispered.

"Chase, too," Aria said, chewing on her bottom lip.

"Where do you think they are?' Jude asked, looking quickly out the peephole.

"I don't know, but we're going to look for them," Aria said, pulling a hoodie over her head and tossing a black one to Jude.

"We can't go out there! We don't even know where Garcias is!"

"Ted, his name is Ted, and he…" Aria trailed off, Jude shrugged as if that distinction didn't matter. Which it probably didn't.

"Fine, Ted. Anyway, Drew's bar is close, and if they started that, then one of them is nearby," Jude said in a rushed panic. Jude nervously peeked out the peephole again and nearly screamed when he was met with another set of eyes. "Goddamnit," Jude grumbled. Aria tensed but watched as Jude unlocked the door, and Jonah slid in.

"See? It isn't nice, is it?" Jonah whispered to his brother; Jonah nodded at Aria, "Chase is fine," he said, irritated; Aria couldn't help but exhale in relief, "yeah, I'm fine too, by the way," Jonah snapped. "He's in the car, Stokes fucked him up pretty bad, so we gotta go."

Aria ran to her bathroom and tossed all the medical supplies she had in a nearby bag then rejoined her cousins at the door.

"Okay, let's go," she said, nearly shoving them out of the way.

"Hold on," Jude said, checking the peephole again. "I don't see anything, but they're close, so stay low and close," Jude pointedly looked at Aria.

"I'm getting to Chase… move." She stepped around Jude and slowly opened the door. She wasn't sure if it was the ringing or the blood pounding in her ears, but she strained to hear if there were any approaching attackers. She took a deep breath and tried to calm the trembling in her hands. Chase needed HER now. She had to get to him. She motioned for the twins to follow her, and together, the three headed out into the darkness, Aria had no idea what time it was, but it wasn't even close to midnight, and she felt like she'd been running for her life for days. She pulled her bag across her body and held it close. They veered left out of her door and walked along the narrow path to the small parking lot behind her building. A sedan was pulled haphazardly across three spots, one tire on the curb but Aria could see Chase's form in the back seat.

"You got him here?" Aria asked, suspiciously.

"Yes! Why is everyone so shocked by that," Jonah said, throwing his hands in the air.

Chase was stretched out against the back seat, his back against the far door, looking pale and exhausted. His eyes brightened when he saw her, and he held his hand out to her. Aria looked Chase over and saw the hasty splint securing his arm across his chest and the blood caked on one leg. She sucked in a breath but took his hand, sliding into the back seat. Carefully, she pushed his bloody leg forward, eliciting a hiss from Chase, laying it on her lap.

"Shit, sorry," she whispered. Aria rolled up Chase's pant leg grimacing at the deep gash into the meat of his calf. Aria's stomach turned, and her vision swam for a second, but she shook her head and took a deep breath. It was just blood. At least she wasn't wearing it this time, she thought grimly. Jude and Jonah had settled into the front seat and Jonah took the wheel again, turning the car around sharply in the parking lot but turning the headlights off as he did so. He didn't want to call more attention to them than necessary.

In the backseat, Aria dug through her bag, swaying back and forth with the movements of the car. She didn't have much more than basic bathroom supplies, but she did her best with the peroxide, bandages, and antibiotic ointment she took from under her sink. She took a steadying breath and then met Chase's eyes,

"You ready?"

"Yep," he said through gritted teeth.

Aria poured the peroxide on the wound and waited. It took a few seconds for the bubbling to start, and then Chase flinched and swore.

"Sorry, sorry, sorry," Aria whispered; she waited a moment to let it cleanse the wound, so she didn't have to worry about infection - yet. She gently dabbed the excess liquid then squeezed a glob of antibiotic cream on the wound, and then carefully laid her only two gauze pads on it. She secured it with band-aids and a small strip of medical tape… it was all she had, but it would have to work. After she finished, she rolled his blood-soaked jeans down to hopefully add another small layer of protection over that nasty gash. When she was done, she threw everything back in her bag and leaned back with a sigh. Chase reached over and wrapped his arm around her waist, pulling her closer to him - causing them both a little pain.

"You're alive," Chase sighed.

"I'm alive." Aria confirmed, "And so are you," she closed her eyes as she laid her head against his shoulder. Thanking whatever deity was out there for that fact.

"What happened to you two?" Aria asked louder to Jonah, opening her eyes again.

"We got separated, and I basically just dodged bullets until they weren't following me anymore. I found this car and went back to see if any of you guys were still by Chase's place," Jonah motioned to Chase, "Then I found this dude about to take a bullet to the face, so I hit Stokes with the damn car. I can add vehicular homicide to my growing list of charges," Jonah joked darkly as he pulled into a local park two blocks down from Aria's apartment. The park sat at the corner of Reynolds and Saphire streets and a small trail traversed from one street to the other through the trees of the park. Over the years people had slowly worn smaller trails into the trees for privacy. Jonah turned into a well-hidden path, and the car was swallowed up by the shadows.

"Yeah, but then he got up. Stokes fucking got up after Jonah threw him 20 feet with a car. Whatever that shit was… It made them like…"

"Terminator," Jude whispered.

They all stared at him, silent for a moment.

"Terminator?" Aria choked.

Then it was like something released, and they all began to laugh. It was that uncontrollable, hysterical laughter that escapes when you've had too much but can't stop yet. If you don't laugh, you'll cry, and they didn't have time to cry. So, they laughed. They cackled until tears filled their eyes, and Chase begged to stop because it hurt so much.

Slowly, the laughter faded, and the car filled with the silence of dread.

"What are we gonna do?" Aria asked.

Everyone sat in silence as the dark settled in around them. The smell of smoke filled the air, and then they heard another gunshot. They all sighed in exhausted resignation.

"What do we have for weapons?" Chase asked.

"I have a bat," Jude said hopefully, and Aria burst into laughter again. The absurdity and the absolute sincerity with which he said it just broke whatever thread had been holding

Aria together. She couldn't stop again. A bat! A BAT! What the fuck were they going to do against these monsters on Alice with a BAT!

"What?" Jude hissed, still trying to be quiet, "It's a legitimate weapon!"

"Is it, though?" Jonah chuckled sadly.

As they settled back into silence, wiping the tears of laughter from their eyes, Aria asked again.

"Seriously guys… what's the plan?" Aria whispered.

"We lay low until help gets here," Jude said.

"They could kill more people," Chase countered.

"We need to hide and wait it out," Jonah said.

"You don't get a vote," Aria snapped.

Jonah scoffed and shook his head.

"What?" she pushed.

"Nothing…" he mumbled.

"No," her temper was swooping in to cover the fear lacing her entire body, "Please, tell me what you have to say."

"That's not," he tried to interject.

"Not another word!" Aria almost snarled, "I can't hear any more excuses,"

"I'm sorry!" Jonah yelled suddenly. Everyone silenced, "I don't know why I did it. There's something wrong with me…" his voice cracked.

Aria's anger departed as fast as it had come. She wanted to reassure him and tell him that he was fine, that everything was okay… That HE was okay. But she couldn't do that anymore. She couldn't keep denying he needed help.

"We'll help you," Aria whispered, "Okay?"

Jude was nodding in the passenger seat; Chase was holding fast to Aria's hand but he didn't object. Jonah nodded and took a deep breath.

"I…" Jonah started, "I have half a box of bullets for the rifle," he said, clearing his throat.

"I lost my rifle back at Chase's," Jude said quietly.

"It's okay, Jude. I haven't used the pistol in my pocket yet," Aria offered hopefully.

"I've got a handful of shells for the shotgun," Chase rasped.

That was it. That's what they had against the murderous men hunting them through town. Three guns with slight ammo and a bat.

"We could head up Fox Canyon," Chase suggested finally, "There's a fire tower up there, we can call for help and maybe get someone up here before morning."

"How the hell do we get across the river though?" Aria asked.

"The train bridge…" Chase whispered somewhere in the dark.

"Oh shit, I forgot about the old train bridge," Jonah said.

"Is it even still standing?" Jude questioned.

"I can't remember," Aria said, trying to visualize the river and the destruction they'd seen earlier, but she couldn't picture anything past the crumpled bridge that served as the roadway. "There was so much going on… I can't remember,"

"If it's still intact and if we could get across…" Chase started.

"That's a LOT of 'ifs,'" Jonah scoffed.

"We don't have a lot of options. We follow the river down and try…"

Suddenly, a blood-soaked figure slapped against Aria's window, her hands clawing at the glass as if it might give way and let her escape within it. Aria screamed jumping towards Chase, the twins barking in horror. The blood-covered woman tried to gurgle words out to Aria, but slowly, she dropped out of sight, leaving streaks of rust-colored blood on the glass.

"Shit," Jonah breathed as his eyes widened in the rearview mirror. Jude spun in his seat, Aria and Chase sat up and peered out the rear window.

"Shit…" Chase concurred through clenched teeth, "How'd they find us so fucking fast?"

Stokes and Ted roamed the edge of the trees like animals hunting for their next meal, eyes raking slowly across the scenery. It was like they knew they were there, hidden within the dark foliage.

"How are they everywhere?!" Jonah hissed.

"This town is fucking small, man…" Jude whispered.

"It's not that small, Jude," Chase rasped, "They know we're here,"

Aria shushed them softly as she stared in horror at the two men walking in a way that wasn't quite human through the hazy night. Staggering gaits and twisted forms that moved ever towards them. This was the shit nightmares were made of. The figures appeared and reappeared amongst the fog in the darkness, glitchy movements the only evidence that they weren't pieces of the night itself. The car was silent except for their rapid breaths and Aria's stifled sobs as they all stared out the back window in horror. Chase's hand squeezed hers in reassurance. But they were trapped. Stokes opened fire blindly into the forest around them as the bullets lit up the night. Then Ted noticed the reflection of the car, and his eyes fell on them. Aria's stomach sank.

"Jonah," Jude urged, "start the car," but Jonah was already turning the key and revving the engine.

Jonah threw the car in reverse and slammed his foot to the floorboards lurching the car backward. Ted didn't react quickly enough, and his body hit the back window, cracking against the impact. Aria and Chase covered their heads as the car burst from the woods across the park drive, careening into a retaining wall on the other side of the park. Ted flew from the back of the car over the small brick wall onto a cement walkway.

Aria's back exploded in pain from the jolt of the wreck, but she managed to throw open her door and tumbled from the car. Chase screamed in pain as he fell from the car on the other side, yelling for Aria as he did. Jonah and Jude were crawling across the grass, staying low, trying to get back to the cover of the trees. Aria scuttled around the front of the car and met Chase, throwing his arm over her shoulder. As they neared the tree line, a gunshot rang out behind them. Aria pulled Chase to his feet with everything she had but he was twice her size and struggling to even stay vertical. After a few steps he seemed to steady and was limping low next to her. They all ducked back into the trees, scrambling into the undergrowth to hide. Ted was up and hunting them again, running with that unnatural, jerky gait. They all froze in their hiding spot as Ted emerged from the darkness into the beam of a streetlight. He stood illuminated in the road like an ethereal nightmare. They watched, horrified, as his body was racked with spasms as he stood to his full height.

Clicks and crunching sounds coming from his joints as he seemed to reassemble himself. Finally, he stilled, and his eyes seemed to land right on them.

"Split up and hide!" Chase yelled.

They ran from shadow to shadow, using the forest to hide them; Aria looked back as Chase stumbled and winced, unable to put much weight on his injured calf. Blood soaked his pant leg, and his face was covered in sweat from the effort. Aria turned and wrapped her arms around his midsection, dragging him with her by sheer will.

"I got him," Jonah said.

Aria looked up at her cousin and saw HIM for a moment, the Jonah she could trust and depend on. So she released Chase.

Gunshots ripped apart the night again, this time close enough to spray foliage and shrapnel at them, splitting the group down the middle. Aria dove to the right as the twins scattered into the trees with Chase in tow.

With her heart hammering in her ears, Aria crawled past a fallen tree, pulled up by the roots, with giant chunks of earth and grass still hanging from them. Though many of the trees in the park still stood, several in this section had been uprooted by the mudslides, an offshoot of the larger one had taken out a chunk of the forest here. Aria tucked herself in amongst the roots, disappearing into the tangle of branches and mud. Footsteps emerged out of the darkness, shoes sinking into the grass, then twigs breaking beneath police-issued boots. Ted passed Chase and Jude; Aria released half a breath. Where was Jonah? Ted seemed to be reacting like a feral animal, attracted to noises and motion… if the four of them could just stay quiet, they might survive this. Then Ted's boot was inches from her.

Aria clasped her hand over her mouth, tears spilling over her knuckles and ragged breaths escaping through her nostrils. She willed herself to fade into the tree around her. Suddenly, Ted appeared around the edges of the bank of dirt left by the upturned tree, feet from Aria's hiding spot. Still concealed by the roots of the tree, Aria pushed back into the tangle, desperate to fade away. Ted was talking to himself in a fervor, she could see his silhouette grabbing at his hair and arms like something was pinching him. He twitched as he fumbled with another shotgun shell, staggering away from her. She watched him stumble away and released the smallest breath. As she did, pain seared across her scalp as she was grabbed by the top of the hair and yanked out of her hiding place, hair parting flesh. Her shoulders caught amongst the roots, effectively trapping her in a cage of earth and wood, Stokes leaned down to her ear and whispered,

"Gotcha,"

Chapter Forty-Eight

Chase

NO. Dear God, no.

He's got her.

No!

Chase exchanged a glance with Jude, whose eyes pleaded with him to stay put, but Chase was already pushing himself to his feet with his one good arm, ignoring the dull ache in his ankle; it was a mere annoyance compared to the absolute agony burning in his calf.

Stokes was crouched on the trunk of the enormous tree, Aria hanging at an odd angle from her hair, her body wedged against the tree and stuck amongst the upturned roots.

"Stokes!" Chase yelled hoarsely, Aria looked up and met Chase's eyes. Horror and protest filled her gaze as she realized what he was doing.

Stokes turned his pistol toward Chase and squeezed as Aria reached up through the branches and grabbed the gun, pulling it down as it discharged. Before Chase could even exhale, he saw the gunfire down at Aria. Aria screamed, and Stokes stumbled, losing his grasp.

"Aria!" Chase screamed; Jude was suddenly at his side, running towards her.

Stokes fell to the side as Aria collapsed to the ground beneath the roots. Stokes was already getting back to his feet when Jude barreled into him, swinging the bat over and over again.

"DIE! JUST DIE!" Jude screamed in a raw, tear-choked voice.

Stokes was unconscious, but no one knew how long that would last. Chase crawled the last few feet to Aria who was dragging herself desperately out from under the tree. Chase reached her, and when she looked up at him, he saw nothing but terror in her grey eyes. And blood. Blood poured down her face in dark ribbons.

No...

"Chase..." she started as she fell forward into his arms.

Chase cradled her and tilted her head down to reveal a mangled, bloody scalp. The bullet had grazed her head just inside her hairline, but the powder burns from the close-range shot were horrific. Her hair was smoking in places still, and the head wound bled uncontrollably. Aria began to gag, and Chase turned her to the side quickly as she vomited.

Shit. She has a concussion.

"Hey, it's okay, it's okay," saying it as much for himself as for her.

There's so much blood.

"My leg..." she gasped.

Shit

Aria was wearing a pair of his shorts that hung well below her knees, they were ripped at the thigh. Chase tugged her pant leg up to reveal a bullet wound that seemed to go clean through the side of her thigh, but blood oozed from the hole, dirt and leaves sticking to the blood on her. Chase ripped the sling over his head and pressed it to Aria's head, trying to staunch the blood. Aria whimpered but didn't cry out. She looked up at him with those eyes, giant gray pools gazing up at him, and then they focused on something behind him, and they widened in fear.

Aria screamed his name seconds before the tree above her exploded into splinters and dirt, a shotgun blast shattering the night air. Chase threw himself over Aria, shielding her from the shrapnel. Chase spun as Ted dropped the shotgun and reached for the rifle slung over his arm. Chase dove for Ted, not waiting for him to take another shot. Chase grappled for the rifle, fighting him with everything he had but at a wicked disadvantage with one good arm. Chase whipped his head forward, slamming his forehead into Ted's nose, who stumbled backward and released his grip on the rifle; Chase snatched it away and turned it on his friend. Finger on the trigger.

This isn't Ted.

This isn't Ted.

This isn't Ted.

Chase aimed for the heart and pulled the trigger.

Garcias was thrown backward into the dark forest. Chase turned wildly, searching for Aria, and found her on her side, unconscious, blood spilling from her head. Her bloody leg in the mud. Jude ran from the foliage, pushing Chase aside he scooped her up and cradled her head. Jonah emerged from the other side of the tree and crouched behind his brother.

"Jude…. Is she…" Chase couldn't go any closer; Jude was cradling her head, tears streaming down his face, "she's breathing, but…" he shook his head. Jonah was stoned faced and panting. He shot to his feet, suddenly making Chase jump. Jonah was unhinged on a good day; with Aria at death's door, Chase didn't know what he would do.

So much blood so much blood so much blood

"Chase, what do we do?" Jude's voice sounded like it was in a tunnel or like there was cotton in his ears.

She's going to die…

Her smile.

Her laugh.

"Chase?"

Her touch the night he came back.

Her smell.

There's so much blood.

The piece of fabric on her head was already soaked through.

"Chase!" Jonah screamed, shaking him by the shoulders.

Chase came crashing back into reality, adrenaline bringing everything into hard clarity.

"Yeah," Chase said, shaking Jonah off, "We need to go," He heard Stokes thrashing in the undergrowth nearby, already up. Chase stood, raising the rifle and firing a shot into Stokes' chest, knocking him back again. Chase slung the rifle over his shoulder and reached for Aria, but Jonah stopped him. Chase tensed, but Jonah wasn't posturing.

"You're hurt… we got her," he said firmly but with a tone that reminded Chase that they loved her too.

Yeah… Jonah a little too much.

Chase thought bitterly.

Not the time.

Jude helped Jonah cradle Aria as he ran ahead to the car. Chase wasn't sure if the damn thing would even drive after colliding with the wall, but they had to try. Jude climbed into the driver's seat and turned the key. Chase exhaled in relief as Jude punched the gas, and the car revved; he put it in gear and then plunked the back tires down on the pavement again. Waving them in.

I'm buying this car when this is done.

Chase slid into the back seat, and Jonah folded Aria into his arms, carefully laying her head against Chase's chest, trying his best not to touch her leg. Just as Jonah was letting go, Aria opened her eyes, and they fell on Jonah.

"Hey there…" Jonah smiled, obvious relief flooding him, "Chase's got you okay?" Jonah looked at Chase, hesitating for a moment, then shutting the door and got into the passenger seat.

Behind them, gunshots sounded again.

"Let's go!" Jonah shouted at Jude.

"Drive! Come on, Jude!" Chase yelled.

"Fuck! I'm trying!" Jude snapped anxiously, slamming his foot down on the accelerator, kicking out the back tires as they tore off the wet pavement, skidding onto the road and turning towards downtown. Jude swerved to miss abandoned cars and two dead bodies. The fire at Drew's was still raging despite the incessant rain. An explosion shook the earth as what looked like a gas line exploded a few blocks over, orange flames lighting up the night. There was no fire department to fight that fire tonight. The valley would lose at least half of what remained of downtown before the rain staunched the flames.

"Head up the other side of town. I know someone who can help," Chase told Jude.

"Chase…" Aria whispered, shivering. Chase looked down at her, realizing how badly she was shaking.

"Hey… I'm right here," Chase cupped her face, stroking her bloody cheek with a thumb.

"I can't…. Feel….," she said between chattering teeth. Chase furrowed his brow as he assessed the rest of her scalp; there was one large round burn across her scalp, culminating in the rip across her skull. The closer to the actual wound the rawer the skin became. Further away, her hair was simply singed in short chunks across her head. But the pure force behind that bullet had given her a concussion, and he had to keep her awake.

Her leg was a whole other matter. He didn't think the bullet was still in her leg, but the risk of infection was incredible with the dirt and mud caking her clothes and skin.

"Aria, I need you to focus on me. You can't go to sleep right now," Chase said sternly, "Jude, head towards my house; there's an apartment about two blocks from there, above some shop. There are civilians there, and one is a nurse. Fucking hurry,"

"Abby Sinclair's place?" Jonah asked.

"How did you…" Chase started.

"You aren't the only man in this car who appreciates freckles, okay? She and I were casual for a bit, I know where her place is. Just keep her awake," Jonah turned and pointed for Jude to turn. Jude was silent, eyes wide with terror.

"Aria, look at me, you have to stay awake…" Chase said desperately tapping Aria's cheek. "Come on, Aria! You cannot go to sleep!"

Her eyes were unfocused and wandered, unable to lock on one target.

"I'm… tired," she breathed. "I'm cold" she shivered.

"Jude, hurry!" Chase yelled in panic, putting his face to Aria's again.

"Stay awake, Aria, do you hear me? Stay awake!" Chase commanded.

"Don't tell me what to do," she said in a haze of pain and blood loss.

"Ha! There she is, there she is," Chase laughed and released the lump in his throat. Tears tumbling down his face, "Aria. I am ORDERING you to stay awake! Do you hear me! You HAVE to do what I say." Aria's anger would drag her through this, if for no other reason than spite. She hated being told to do anything, especially by Chase. He hadn't really had the opportunity to annoy her yet since being back, their reunion had been a whirlwind of sex and laughter.

"Listen to me, you are so strong. I'm sorry I've been a dick, but I need you. I need you to stay awake Aria!" Chase watched with dread as her eyes closed. Slowly, she opened them again with what seemed to be a huge effort. "Good job. There you go. Aria do NOT give this world the satisfaction of beating you!" Chase yelled at her.

Jude skidded the car to a stop in the alley behind Abby's house, Chase threw open the car door and somehow scooped Aria up into his one good arm and hobbled toward the front door.

Jude stopped in front of him, taking in the mangled front door and tensed.

"Looks like someone beat us here," Jude said darkly.

"Nope. that was me," Chase said, kicking the remaining pieces of the door out of his way and heading up the stairwell.

Chase heaved himself and Aria up the steps and slowed by the third step, his leg on fire and throbbing.

"Here, man, let me help," Jude said carefully, taking Aria's legs while Chase cradled her head and shoulders. Together they ascended the steps and came to a halt.

No

"Abby!" Jonah yelled as he reached the top of the steps.

"No, Jonah wait…," Jude started.

"Jonah!" Chase tried stopping him, but Jonah breezed past him then froze mid-stride.

Before then there was a grisly massacre. The couch was thrown across the room, leaning against the far wall. A dark pool of blood spread from the bedroom doorway, soaking into the carpet. Within the bedroom, bodies were piled one on top of the other. Shattered furniture littered the ground from the victims trying to barricade the door. Chase's stomach twisted. He and Jude laid Aria on a rectangular butcher's block table that was barely long enough for her.

Fuck.

I shouldn't have left them.

The guilt crushed against him like a tidal wave. He could've stayed and fought with them; he could've taken them with him, but no! He left them there to be slaughtered. And when they were done; Garcias and Stokes had continued their hunt for Chase and his friends.

Jonah was standing at the doorway, shoulders heaving up and down with his ragged breaths.

"You led that fucker here, and he slaughtered them…" Jonah growled, spinning on Chase with angry tears lacing his eyes. The accusation hit Chase like a punch, but he recovered quickly.

"Me? YOU did this! You can't mind fuck me like you do with Aria and Jude! I see you asshole! You poisoned the entire police department! And those cops killed these people! YOU DID THIS!" Chase snapped, stepping up until he was inches from Jonah's face. The two stared at one another until Jude started screaming.

"ARIA!! Wake up! Aria," he had her face in both his hands, trying to shake her awake.

Chase froze. He was counting on the nurse to help them. He was counting on people being ALIVE here. His chest tightened. He didn't know what to do.

What now?

He frantically searched the scene trying to think, trying not to panic, trying to force that building scream in his lungs down before he completely lost it.

"What now Boy Scout?" Jonah sniped.

I don't know…

"I don't know," he said resigned, sounding far away and muffled.

"Jonah, shut the fuck up!" Jude snapped, "Go get towels and something to clean her wound with! Fuck find some Tylenol! WE ARE ALL SHE HAS!" Jude roared at them. Chase had never heard Jude so forceful. It slammed Chase out of his stupor; he spared a glance at Jonah and then hobbled to the bathroom, his calf screaming with every step. He carefully skirted the blood soaking into the carpet in the living room and averted his eyes from the bedroom. He threw open the medicine cabinet and began grabbing bottles and ointments in a frenzy, throwing anything unuseful over his shoulder. Under the sink, he found bandages and towels; gathering up what he collected, and again carefully made his way around the blood-soaked floor back to the table.

Jude seemed to assess her two injuries and decided her head was the worst of the two.

"Jonah!" Jude shouted, "Help me!" Jonah did as he was told and helped Jude lay Aria flat and move her hair to get a good look at her wound. That meant removing the fabric that started to clot to the wound. "Shit, this is going to hurt Aria. I'm sorry," Jude said, peeling away the fabric from her scalp. As he pulled back the cloth, he could see the places her hair had been ripped away by Stokes. Aria groaned and turned her head away. Jude threw the bloody rag aside as Chase slammed the supplies on the table and took Aria's hand.

"Why is she limp? Jude is she…" Chase began, panic rising in his chest.

"Just hand me that… I need to clean her head," Jude said, pointing to the antiseptic Chase pillaged from the bathroom. Jude studied the bottle a moment and sighed, "This is gonna sting," Without hesitating, he poured the clear liquid on her wound, and her whole body bucked, back arching in pain, a scream squeezing from her chest.

Shit

"Hold her down," Jude ordered. Chase tried to still her shoulders, but with only one good arm, he couldn't hold her. Jonah shoved him out of the way and put a hand on either shoulder and held firm. Chase didn't even care. He threw himself over her thrashing legs on the other side of Jude.

"Sorry, sorry, sorry," Jude whispered to Aria as he dabbed the blood from the injured flesh with a cream-colored hand towel.

Jude worked carefully and excruciatingly slowly, but by the time he finished, the wound was clean, and Aria had stilled again.

"Okay, let's look at her leg," Jude sighed.

"How much can she take, man?" Jonah sighed.

"We've got to clean it, she can rest after," Jude answered quietly.

Jonah and Chase looked at each other in concern but stayed quiet as Jude rolled her pant leg up, inspecting her leg. Aria was coated in sweat and Jude simply touching her leg elicited a whimper that broke Chase's heart. Her breath came in short pants.

"It went through," Jonah said as he splashed the antiseptic on the wounds. Aria stiffened again and cried out in pain.

"Goddamnit man," Jonah cringed.

"Needle and thread, steri-strips something... NOW!" He ordered, sending Chase and Jonah frantically searching the bathroom and every cupboard or closet available. Jonah returned with a sewing kit. Jude took a needle, sanitized it, and threaded it... then sighed heavily.

"Hold her still," he said, resigned.

Chase and Jonah grabbed Aria and held fast as Jude pierced the needle through her inflamed skin. Aria wailed in pain.

"Shit," Jude said, struggling against her writhing body. "Hold her still!"

Jonah leaned into his hold on her shoulders as Chase tried to hold her other leg and hips still, but her spasms were strong.

"Come on, Aria!" Jonah yelled.

Chase laid his body across her legs, desperately trying to hold her still while Jude sewed. He tilted his head down to watch as Jude pulled the bloody needle through one side of the ragged edge of Aria's skin into the other edge of the wound.

"Holy shit…" Chase said weakly, his vision swimming.

"Keep it together Boy Scout," Jonah said, his face paling at the scene too.

"Fuck you," Chase said queasily.

"Fuck you," Jonah said, swaying on his feet.

"Jude?" Chase rasped, wanting to tell him to be careful, to save her, that he loved her and needed her to be okay but he didn't because Jude felt it too. Jude truly loved Aria as a sister, as the sibling he was supposed to have. Jude met Chase's eyes and seemed to read his mind. Jude nodded, leaning over Aria's body and carefully pushing the needle through the next piece of skin. Her head thrashed to the side, another cry escaping her. Chase's heart was hammering in his chest, all he could hear was the roaring in his ears and Aria's cries. He needed her to survive.

"Aria, I will never leave you again. You will have to shoot me to get me to ever leave your side again; I promise, if you will just FIGHT!" Chase begged, "Make it through this and I will never leave again. PLEASE,"

After what seemed like an eternity Jude sat back and sighed.

"Done,"

"Good job, man," Jonah said.

"Yeah," Chase whispered, "Thank you,"

Jude nodded, and after taking a few deep breaths, he wrapped gauze around her thigh and tied it as tight as he dared.

He used a kitchen towel to wipe the blood and dirt from her torso.

They all stood back a minute, just breathing.

Jude was covered in Aria's blood and just stared at his cousin, shell-shocked by what he had just done. Jonah leaned against the wall, bent over with his hands on his knees, Chase could only stand there and just digest everything that had happened in the last few hours. The mudslides, the bridge, Alice, Garcias and Stokes... now Aria. He didn't know how much more he could take before he collapsed from pure exhaustion. His physical state wasn't great either. He shook his head, snatching the Tylenol from the medical supplies and pouring some into his mouth straight from the bottle.

"I thought you didn't do drugs," Jonah said quietly; they were quiet for a moment, and then Chase laughed.

"Feeling adventurous," he chuckled as the twins both gave into exhausted laughter.

After a few moments, they went quiet again; Chase walked over and closed the bedroom door.

Chapter Forty-Nine

Aria

ARIA'S body was nothing but pain.

Searing white hot pain. But the nausea had subsided, and the world wasn't spinning anymore.

She was so thirsty.

She opened her eyes, her head roared in pain, and the world spun. As she let the wave of pain pass, she looked around and found herself on a small rectangular kitchen table in a darkened apartment. Her leg was bandaged, confirming the pain throbbing from the wound. She turned her head slowly to the right and found Chase dozing in a nearby chair. Arm re-slung in a new sling that seemed to be made out of a bedsheet. Behind him, she could see a set of shoes she knew belonged to one of the twins, pacing in the small kitchen. She tried to sit up but groaned when a wave of pain rolled across her thigh and knocked her back down, waking Chase.

"Hey, take it easy," Chase said, standing to help her sit up. "Here," he whispered, "I found some pain meds and some expired antibiotics… better than nothing," Aria saw the tremble in his hand when he put the pills in her palm. Aria took the pills and swallowed them with the water he handed her, the cool liquid was like heaven. She wanted to drain the entire glass but knew she'd regret it, so she forced herself to stop.

"How are you feeling?" Chase said softly, stroking her cheek.

"Everything hurts..." her own voice sounded far away.

Chase exhaled, and he brought her hand to his lips and kissed it gently.

"Why did you do that?" Chase exhaled a shutter, and he squeezed her hand like she might slip away from him if he didn't hold on tight enough. "You grabbed his hand right as he pulled that trigger, and he hit you instead of me," Chase's eyes welled with tears.

"Well yeah!" She tried to laugh, but her head was one giant ripping pain. She gingerly reached up, feeling the bandage and patches of burnt and torn scalp. Aria looked back at Chase; his eyes were dark, and his face drawn.

"Are *you* okay?" she asked, examining his arm. When she looked at his face she saw utter exhaustion.

"Um..." he said in a quivering voice, "I thought you were going to die. I... there was so much blood." he swiped at his eyes angrily. "I uh... got a whole apartment of people killed," he motioned toward the bedroom, "I..." he finally met her eyes. "I love you. I cannot do this without you. Please don't ever scare me like that again," he said, leaning down and kissing her on the cheek.

"I'm okay. I'm not going anywhere," she said into his neck now, "I'm sorry I scared you," she straightened and kissed Chase softly on the lips, smoothing the worry out of his face with her hand. He covered her hand with his and leaned his face into it. He looked so tired. Chase kissed her again and again. Gently but earnestly because the gunshots in the distance signaled the night wasn't over yet.

"Aria?" Jude's quiet voice drifted from the kitchen, his eyes were wide with fear and tears. Aria smiled and held her hand out to him.

"I'm okay," Aria said reassuringly as Jude took her hand and squeezed.

"Jude saved your life," Chase said, absentmindedly putting a hand on her outstretched leg. Aria looked up at Jude and saw the welling of tears in his eyes.

"I thought you couldn't stand the sight of blood," Aria laughed, wincing again at the pain. Jude's brow knitted tightly together at her joke.

"Yeah… but it was YOU," Jude rubbed his hand over his face, sighing heavily. "Let's not do that again,"

"Agreed," Aria said as she moved to sit up with Jude and Chase's help. Her leg screamed from the pain, but she leaned on Chase to ease the pressure.

Aria surveyed the apartment, her eyes landing on Jonah, who sat on the floor staring at the bedroom door. An enormous pool of blood soaked into the floor in front of him. "Jonah?" Aria rasped.

"We're all going to die here…" Jonah said darkly.

"Don't say th…" Jude started but Jonah was already shaking his head, rising to his feet.

"Because of me," he finished quietly as he turned and looked back at the group of them, huge tears falling down his cheeks. Aria's heart broke, this was it. This was Jonah's rock bottom. Maybe they could help him now.

They just didn't have time right this second.

"Jonah, we'll get you whatever help you need, but you can't check out now, okay?" Jude whispered from the kitchen. Aria felt Chase tense slightly.

"Yeah… we need you if we're going to get out of here alive," Chase said, releasing the rest of whatever resentment he had towards Jonah. Jonah didn't move, he sighed and closed his eyes. Aria knew she needed to push him back to the now, or he wouldn't survive the rest of the night.

"Jonah, look at me…." Aria whispered. After a moment Jonah opened his eyes and lowered his eyes to hers.

"I need you, okay? I need you to help get us out of this. Please don't leave me now," Aria pleaded.

Jonah stared at her for a long time. The entire world seems to hinge on whether Jonah succumbed to his demons or chose to keep going with them. With her.

"Okay," Jonah finally said, "What now, Chase?"

Chase took a beat at the sound of his actual name from Jonah's mouth, no Boy Scout or Pretty Boy said with malice. Chase released a breath and answered.

"We've got to get the fuck out of town,"

Chapter Fifty

Chase

THEY all sighed heavily.

The sigh of the defeated and exhausted. Aria was still covered in blood and looked too pale. Jonah had a dark glint in his eye, but Chase saw real fear and regret there. And with Abby's body lying dead in the next room, Chase couldn't meet his eyes for long.

I shouldn't have left them.

Nope… not now… can't think about that now.

If they could put some distance between them and Stokes and Garcias, maybe, MAYBE they would have a chance to survive until daylight. They seemed to find them no matter where they went so the further away from the surrounding houses they could get, the better. The ranger station offered the best chance of being rescued, and from what they'd seen earlier in the night, the train bridge was their best route across the river. Chase didn't even know if it was safe to cross or still whole. It was all he could think of. They had to try.

She's going to be pissed.

"Look, I think Aria and Jude should stay here. Jonah and I will go.,"

"What?!" Aria balked, "Absolutely not! We are not splitting up again!"

"I agree with Boy Scout," Jonah rasped, "You two need to stay here."

"Not happening. I'm not sitting here just waiting to see if you two die or not," Jude countered. "Plus, Chase is all fucked up too!"

"Aria you can barely stand and if something goes sideways, Jude is here to help you." Chase looked apologetically at Jonah, "Jonah and I can do this,"

"You said you wouldn't leave me again," Aria rasped.

I did say that like an hour ago.

"Aria, you're too hurt! I need you to survive this," Chase begged.

"And I need you to keep your word and not leave me," Aria challenged.

He wasn't winning this.

I had to try.

"Fine," he pushed his fingers into his eyes, trying to visualize the best route to take to the train bridge. It was still dark outside, but they had an hour, two maybe, before dawn, which would make travel through town exponentially harder in the light. As it stood, if they stuck to the shadows of the buildings and made it to the river, they could follow that west to the train bridge. The rain had subsided, but crossing the train bridge was hazardous on a normal day, at night during a storm?

There's no way.

But that's all they had.

So that's what they'd do.

Jude and Jonah helped Aria get up, and she seemed fairly steady but leaned heavily on Jude. They fed her granola bars they found in the kitchen and water. They cleaned most of the blood off her face, but her hair was utterly caked with it. Chunks of her long auburn hair were singed down to the scalp from the powder burns, streaks of red still ringed her face and down her neck.

Chase turned away, careful not to draw their attention. He stared at the door for a moment, sighing heavily, then pushed the bedroom open quietly. He knew they had weapons in there, he'd made sure of it when he'd left. Their own weapon stores were running dangerously low; the fact that they had managed to hold on to any of their weapons was a miracle. Chase stepped around the blood congealing into the carpet and around the dresser that had been kicked aside. They'd braced it against the door, but it hadn't mattered. Bodies littered the floor and bed, lying at odd angles and impossible positions.

Don't look at their faces.

Chase closed his eyes, clenching his jaw and breathing tightly through his nose as bile rose up his throat.

Breath.

Guns... find the guns...

Slowly, he opened his eyes and tried to scan the room with the eyes of a machine. No emotion. No personal ties. Just a searchlight looking for...

Guns!

He spied a shotgun (singular) on the opposite side of the room, leaning against the bed across from the... collection... Chase's resolve was waning. He tried to blur the image in front of him with only the gun in focus, but the forms were becoming people shaped. Their hair was individualizing, and their faces were becoming clear. Chase slammed his eyes closed and again tried to breathe through the panic and the horror. He just had to reach across the bed and grab it. That was it.

I got this.

He sidestepped to the head of the bed, leaning forward with his good arm out, he reached for the barrel. As his hips and thighs leaned against the bed, the mattress shifted, and so did the bodies upon it. A head lolled to the side, the empty eyes of Erica falling upon him.

Fuck

Chase suppressed a scream and squeezed his eyes shut. His heart was racing, and he panted through his nose, trying in vain to get ahold of himself. He was pulled upright again, Jonah pulling him back into the main room, closing the door reverently behind them. Jonah released him and they both stood awkwardly for a moment.

"I'm…" Chase started.

Fuck

"I'm sorry about Abby… I didn't… I should've…"

Jonah held up his hand.

"I know you didn't want this." He sighed heavily, staring at the closed door for a long moment. "Remember when our biggest problem was that we were both in love with the same girl?"

Chase chuckled despite the pit of anger that lit at the memory of that kiss, the kiss Jonah had stolen from Aria. But even that utterly paled to the shit storm they currently found themselves in.

"Yeah…" Chase shook his head.

"That was like less than 24 hours ago," Jonah proclaimed.

"No shit?" Chase said in disbelief, thinking back on the timeline of their day.

This has been a hell of a day.

"And we still gotta cross that damn bridge…" Jonah groaned.

"No rest for the weary," Chase said, slapping him on the back.

"Wicked… it's wicked," Jonah corrected.

Chapter Fifty-One

Aria

THEY set out into the night, tired, beaten, and resigned. Defeat already weighing them down. They stayed low against the buildings, Aria leaning against Jude for support. Her head throbbed, but it seemed the more she moved, the less she felt it; whether that was resilience or shock, she didn't know. Her leg, however, was on fire. Pain ricocheted through her thigh with every step.

They clung close to the buildings, avoiding streetlights as best they could. Chase was leading the way, limping severely, and breathing heavily. His shirt was soaked in sweat, and she wondered how much longer he could go like this.

The end of the block stopped at the T of two roads bordered by a guard rail to stop cars from careening off the hillside into the river. Below them, the river raged higher than normal due to the rain and sediment. The water sloshed over the broken barriers of the highway and onto the fractured bridge and roadway downriver. Aria had never seen such destruction. They all stood in awe of the broken roadways, the giant boulders, and the slides of mud sloping from the mountain. The earth itself had been reshaped, and this was what was left.

Aunt Marnie had loved the mountains, she'd be okay with being among them if she had to go. Aria swallowed hard around the lump in her throat and leaned harder into Jude.

Carefully, they slid down the small embankment until they were hidden from the street above. They stayed low but ran along the river until they neared Main Street, the broken bridge to their right hung over the river, dipping down into the water like a wounded beast. The bridge was the main road through town, and due to the destruction, they were left with no other recourse than to cross the wide, well-lit street to continue along the river. But doing so would expose them to Stokes and Garcias.

They're only two men, Aria reminded herself. But tonight, it felt like they had always been one step behind them. They were everywhere at once. They all looked at Chase nervously.

Chapter Fifty-Two

Chase

THEY'RE waiting for you.

Shit.

Chase was exhausted, he tried to keep up with the growing demands of his body, but he was running on empty and had three people depending on him. Jude was huffing, holding up Aria, but standing straight and fairly unscathed. Jonah's head was on a swivel, constantly surveying the town around them for the next attack. And Aria, blood-soaked and disheveled, still stared up at him with trust. After everything they'd been through, everything SHE'D been through she still looked to him to get her through this. To save her. His heart swelled with love… and terror. He didn't know if he could do it; he didn't know if he could keep them all alive and make it out of this. He'd been pushing through pain and exhaustion for hours and would continue to for her and Jude (fuck, even Jonah) for as long as he could. He just didn't think it'd be long enough. He had a sinking feeling they weren't going to make it. There was too much against them. They were too tired, too wounded, too out of options…

But she's looking to you.

Don't let her down.

"Just stay low and RUN for the other side; get down by the river on the other side; the bridge isn't far. A quarter of a mile, that's it; we get to the bridge and get across. Hopefully, those fuckers can't follow us," Chase sighed.

We're not going to make it.

"This is crazy." Jude worried.

He's not wrong.

From somewhere above them, they heard the telltale *wup-wup-wup* sound of helicopter blades; they all looked up to see a rescue chopper swing over the north side of town, surveying the damage. The helicopter then swung around and headed over the river and over downtown, a giant spotlight roaming over the town. Right over their heads!

We just gotta get to somewhere open!

From somewhere to their left, gunshots erupted again, sparking off the metal sides of the helicopter. Chase couldn't tell how far away they were, but he didn't care. They had to go now.

"They're distracted! Go now! Fuck the bridge. Go for the mud field past it," Chase hissed, then stood as quickly as he was physically able and pushed himself over the chunks of cement and boulders caked in mud. Jude pulled Aria to his chest and followed with Jonah bringing up the rear. They ran and stumbled for the other side of the street with the same panicked feeling of running up the basement steps at night like something was a whisper away from grabbing you.

Except this time, the monsters are real.

Main Street stretched out before them like a football field lit up by surrounding streetlights and bared for the world to see. They all hesitated at the edge of the shadows, and–Chase watched another bullet ~~gun shot~~ fly at the helicopter, as it swung away and headed toward the destroyed west end of town across the river.

Shit! No! They can't leave yet!

"We gotta run now!" Chase said, pushing his body past its limits and into a run.

Every muscle screamed for a reprieve, but he focused on the opposite sidewalk. They walked across the open road, the squad car and carnage from earlier in the evening to their left, the crumbling bridge to their right, above them, streetlights illuminating their every move. Another gunshot echoed off the hills, sending all four diving to the ground. The helicopter still hung in the distance, light roving. Chase pushed himself up on shaky limbs staggering forward, glancing back to make sure the twins and Aria followed.

With a collective sigh of relief, they stepped onto the opposite sidewalk, disappearing behind a building and carefully descending the ruined bank towards the open debris field and old iron bridge. The water looked like an inky slice cutting through the night, passing over the crumbled roadway and under the old train bridge which now hung broken above it. The earth had flooded down the slope and dislodged the bridge at the base causing the far side to break off and fall into the rushing river below. The old rusty structure had crumbled sometime since yesterday, and their hopes with it.

Chase kept his eye on the chopper but almost wept when it swept away from them and disappeared over the crest of the mountains across town, and the gunshots stopped. Garcias and Stokes would be on the move again. Chase motioned for Aria and the twins to follow him behind an outcropping of jagged hunks of rocks scraped from the mountain. Jude laid Aria back against the rock, and Chase saw her panting; she looked pale again.

She shouldn't have come… she's too weak.

"What now, Boy Scout?" Jonah quipped.

"Not now, Jonah," Jude said, exhausted, handing Aria a bottle of water he had stowed in his coat.

"The helicopter is GONE, we have minutes until morning, the only way across the river is gone, and then they're going to find us, so WHAT THE FUCK ARE WE GOING TO DO?"

Motherfucker.

"I don't know, Jonah!" Chase yelled, losing the last of his grip on his sanity at Jonah's instigation, "Why don't you fucking take over, man? You started all this!" Chase motioned with his good arm at the destruction. "Everything is because of you and Alice!"

From behind a block of buildings to the east, the helicopter emerged like a giant creature, kicking up the air around them. The four screamed and waved their hands over their heads, desperately trying to get the pilot's attention. The helicopter stopped overhead and trained its light on them as they furiously flailed their arms. The helicopter swiveled side to side, and Chase exhaled in relief at the recognition.

They saw us.

They saw us.

It was like someone released all the air out of him, he deflated and was suddenly weak. His eyes blurred, and he stumbled to the right a little, unable to find the earth beneath him, and then he crumpled to the ground.

"Chase?" Aria shrieked.

Chase tried to answer, but he was so drained that he couldn't make his mouth work, and he couldn't make words make sense. Jude was hovering over him, his brows knitted together in concern.

"He's pale," Jude said, but he sounded far away, like they were underwater, "oh shit… he's hot. He's got a fever,"

Chase felt Aria's small, cold hands on his forehead and cheek, and a huff of worry escaping her.

"His leg," she hissed.

Something is pulling on my leg… get it off of me.

The pain ripped up his leg as someone removed the bandage.

"Oh god," Aria gasped; Jude sucked in a breath.

"That's infected," Jude cursed. "Shit… that's bad,"

"It's okay, it's okay. They'll come get us!" Aria whispered desperately.

More gunshots.

Closer.

Chase tried to form words to tell them to run, but his head was spinning. Jude was pouring water into his mouth, but he couldn't make his throat work either. He coughed weakly.

Is this dying?

"Oh shit!" Jonah yelled, "They're here! They're fucking here already!" Chase heard Jonah hit the ground and scurry closer to him, then Jonah was at his ear.

"I don't want to waste this… but we need you, asshole,"

Chase felt a stab in his bicep followed by a rush of something - his heart jumped back into formation, and his body lept from the ground. Blood rushed to his head and arms, and all he felt was one massive heartbeat.

"What the hell was that?" He said, eyes wide.

"Adrenaline… I swiped it from the nurse at Abby's," Jonah said, revealing the retractable injector.

"Shit, I'm glad you did," Chase laughed.

Suddenly, bullets ricocheted far too close, and Chase and Jonah ducked behind the lumbering chunks of rock and cement from the destroyed roadway. Behind them was the broken bridge, as Stokes and Ted approached from the road, they had nowhere to go. They were being herded away from the open land to the inescapable bridge.

I don't know what to do.

I'm going to get them killed.

I failed.

Chapter Fifty-Three

Aria

ARIA could just see them rounding the corner in their staggering, convulsive gate; Both soaked through with Alice's blue/black oozy sweat. Stokes was reloading a massive shotgun as Garcias slammed a clip into a gun Aria couldn't name.

"Oh my god, what do we do?" Aria whispered.

"If we can disarm them, we might have a chance," Chase said in a weird, rushed tone; his color was better, too.

"You SHOT both of them multiple times, and Jonah hit them with a car! How do we stop them?" Aria countered, feeling the well of panic begin to bubble up.

"What about the water?" Jude said from behind her, "Maybe if we deprive their brains of oxygen, it will stop them."

"We need to drown them," Jonah said in agreement.

"Okay…" Aria saw a plan, but it was insane, "They're clumsy and twitchy… we need to get out on the bridge and get them to follow us. Most of the boards are gone, and those beams are crisscrossed; they'll never be able to navigate that shit. They'll…" She looked at Chase, "Fall,"

They paused for a moment, and they all seemed to silently agree with her.

Crouching, they all turned and began scrambling for the remnants of the bridge. The decrepit train bridge was a long rectangular structure with four open sides, save for the crisscross support beams and the scattered wooden planks of the long-ago bridge, all ending in an abrupt break. Shots rang out around them, and the ground exploded to the left of Aria. The pebbles and dust peppered her face and coated her tongue.

"Go! Go!" Chase screamed as they all clamored to their feet and ran the remaining distance to the bridge, Jude reached the bridge first, but Aria was a step behind. Jude spun and grabbed Aria, tossing her onto the metal following quickly behind, Jonah jumped up behind them and Chase crawled up after.

"Chase? Are you okay?" Aria called back.

"I'm good! Go!" he yelled back.

Aria stood and limped over the two panels of steel that were still intact then slid to a stop when the rushing water opened below her. She felt the others at her back and suddenly seized. She couldn't lead them, she couldn't move. The beams were too thin, the water was too cold and going too fast, making her head spin like she was moving. She couldn't breathe because all she saw was death in front of her and death behind her, signaled by another gun shot. Jonah stepped up next to her and looked her in her eye.

"You got this," he said. Then, bending at the knee, he lowered himself to a crawl and began making his way down the beam to the right of her.

The vise releasing around her heart, she did the same, lowering herself to a crawl. She screamed when she put weight on her left leg but pushed through it even as tears collected. The metal was hard against her knees and her arms shook with fear. The iron creaked and groaned beneath them, rust covering her hands as she inched along. Spray from the river misted the already damp beam, leaving icy water covering every surface. The further out they got the more the bridge degraded into jagged hunks of rust.

"This is as far as I can go," Aria gasped at the broken beam in front of her. Carefully, she turned around, keeping one hand on the beam at all times. The group was trapped. They could do nothing but watch Stokes and Garcias walk their erratic gate up the bridge towards them. They didn't even stop to assess the danger at all, and with uneven steps, they stepped up onto the iron bridge. As Garcias crossed the second panel, the corner caved in, and his right leg sank to his shin, the jagged metal slicing into his leg like paper, bone scraping against metal. Without taking his eyes off of the group, he dragged his leg back up through the hole, peeling skin and muscle back from bone as he did. Bile rose in Aria's throat, watching the skin stretch and snap. Chase looked away, and Jude gagged; Jonah stayed silent in horror. Another gunshot broke the spell of the grizzly scene; Stoke's unsteady hand was already reloading. Luckily, he'd hit the cross beam between the two pairs.

"We're sitting ducks out here," Jonah yelled over the roar of the river.

"They just need to fall," Aria said, "Please just let them fall,"

Garcias hobbled forward on his decimated leg as Stokes mechanically reloaded his gun to the left.

"Chase…" Aria whispered. Chase cocked the gun and shot Garcias in the shoulder, trying to spin him to the left towards the opening between crossbeams. Garcias spun but not enough, stumbling backward a couple of steps.

"Shit!" Chase hissed, reloading.

"Come on, man," Jude pleaded.

"I've got two shots, you guys, if I can't… I'm going to have to…" Chase started, but Aria's heart seized, and she felt that panic of losing him rise in her again.

"No!" she snapped, "Don't miss," she ordered.

Chase opened fire again, and Garcias fell to one knee as the remainder of his right leg exploded in a plume of red.

"There you go!" Jonah cheered. "That's what I'm talking about Boy Scout!"

Aria watched Stokes, though, and he was already raising his shotgun and looking suddenly steadier.

"CHASE!" She screamed, "Stokes!"

Chase swung on Stokes and shot him directly in the head; Stokes' head jerked backward, then his whole body tumbled over the side of the beam and fell into the churning waters below them.

They turned their attention back to Garcias who still raised his weapon, still came for them. He'd been shot so many times; he had a mangled leg and half a face, but STILL he came for them. Chase trained his weapon on Garcias, but the audible *CLICK* of an empty chamber made Aria's stomach sink.

Garcias smirked.

Chapter Fifty-Four

Chase

THIS isn't a good idea.

If he pulls the trigger, he'll shoot me in the face.

Best case scenario… I hit him and get his ass off the bridge, and I fall into the water and…

Welp… too late

Chase charged at Garcias with every ounce of strength he had left in him. A shot rang out, and Chase slammed into Garcias, hitting him in the sternum with his wounded shoulder, pain exploding across it. Chase wrapped his arms around his friend and threw them both into the water below. Tumbling between the rusted scraps of crossbeams, they hit the icy water with a jolt.

Garcias peeled off of him as they sank below the surface, Chase kicking him away. Chase watched his body twist and disappear into the churning rapids. Chase kicked to the surface and gasped for breath. Chase's body was rigid from the cold water, but he forced himself to breathe, forcing his body to relax and stop fighting the water. He spun, putting his feet downstream and leaning back into the current. He spotted a piling about 50 feet downstream; if he could angle himself toward it, he could climb out of the…

Tired… so tired…

Nope… not now

Chase angled himself as well as he could as his vision began to swim again. Just as the dark edges of his vision began to overtake him, he felt his legs hit the piling, the water pushing his upper body to the left against the rough cement—like he was a doll. The water pummeled him, but he was close to shore; someone would get him.

It's fine.

This is good.

I'll wait here.

And his vision faded to black.

Chapter Fifty-Five

Aria

SHE didn't know if she stopped to breathe after Chase fell into the water. She was on her feet, sliding and sprinting down the bridge. She rounded the side of the bridge toward the water, sidling down the small, muddy embankment. She groaned in pain as the motion rocketed through her thigh. Once at the river, she ran alongside it, frantically searching the churning blackness for Chase.

"Aria!" Jude yelled from behind her. When she turned, he was pointing ahead of her towards a hunk of cement and rebar broken into the edge of the water. Jude and Jonah reached the debris first, and Aria almost balked when Jonah threw himself out onto the piling in the water, grabbing Chase with an outstretched hand. Jude followed, and Aria watched them drag Chase to the shore. Tears sprang to her eyes, a lump in her throat strangled the breath from her lungs as she knelt at Chase's.

"Is he alive?" she sobbed.

Jude put his fingers to Chase's throat, waiting for a pulse. After what seemed like the longest minute of her entire life, Jude nodded, and they collectively let out a sigh. Even Jonah. With tears streaking down her face Aria took Chase's face in her hands.

"Wake up, please," She turned his face up towards her and leaned her lips to his. "Please wake up," she said, Laying her forehead against his.

To her utter amazement, Chase coughed then wearily sighed awake.

"I just needed a nap," he joked weakly.

"Oh my god, please quit almost dying!" Aria yelled.

"You first," Chase said, attempting to sit up.

"Stay down," Jude ordered taking a deep breath himself. "You scared the shit out of us, just stay fucking still for a second,"

"Okay, okay," Chase sighed, laying his head back on the ground, "Help should be here soon,"

Then, Aria felt the air shift.

Something was off. Then Jonah got eerily silent.

"What?" Aria said looking at him suspiciously, getting to her feet.

"I can't be here when the cops get here..." Jonah said quietly.

"Jonah... you can't leave us here! Where are you going to go?" Aria snapped at him, an accusation hanging in the air.

"You could come with me," Jonah said quietly.

Jude and Chase stilled behind her, but she wasn't sure if she had heard him correctly.

"What?" she said in a barely audible whisper.

Jonah took a couple of steps towards her, closing in on her and looking down at her with that intensity she wanted to shrink away from.

"You could come with me," Jonah said again, reaching down and taking her hand in his. "No one would know us, they wouldn't know how we met or anything. We could be together…"

"What?" Aria said horrified, taking her hand back but finding his other hand shooting out to take her by the forearm.

"This is easier. Now we won't have to hide, the town is gone we can just go," when Aria didn't respond, he rushed on, "You felt it too when I kissed you… I know you love me. We can just go. I won't have to… we can just go," he said, desperation lacing his words.

Aria backed away from him.

"Jonah…" Jude said sadly, also getting to his feet.

"Shut up! YOU DON'T UNDERSTAND! You've never understood. I LOVE her! I need her!" Jonah shrieked in his twin's face. Spit flying from his mouth as he seethed at his brother. He turned back to Aria, the earnest pleading returned to his eyes, "We can just go, we can…"

"No…" Chase rasped from the ground. Aria was swimming in confusion, and something sharp hung in the air. There was something new in Jonah's face that set her on edge. Fear.

"It wasn't the first time," Chase coughed as he sat up shakily on his elbows.

"Don't listen to him," Jonah said panicked, turning to put himself between her and Chase.

"That kiss wasn't the first time Aria," Chase said louder.

Aria suddenly felt cold, and a pit in her stomach suddenly formed, plummeting to somewhere deep inside her. That wasn't the only time Jonah had tried to kiss her then… when was the other?

"What does that mean?" Aria whispered, "What does he mean?"

"Lindsey's house party.... Senior year," Chase breathed through the pain. Jude looked frantically between his brother and Chase.

Aria rewound time in her head, visualizing the party, her anger, the alcohol, so much alcohol.... She remembered wandering the house. Seeing Dana and then she found a quiet room and curled up on the bed wanting to simmer in her anger alone. She woke up at Chase's house. Then... Chase's bloody knuckles. Jonah's battered face, that no one ever gave her a straight answer for.

"What... happened?" She asked them all. Jude stood silent, tears welling in his eyes as he realized what his brother must have done.

"He..." Chase started, wincing at some unseen pain, "I found him on top of you, he had his hand down your.... He was kissing you...." Chase kept talking.

But for Aria, the world itself stopped.

She couldn't hear anything except the hammering of her heart in her ears. The only thing she felt was the rush of adrenaline surging through her veins at the injustice. The violation. She could never trust Jonah; she had protected him, defended him, and continued to be his cousin, his sister, but she had never been safe.

Jonah put his hand down and began to speak quietly. Nature itself stilled, and his words hit her like acid.

"You were laying there so still, and you were... are so gorgeous... I thought no one would know." Jonah said.

"YOU would know, Jonah!" Aria screamed.

"I love you!" he cried, "I thought eventually you would see that we should be together,"

"You don't get to decide!" Aria screamed, "You refused to believe I wasn't in love with you, so you just waited; you lurked and waited for your opening." Aria said, shoving him hard in the chest and then stalking towards him. Chase tried to scramble to get to his feet but fell back to the dirt again. Aria threw her fist out, and her knuckles burned, her hand screaming when it connected with Jonah's face.

"And THEN your actions killed HUNDREDS Jonah! All because you didn't want to face the consequences… AGAIN!" She threw another punch, pain exploding again in her fist. She was breathing heavily and sobbing again, "Why couldn't it be enough to be my cousin." Aria screamed at Jonah, "My BROTHER! My protector. My friend?" her voice grew sad. "You… tried to… take something from me I didn't want to give you. How could you?" Aria whispered.

"I wanted to," Jonah said flatly.

Aria suddenly withdrew the gun she'd been carrying since leaving Chase's apartment earlier on this hellacious night. It had been weighing down the pockets of the oversized basketball shorts she still wore. She raised the gun and pointed it squarely at Jonah.

Chase and Jude both sucked in a breath.

"You're sick, Jonah. I think you have been for a long time, but I can't anymore," Aria said.

"Can't what?" he responded incredulously.

"I can't pretend we don't all feel you sucking the life out of us. Keeping us away from anything that might take us from YOU!"

Jude sniffed, then joined Aria, quietly with her. Her true sibling, the brother she got to choose.

"Jonah, you need help. We can't protect you anymore. They have to know what happened here. And how could you do that to her? She trusted us! She trusted YOU! You have to let her go, Jonah," Jude stared at his twin a moment, then continued, "You poisoned an entire police force, who then killed half the people we grew up with. And you still expected Aria to bail you out and leave with you?"

"None of you are innocent," Jonah laughed, "Don't forget about what the boy scout here did to Miguel,"

"What is wrong with you?" Jude said in disappointment.

Suddenly, Jonah jolted forward, shoving Aria backward, her back hitting the earth hard enough to knock the wind from her lungs. Aria could do nothing but gasp for breath and watch as Jonah pulled a gun from his jacket and shot his brother four times.

Every bullet was in slow motion. Every drop of blood that spattered to the earth echoed in Aria's mind. Jude hit the ground with a dull thud. The light leaving his eyes.

Chase screamed to her right, but Jonah was already raising his gun at him.

A single gunshot rang across the mountains.

Jonah staggered backward, looking at the plume of red spreading across his sternum and down his abdomen. He looked up at Aria, whose gun was still smoking from the discharge. Jonah's eyes widened in surprise, then anguish as he exhaled and crumpled to the ground.

Chase pulled himself to Jude, screaming his name, his voice sounding far away as Aria dropped the gun to her side and sank back to the ground, staring at the sky.

That was it.

That was the final piece of her heart breaking.

Chapter Fifty-Six

Chase

THE roads were finally passable for emergency vehicles at ten the next morning.

Police descended upon the valley only to find the remnants of a massacre. Ted and Stokes were found downriver caught on debris from the mudslide; their bodies were taken away in biohazard bags. Survivors were found in several apartments downtown, one little boy waved at Aria. Chase found out later she had told him to hide.

It took weeks to process all the bodies and find all the survivors. Aunt Marnie's body was found amongst the wreckage by volunteers a week into the search. Many of the bodies were unrecognizable, so the fact they had identified her was a small mercy.

Jonah's death was minimized by his crime, his face looked back at Chase from the TV screen as the face of the Serenity Springs Massacre. The news called it "a series of unfortunate events" that led to the perfect conditions for the events of that night.

Funerals were nearly back-to-back for a month and finalized by a memorial ceremony complete with a plaque downtown by the river where the temporary bridge had been put in. It'd be at least a year before a proper bridge could be constructed.

The North and West sides of town were utterly decimated by the mudslides; subdivisions, restaurants, the hospital, and the post office gone to mother nature. The rest had been lost to Alice.

Including Aria.

In the weeks since shooting Jonah, Aria hadn't been the same. She'd endured her parents' death, had pushed through the guilt of Miguel's suicide, she even processed Aunt Marnie's death by holding a beautiful ceremony for her near the river. But she couldn't forgive herself for what she did to Jonah.

Officials from Denver had set up a temporary hospital in the high school; beds separated by sheets and blankets were all the privacy they were afforded. Chase didn't remember the first day or two; his leg had gone septic, and he'd needed a blood transfusion. When he woke, he found Aria in the bed next to his, awake and healing. But she barely moved. She barely spoke. Chase had laid next to her for days without saying a word or hearing one in return from her. She squeezed his hand like it was a lifeline, though, so he stayed by her side. The only time Aria left the bed was to visit Jude in the makeshift ICU set up in the old chemistry lab.

Of the four bullets Jonah shot into his brother, only one did any damage, but it had taken almost everything. Jude would never walk again.

Aria's head had been nearly shaved to treat her bullet wound and scalp burns. Chase watched her sit like a zombie as the nurses cut her long red locks, hunks falling from her head onto the gymnasium floor. Most of the medical staff were from the city but all handled her like glass, like the slightest misstep might cause her to shatter into a million pieces. They apologized as they took chunk after chunk of her hair. They stroked her arm and spoke to her encouragingly yet gently. When they were done, Aria returned to her bed.

Due to the sheer mass of bodies, Jonah's remains weren't released for almost two months. Aria had been released after a month, but she rarely left Jude's side; Chase had gone home and tried to piece together his house.

Now, Aria accepted the ashes with shadowed eyes and shaking hands, asking Chase to drive her to the mountains. Jude couldn't even look at the ashes. He couldn't separate his anger at Jonah from his grief for his twin, so he told Chase and Aria to go without him. Chase didn't hesitate, but during the long, quiet car ride, he found his eyes falling to her small frame, sitting blank and pale in his passenger seat. He felt helpless and didn't know how to reach her, so he just kept driving.

Aria stood on the ridge overlooking the devastated valley whose shape had changed since the mudslides. Chase put an encouraging arm around her shoulder and squeezed gently.

"You got this," he whispered before giving her some space to say what she needed to say.

Chapter Fifty-Seven

Aria

WHO knew finding out you were a victim would break you?

Who knew killing the person who victimized you would be what pushed you into the dark abyss?

Who knew losing everyone could kill you from the inside out?

She couldn't stop seeing Jonah in those final moments. Twisted and cold as he turned on his brother. The Jonah she thought she knew would have never hurt Jude. Jude was good and pure and everything that was right about all of them. Jonah tried to deny the world of that light.

She sighed raggedly.

"I don't know what to say to you, Jonah…" she said to the open air, the box of Jonah's ashes in her hands, "I've lost so many people, and you're the one that broke me, I can't… I can't forgive you for that." tears started to collect in her eyes, "But…. I can choose to remember the times that you were a brother to me. Helping Aunt Marnie paint my bedroom so I felt at home, walking me into school on the first day, listening to me cry every night, and never telling a soul…" she coughed out a sob. "Why couldn't that be enough, damnit!" she screamed into the mountains.

Nothing answered, but the wind.

"I'm sorry I couldn't be that for you," Aria sighed, "Wherever you are… I hope you find the love you were looking for because you deserved it, Jonah. It just couldn't be from me." She looked up at the sky, begging for vindication from above.

She unraveled the bag within the box and stood with Chase, quietly waiting behind her.

"Goodbye," she said simply and then released the ashes into the wind watching them catch a breeze and swirl into the air over the valley.

She wiped her tears and returned to Chase.

"I want to go sit with Jude for a while. Is that okay?" Aria asked her eyes a well of sadness.

"Of course. Do you want me to come?"

"I just want to be alone with Jude for a bit," her throat was tight as she tried to squeeze out the words.

"Okay. C'mon, I'll take you," Chase said putting his arm gently around her waist. He'd been worried about her, but he'd never said it. She could tell in the crease in his forehead and set of his jaw.

They drove in silence for a moment, and then Aria reached over and took his hand; he smiled and squeezed it gently. She felt tears welling but took a deep breath and willed them back in. She couldn't let them fall yet.

When they pulled up to the high school, Aria pointed to a parking spot near the front, she could hike a mountain but hated walking further than she had to in a parking lot. She turned to Chase and just watched him for a moment making Chase blush.

"What's up?" Chase chuckled, cupping his hand to her cheek. She put her hand over his and leaned into his touch.

"I… Love you, Chase," Aria said, looking him in the eye.

Chase was quiet for a moment then smiled the sweetest smile Aria had ever seen.

"I knew it!" he joked quietly, then touched his lips softly to hers.

"I love you too," he whispered as they parted.

Aria leaned across the console kissing Chase one more time, parting carefully, her lips hovering near his. She breathed him in, knowing this was where her heart would always call home. She smiled and then slipped out the passenger side door.

"I'll see you later?" Chase called after her.

"Yeah, come by and see Jude in a couple of hours," Aria smiled at him, then turned and headed up the steps to the school.

Chapter Fifty-Eight

Chase

CHASE knocked lightly on the door of Jude's makeshift hospital room 4 hours later. His current room was the old freshman English room, it was small, but he didn't have to share it. Chase had also snuck in a bag of contraband donuts.

"Yep! Come!" Jude yelled from inside.

Chase pushed the door open and surveyed the room.

"Where's Aria?" he asked as he made his way over to the chair and plopped down, tossing the bag to Jude.

"Nice! Awesome man, thanks," Jude sounded dull even as he tore into the bag of pastries. He wouldn't meet Chase's eyes.

What's happening?

Something's off.

"What's going on Jude?" Chase asked hesitantly.

Jude shifted uncomfortably and then retrieved a letter from his side table.

Oh no

Chase took the letter with shaking hands and opened it:

Chase,
I love you…. I always have.
Please don't try and find me.
I'm sorry.

Aria

"No no no nonono," Chase's chest tightened.

She can't leave.

We didn't survive this to be apart.

Chase's eyes flew up to Jude who sat awkwardly in his hospital bed.

"You just let her go?" Chase said around the lump in his throat. Jude sighed and motioned for Chase to sit down. But Chase wanted to sprint from the room, catch her before she could leave town… leave HIM! He looked toward the door.

"Chase, don't," Jude said softly.

"Jude, what the fuck?!" Chase yelled, not sure what to do with all the emotions roiling inside of him.

"She was drowning. I've never seen her like…. Like how she's been. She needed to get out, and she knew you wouldn't let her go," Jude said plainly.

"I would've gone with her!" Chase screamed, his voice breaking.

"And how would that have helped HER," Jude asked quietly.

Chase looked down.

Fuck…

"Look, Chase… We've all been bound to one another by misery since high school. You and Aria being together was the only positive thing to come out of it, so we all just kept moving… except Jonah…" Jude trailed off for a moment, his eyes sad and looking at something far away. "You and Jonah both latched on to her as your only lifeboat, and that wasn't fair to her. Let her go. Let HER decide."

"And if she decides not to come back," Chase rasped sadly after a moment, "to me…"

"Then, at least you know what's real. IF she does, then you know it wasn't some traumatic event tying her to you. Then you know for sure. If she doesn't, then you can move on too,"

I don't want to move on from her.

All I want is her.

We were supposed to do this together.

Chase sighed heavily. His heart was broken, his home was demolished, Ted was dead…

Then he looked at Jude. His eyes weren't angry or bitter. They were calm and compassionate like they always were. Chase was crying about heartache to a guy who just lost his entire family plus the use of his legs.

Fuck that.

"Okay then," Chase said, wiping his eyes, "What about you? How do we get you better?"

"Doc said I should get out in the chair today to get a feel for it, but…" Jude's eyes dropped to the chair parked near the door. Chase saw the fear there. Jude had lost as much as anyone, and now, they were the only ones left holding the mantle of this disaster. But they didn't have to do it alone, and Chase needed to get his head out of his ass.

Chase walked to the door of the room and grabbed the wheelchair, wheeling it over to the bed.

"Let's go," Chase grinned. "In the chair, let's go!"

"I don't need to be your project, Chase," Jude said, shaking his head.

"You're my friend, Jude fuck off," Chase locked the wheels and patted the seat "Come on. We're doin' this."

Jude stared at him for a minute, and a thousand emotions seemed to cross his face, but he took a heavy sigh and nodded. Chase helped him sit up, and together, they moved his legs over the side of the bed. Then Chase lifted his upper body up and carefully onto the chair. He waited for Jude to make himself comfortable, then he leaned down, unlocking the wheels and rolling him through the doorway. Jude tensed in the chair as they entered the more public space, but Chase pushed him forward.

"Here's what we're going to do Jude… We are going to take this shit one day at a time. Okay? We got this,"

"We got this," Jude agreed.

"Good evening, I am Rhonda Stillerton and this is WGRT news. Tonight, we are doing an in-depth look at the Serenity Springs Massacre and the now-infamous Jonah Forrester. Officials say the variant of Alice used by Forrester in this attack was extremely concentrated, so when Officers Theodore Garcias and Jeffrey Stokes ingested a small amount with their daily coffee, the effects were unlike anything witnessed before. Officials are looking into who supplied Forrester with this dangerous compound and urge anyone with any information to reach out to their local law enforcement. This senseless tragedy was only intensified by the cataclysmic mudslides that cut off retreat from the secluded town. Efforts are now underway to fortify the town's infrastructure and create a bypass that would add an additional route to and from Serenity Springs.

So, who was Jonah Forrester? Sources close to Forrester called him "fun but had a dark sense of humor" and "devoted to his brother and cousin,"

But why would someone so charismatic do something so vicious? Recovered journal entries reveal a boy obsessed, driven mad by unrequited love. Aria Delgado was Forrester's cousin by adoption and, after her parent's death in 1999, was adopted into the Forrester home. Sources say the teens were as close as siblings, but these journal entries show that Jonah Forrester was in love with his cousin and had plans detailing her abduction and confinement. Records show he recently secured a storage facility in East Serenity Springs, and when officers searched the premises, they found it soundproofed and furnished with a bed, chair, canned food, and chain bolted to the floor. It seems, in the end, Forrester foiled his own plan by poisoning Serenity Springs police and ushering in a night of absolute horror for residents.

Today survivors thank the heroes they did see when times looked their darkest. Aria Delgado herself is credited with saving a family of 4 and their neighbors.

'I saw her running by, and she told me to hide, and we did... the people next door all died, but we hid because we had time... she saved us,' Sebastian Clemons said of Delgado. Others credit the only unaffected officer on the force in town at the time, Chase Gorski.

Neither could be reached for comment..."

Epilogue

CHASE jogged up the front steps, juggling his keys in one hand and a bag of takeout in the other. His key turned in the lock, and as he pushed the door open, he tossed his keys on the table to the right when he felt someone behind him.

His heart rate spiked, and he turned, ready to fight. A phantom pain rocketed through his leg.

All this time and I'm still jumpy as fuck.

But as he spun, his gaze landed on a face he never thought he'd see again.

"Hi, Chase," Aria said.

Her eyes.

"H… Hi…" Chase stuttered, his brain halting in her presence.

She laughed a little at his shocked face.

"Sorry to sneak up on you,"

Her voice.

"Its… fine…" Chase stuttered.

"Jude told me you were still living here," Aria fumbled with the strap of her bag. Her hair had grown out to a cute chin length, red strands falling in her face. A small scar peaked out from her hairline, a white mar against her freckled skin.

"Yep, still here," he didn't know what to say; they hadn't talked in years. Jude had been in contact with her but would only ever tell Chase she was safe and to let her be. So, he had moved on.

Well… tried.

"Um… Can I come in?" Aria said expectantly.

Dumbass

"Yeah, sorry. Come in," Chase stammered and stepped aside, motioning her in. She entered and looked around.

"It looks the same," she said lightly, sighing.

Chase didn't respond. He closed the front door and then remembered the greasy bag in his hand. He stepped around her and dropped it on the table. They stood in silence for a moment as Aria took in the house. She hadn't been here since that night. It was like she had to abandon anything tying her to that night, to this town. She'd left most of her belongings at her apartment when she left town.

"Is that my chair?" she asked, smiling.

Chase blushed as his eyes landed on the purple and orange monstrosity.

Shit… that's embarrassing.

"I… helped clean out your apartment. Jude said it was fine…" Chase started, embarrassed.

"No…" she laughed, "I'm glad you have it,"

Chase exhaled.

What was she doing here?

As if reading his thoughts, she sighed and started to talk again.

"I um… just got back. I haven't even been to see Jude yet," She started to pace slowly, wringing her hands in front of her, "How is he… really?" she said, stopping to look at him.

"Jude is good," Chase said honestly, "It was rough for a while, but he got through it,"

"He got through it because of you," Aria said seriously.

"Nah, nothing keeps Jude down. He's, uh, actually dating a new guy at the station; I set them up," Chase was pretty proud of that, actually.

"Of course you did," Aria laughed, "He told me about Triston, he sounds great,"

"I think he's been good for Jude," Chase agreed, smiling.

They lapsed into silence again, and Aria started wringing her hands again.

When did she start doing that?

"Chase…" Aria started.

This was it. Whatever she came here to say, she was going to say it.

"I… I'm sorry I left the way I did. I didn't think I could tell you I needed time without breaking your heart and you blaming yourself."

Yeah, that checks out.

"I get it," Chase said genuinely, "I'm not mad, you don't owe me anything…" Chase began.

"Yes, I do," Aria countered, "I *left*; I know that hurt, and I am sorry," Aria said sincerely, taking a step towards him.

Something in Chase needed to hear that, and a knot in his heart let go.

"Thank you," Chase nodded.

"And I needed to see you so that I could see if it was still there," she said quietly.

"If what was there?" Chase's heart was pounding.

"The pain,"

So much of what tied them to each other was rooted in her pain; her parents' death brought her to the valley, Miguel, Chase's dad, Jonah, Alice… all dark laces that led back to Chase.

Chase had been put in mandatory therapy after Alice and what he found there was a way out of the suffocating sadness without clinging to Aria or running. He talked about his dad, his childhood, Aria, Miguel, Jonah, Jude, all of it. It had felt good to purge the poison of his life. Then, he and Jude set up a Non-profit for the survivors, helping them get new homes or put on lists for rentals in nearby towns. They had an army of grief counselors descend upon The Valley, offering services to all that needed it. Jude felt like he owed the town for what his brother had done, whereas Chase just needed to pour himself into something meaningful. He found it healing to help. Chase stayed because he could. He found a way out of that darkness, but Aria had to run to survive, and Chase couldn't begrudge her that.

"So… Is it? Still there?" Chase asked, holding his breath.

You can do it without her. She deserves to be happy. And if that's without you, that's okay.

Aria walked over to him and stopped a breath away from him.

"No," she smiled, "I don't see it anymore. All I see is you,"

Another knot released in his soul.

"But… I understand if you can't do this again. I left. I get it if you don't…" Before Aria could finish, Chase stopped her.

"No!" Chase said hastily, then he took a breath and took a small step back "Let's… Start over. I'm Chase," His heart was racing, but he extended his hand to her.

Aria smiled.

"I'm Aria," she shook his hand, "Nice to meet you, Chase. Could you help me find my locker?" they both laughed softly, then fell into silence and stared at one another for a moment, Chase simply feeling her hand in his.

"Can I buy you some real dinner Chase?" Aria said, motioning towards the greasy bag on the table.

"That would be lovely," he said, offering his arm to her.

Together, they stepped out into the sunset-washed town to find a future not bathed in blood and heartache but hope.

Aria's car was parked at the curb, and in the front seat, a short-haired tan and brown dog bounced up and down happily as they approached. Aria opened the door, and the dog bounded to Chase, nuzzling her dark nose into his hands.

"Who's this?" he laughed, bending down to meet the wiggly butted dog before him.

"I adopted her in California," Aria smiled wryly, "Guess what her name is."

He looked up at her quizzically, scratching the dog's ears.

"Chase, meet Alice,"

THE END

Afterward

This book was born from a dream I had when I lived in Glenwood Springs, CO at the age of 19. It consisted of me hiding in the woods from a man with a gun who was hunting everyone in the town, a mindless zombie taking lives. Over the years since that dream, I wanted to explore that feeling of being hunted and along the way this story morphed into an apocalyptic look at being trapped in a secluded town after a natural disaster. Unlike my other books where the characters were well planned before the book began, I let these characters show me who they were. Where Aria was supposed to be a ball of fire and sass, she revealed herself to be a broken girl who used anger to hide her deep well of sadness. All she wanted was safety and people who loved and accepted her. I think we can all identify a little with that. Chase was supposed to be a lighthearted football player who made Aria smile, but overtime he became more defined as a boy struggling to survive an abusive home, looking for a reason to stay afloat. The character Jonah quickly became my favorite as he grew into the monster under the bed, twisting up the concepts of familial love and protection for possessiveness and obsession. He's not based on anyone real but the fear and uneasiness he instills very much is. He was a fun character to explore and I'm going to miss him. Jude was my little ray of sunshine who had to take a hit for the story, but I couldn't bare to kill him either. I think we all need someone like Jude in our lives and I wish him and Tristan well.

If you or anyone you know is struggling with suicide please call 988 (in the US) for help and resources.

Miguel was missed, and you would be too.

Visit 988lifeline.org

Acknowledgements

This book was made from a fever dream but it would not be what it is today without my amazing publisher, Amanda Lamkin at Line by Lion Publications. She has helped me grow as a writer in ways I cannot describe and has given me the freedom to figure it out as I went along. Also, Thoman Lamkin for his epic artwork! I am always complimented on my covers and that is all thanks to his amazing skill, my books catch they eye because of your wizardry. They are both amazing souls that I am honored to know.

Thank you, Susan Travis, for all the time you devoted to Alice and making her into what she is today. You offered the best insights, and one day I will give you the biggest hug for all of your help and advice.

Thank you to Line by Lion for giving me a chance

Thank you to my readers.